Murder of the Ninth Baronet

J.S. Fletcher

Originally published 1932
Harrap, London, U.K.

This edition published 2023 by

OREON

an imprint of

The Oleander Press
16 Orchard Street
Cambridge
CB1 1JT

www.oleanderpress.com

ISBN: 9781915475244

Sign up to our infrequent newsletter
to **receive a free ePub** of
Fatality in Fleet Street
by Christopher St John Sprigg and get
news of new titles, discounts and give-aways!

www.oleanderpress.com/golden-age-crime

A CIP catalogue record for the book
is available from the British Library.

Cover design, typesetting & ebook: neorelix

Contents

Chapter 1

GONE! – BUT WHERE?

CHANEY AND I FIRST heard of the mysterious disappearance of Sir John Maxtondale on the morning of May 16, 1923. About half past nine o'clock, just as we were settling down to a discussion of our day's business (in which, as it happened, there was nothing of any particular importance), Chippendale came into our room and announced Mr. Ellerthorpe. We knew Mr. Ellerthorpe; he was a well-known solicitor of Lincoln's Inn Fields, having a considerable practice amongst county families, and we had occasionally done business with him. Up to that time, however, it had never been of any serious nature; none of its occasions, certainly, would have caused Mr. Ellerthorpe to present himself in person at our offices at that early hour of the forenoon, and hearing that he was there, we glanced at each other and at Chippendale with questioning eyes.

"He's got a gentleman with him," added Chippendale. "Swell!"

That was Chippendale's way; he always sized up any stranger before approaching us as to entry.

"Bring them in," said Chaney.

Mr. Ellerthorpe entered – hurriedly. He was a little inclined to be fussy, and he lost no time in wheeling round and indicating his companion, a tall, elderly man of the country-gentleman type, who looked at us and our surroundings with a detached, speculative air.

"Morning, morning!" began Mr. Ellerthorpe. "Glad to find you here – both. This is very urgent, important business. Allow me – Sir Stephen Maxtondale."

We made our obeisances to Sir Stephen Maxtondale. Chaney rose from his desk and placed chairs.

"Yes, Mr. Ellerthorpe," he said, resuming his own. "What is it?"

"Sir Stephen," replied Mr. Ellerthorpe, "is a client of mine – a very old client. He came up to town last night to consult me. What he wished to consult me about – and did consult me about – is, well, a mystery! I am no good at the solution of mysteries – not in my line. So—"

"You came to us, Mr. Ellerthorpe," said Chaney. "Well – and the mystery?"

Mr. Ellerthorpe glanced at his client. But Sir Stephen made no response.

"Well," continued Mr. Ellerthorpe, "the fact is, it is a case of disappearance. Of – of somebody vanishing. Clean gone!"

"Yes?" said Chaney. "And – who is it that is clean gone?"

"Ah!" exclaimed Mr. Ellerthorpe. "Now, to give a really truthful reply to that question is beyond me! Not possible, at present. At – present, you understand? May be possible later. But – well, the disappearance is that of a – a person who says he is Sir John Maxtondale, elder brother of Sir Stephen."

"Says?" questioned Chaney. "But – is he?"

Mr. Ellerthorpe and Sir Stephen Maxtondale exchanged glances.

"Er – he might be," admitted Mr. Ellerthorpe. "Might!"

Chaney reached to a shelf at the side of his desk and took down a copy of the current *Who's Who*. Silently he turned over its pages and presently looked up at Sir Stephen.

"I see you are the ninth holder of the title – the baronetcy?" he said.

"Yes," replied Sir Stephen.

"Then – supposing this man of whom Mr. Ellerthorpe speaks to be what he claims to be – where does he come in?" asked Chaney.

"He would be the ninth," replied Sir Stephen. He hesitated a moment. "If – if he is really what he says he is, he is the ninth baronet! I – in that case – have no claim. You see—"

He hesitated again, obviously at a loss. But, no one making any observation or asking a question, he went on:

"You see, we don't know whether he ever did succeed or not. I mean, I don't know if he succeeded his father—"

"Your father?" interrupted Chaney.

"Exactly! Perhaps I had better explain? The whole thing is a bit muddling to anyone not conversant—"

"That would be excellent, Sir Stephen. If you can make things clear—"

"Well, it's like this. My father, Sir William Maxtondale, the eighth holder of the title, had two sons, my elder brother, John, and myself, Stephen. When John was about twenty-five years of age, and I three years younger, he had a very serious quarrel with my father; so serious that he left home—"

"A moment, Sir Stephen," interrupted Chaney. "I am making mental notes – so, too, is my partner, Mr. Camberwell. Let us have all the details clear. By home, you mean your place in Warwickshire – Heronswood Park? Very well – now, what was the cause of the difference between your father and your brother?"

"This!" continued Sir Stephen. "John had fallen in love with, and wanted to marry, the daughter of one of our tenant farmers. My father positively forbade this match and no doubt threatened my brother with all sorts of dire consequences if he persisted in his intentions. So—"

"Again a moment. The estates – were they entailed?"

"No! They were absolutely at my father's disposal."

"Then he could have penalised your brother pretty heavily?"

"Yes, but since his coming of age John had been quite independent of my father. Our maternal grandfather had left him a lot of money, and in addition to that he had inherited my mother's private fortune. He was well off."

"Could – from a monetary point of view – do as he liked, eh?"

"Exactly. And – he did! As I say, he left home – for good. Disappeared! – without a word to anyone."

"And the girl?"

"She disappeared, too, at the same time."

"To join him, of course. Well?"

"Well, time went on, and we never heard anything of John. Nor did the girl's people ever hear anything of her. Inquiries – of a tentative sort – were made on both sides, but nothing resulted. Then, eventually, my father died, and we began to search for John in earnest. We left no stone unturned—"

"I can speak as to that," interrupted Mr. Ellerthorpe. "I engineered the inquiries. We advertised in every quarter of the globe; the bill for advertisements was enormous. We employed private inquiry agents – you weren't in business at the time, Chaney, or I'd have employed you – and we never got one single scrap of information!"

"And so – ?" asked Chaney.

"And so," continued Mr. Ellerthorpe, taking up the story in response to a nod from Sir Stephen, "in due course the courts sanctioned an application to presume the death of John Maxtondale, and Sir Stephen here assumed the title. But—"

"What about the estates?" asked Chaney. "I presume Sir William had devised them to Sir Stephen?"

Once more Mr. Ellerthorpe and his client exchanged glances.

"Er – no!" replied Mr. Ellerthorpe. "The fact is, Sir William died intestate. He was always going to make a will, and never did. He died very suddenly."

"Then – if John Maxtondale is alive – eh?" suggested Chaney.

"Exactly!" agreed Mr. Ellerthorpe. "You are quite right!"

"Let me know in plain words if I am right, though," said Chaney. "Am I right in concluding that if John Maxtondale is alive, the estates and titles are his? Is that it?"

"That," responded Mr. Ellerthorpe, gravely, "is it! They are!"

Chaney turned to me.

"Got it, Camberwell?" he asked. "All clear?"

"Clear enough!" I said. "I've got it – all!"

"Well," continued Chaney, facing our visitors again, "this man you spoke of at first? Is he the man you referred to as having disappeared?"

"Exactly," replied Mr. Ellerthorpe. He turned to Sir Stephen. "You can tell that best," he added.

"What I can tell," responded Sir Stephen, "is just this. Yesterday afternoon, about three o'clock, my neighbour Mr. Henry Marston, of Sedbury Manor, who is just about my own age and has known me ever since we were all boys together, came to me with a strange story – he was very much agitated. He said that the previous evening there came to his house, very late, a man who, on securing an interview with him, announced himself as John Maxtondale. Now, my brother John and Henry Marston were old schoolfellows and had always, as boys, been very close friends, and their friendship had lasted until John's disappearance – Marston, indeed, had been the very last person to see John before he went away so suddenly. Of course Marston had believed him dead, and he was of the opinion, at first, that this caller was an impostor. But within a few minutes, according to his own account, he began to think differently. He put certain very searching questions to his visitor, which were answered promptly and satisfactorily; moreover, knowing that John Maxtondale had a very peculiar birthmark on his upper left arm, he got the man to turn up his sleeve – the birthmark was there! Marston came to the conclusion that he had the real John Maxtondale before him."

"Yes?" said Chaney, as Sir Stephen paused. "Well, did he give Mr. Marston any explanation of his movements during the time – a great many years! – that had elapsed since his disappearance?"

"He may have done; I can't say," replied Sir Stephen. "Marston was hurried, agitated; we only had a short interview. You see, he had rushed over to tell me that his visitor had disappeared."

"Ah! – that's the disappearance you came to tell us of?" said Chaney. "Well?"

"Marston says that after becoming convinced that the man before him really was John Maxtondale, he asked if he was staying in the neighbourhood and if he had been to me. He replied that he had come to Marston first – from the Waldorf Hotel in London, where he had been living for two or three weeks since his return to England. He had wanted to see Marston first, he said, before seeing any of his own family, but he proposed calling on me next morning. On that, Marston asked him to stay the night with him at Sedbury. He did so. Next morning – that is, yesterday morning – Marston was obliged to go over to Monkseaton to a meeting of magistrates. He left home just after breakfast, first extracting a promise from his visitor that he would not go to Heronswood until his return, when they would go together. The visitor replied that he wouldn't leave the house till Marston came back. But when Marston came back at one o'clock for lunch, he had gone. Marston's butler said the gentleman had gone out about ten o'clock, saying he would have a look round the park and be back for lunch at one. But he never came in – and eventually Marston rode over to Heronswood and told me all about it. I returned with him to Sedbury, but we got no news, and late in the afternoon I telephoned the Waldorf to ascertain if Mr. Maxton – the name he had told Marston he was going by – had returned there. They replied that though Mr. Maxton's belongings were in his room, Mr. Maxton had gone out the day before and had not returned. So I at once caught the evening train to town, knocked up Mr. Ellerthorpe, and told him all about it. This morning at eight o'clock we called at the Waldorf Hotel; there was no news of Mr. Maxton. They allowed us to see his room. There is luggage there, showing – the labels, I mean – that he had recently travelled from South America to Southampton. We got no other information about him, except that a smoking room waiter was able to tell us that a few days ago Mr. Maxton was twice visited in one day by a well-dressed Jewish man, a sort of prosperous business man, the waiter said. Otherwise he was not known to have had any visitors, and there was no correspondence awaiting him. After leaving the Waldorf I telephoned Marston; he replied that he had not heard anything. And so Mr. Ellerthorpe brought me to you."

Chaney had listened to all this with silent attention. Now he put a straight question.

"It is only a few hours since this man – Sir John or not – disappeared," he said. "Why are you so concerned about it? Tell me – do you fear something?"

"Yes!" replied Sir Stephen, promptly. "Foul play!"

"Why?"

Sir Stephen hesitated; hesitated, indeed, so long that Chaney spoke again.

"Don't keep anything back, sir," he said. "Better let us know everything."

"I don't care to incriminate anyone," replied Sir Stephen, "but the fact is that when my brother left Heronswood, all those years ago, he left a bitter enemy behind him. That enemy is still living – and, I believe, is still as bitter and desirous of revenge as ever."

"Yes," said Chaney. "A man, of course?"

"Just so," agreed Sir Stephen. "In fact, one of our tenant farmers."

"Jilted suitor of the girl your brother ran off with, no doubt?" suggested Chaney.

"You are quite right in your surmise. That is precisely it!"

"What's the man's name?" asked Chaney.

"Robson – James Robson. He is tenant of our Home Farm – it has been in the occupancy of his family for two hundred years or more."

"An elderly man, I presume, Sir Stephen?" suggested Chaney.

"He is about the same age as my brother John," replied Sir Stephen. "Fifty-eight."

"And you say that your brother ousted him in the affections of the girl who, you believe, ran away with your brother?"

"Robson, it was said, was formerly engaged to the girl. Whether she really did accompany my brother I can't say positively. She disappeared at the same time that he did. Besides, John had told our father that he wanted to marry her – was deeply in love with her. Everything was very sudden – it all occurred in a few days. My father heard something – he spoke to John – they had a violent altercation – John left Heronswood. Then we heard that the girl had left her home, too."

"And this man, James Robson? He took it badly?"

"Very! He was, of course, a young man then, and he was noted – and always has been noted – for his violent temper. He set off at once for London, in the endeavour to trace my brother and the girl. Whether he came upon any trace of them in London we never knew, but he went on from London to Paris, in a further search. He was away, trying to track them, for some weeks. When he returned, he preserved an obstinate silence, and he has kept it ever since. But at the time of my brother's disappearance Robson declared publicly, at Monkseaton market, that if he had to wait thirty years, or forty years, or fifty years, he would kill John Maxtondale the first time they met. And – he meant it!"

"Has Robson ever married?"

"No! He is a silent, morose man, given, I should say, to brooding over this. He is a good tenant and a very clever farmer. But – I don't think he has ever lived down his almost insane desire for revenge."

"And you think it quite possible that he may have met your brother – if this man really is your brother, which seems very likely – when Sir John left Mr. Marston's house yesterday morning, and – killed him?"

"I think it very possible. Our property and Mr. Marston's adjoin – if my brother (and, as you say, I think it very likely that the man concerned is my brother) went across the park at Sedbury Manor, he would be on Robson's land. They may have met."

"You haven't questioned Robson, Sir Stephen?"

"Oh, no, I have had no opportunity, and I don't think I should have questioned him if I had. You see, I lost no time in coming up to see Mr. Ellerthorpe."

"Why, now? What was the hurry?"

"I thought that if this man really was John, he might have called on Mr. Ellerthorpe. Mr. Ellerthorpe is our family solicitor. John, of course, knew him in the old days."

"Sir John and I," remarked Mr. Ellerthorpe, "are of an age."

"Sir John hasn't been to see you, Mr. Ellerthorpe? Just so – you know nothing of him – of his return? Very well. Now, gentlemen, what do you wish my partner and me to do?"

"If you would go down to Heronswood and get at the truth," said Sir Stephen. "The matter must be cleared up. I am going down myself by the twelve o'clock from Euston to Monkseaton. Mr. Ellerthorpe is going with we. Will you go with us?"

Chaney glanced at me; I nodded my consent.

"We will both go," said Chaney. "Euston, then – the twelve o'clock train."

A moment later our two visitors had gone, and Chaney turned to me.

"Camberwell," he said, "I know something about this matter that you don't know. That Maxtondale estate in Warwickshire is worth about fifty thousand pounds a year!"

Chapter 2

SEDBURY
MANOR

I PRICKED UP MY ears at that; there was some hidden meaning in Chaney's remark.

"Well?" I said. "What are you after, Chaney?"

"Fifty thousand a year is a lot of money," he replied. "Even in these days, with income tax and death duties and estate duties and all there is in the way of deductions, it's a lot of money."

"Still I don't know what you're after," I repeated. "And how do you know the Maxtondale property represents such an income?"

"I remember the Maxtondale case being before the courts," he answered. "I mean when they got leave to presume John Maxtondale's death. Fifty thousand pounds was mentioned as the annual value of the property. Also, a few years ago, before I knew you, Camberwell, I had a case in that neighbourhood, and I heard a good deal about the family and its possessions. Old, very old family, settled there at Heronswood for three or four hundred years as country squires. Not so well off once upon a time, but of late – rolling!"

"What caused the change?" I asked.

"Coal, my son, coal! Found a splendid seam on the estate – have you never seen trucks with 'Heronswood Colliery Company' on 'em? That's the nugget. And it'll go on producing for many a generation yet."

"Pity to have a coal-pit on a fine old property," I remarked.

"Well, as it happens, Camberwell, the coal-pit doesn't show – it's hidden away from the house by thick woods. Very fine old place, Heronswood – I went over it while I was there. Pictures – books – old china and glass – old silver; that sort of thing. But you'll see it for yourself today or tomorrow."

"Then you knew something about the Maxtondale family history before we heard Sir Stephen's story just now?"

"Knew all about it, my son! But I wasn't going to let Sir Stephen – Mr. Stephen, I suppose we should call him, though if John's dead, he may be Sir Stephen, unless John had a son who's living – know that I knew. I wanted to hear what he'd got to say."

I made no remark on that; Chaney had his own way of doing things. He had also a wonderful store of knowledge of all sorts and was continually digging into it in a surprising and sometimes highly convenient fashion; the fact was that he had a remarkable memory and was always on the lookout for anything to treasure up for future reference.

"I suppose we're going, then?" I said.

"Of course! Let's put things shipshape, give Chip his orders, and get to Euston," he replied. "Last thing, however, we'll just phone the Waldorf and inquire if Mr. Maxton has been heard of there."

We phoned the Waldorf Hotel at 11.30. No, Mr. Maxton had not returned. On that we repaired to Euston and met Sir Stephen Maxtondale and Mr. Ellerthorpe. Over lunch in the train we naturally fell to a further discussion of the disappearance. Mr. Ellerthorpe suddenly introduced a new theory.

"Since John Maxtondale disappeared from Heronswood, the colliery has been started," he said. "It's occurred to me that he would hear of this from Marston the other night. Now, supposing his curiosity led him, yesterday morning, to go and have a look at the pit and its workings? To get there from Marston's place, Sedbury Manor, he would have to go through the woods which lie between Sedbury and Heronswood Park. And I believe" – here he turned to Sir Stephen for confirmation – "I believe that in those woods there are old trial workings – shafts?"

"Yes," assented Sir Stephen.

"Supposing he fell down one of them?" suggested Mr. Ellerthorpe. "Not improbable."

"Not very probable," said Sir Stephen. "Fenced in, those places, or overgrown by now. I think my theory is more likely to be the correct one. Our Home Farm, Robson's place," he added, "is, though on our property, just at the foot of Marston's park. Lonely place, too."

"You stick to the Robson idea, Sir Stephen?" said Chaney.

Sir Stephen shook his head.

"I know Robson," he answered. "He is the sort of man who, having once felt himself deeply wronged, would nurse his feelings of revenge assiduously. Instead of growing fainter with the passage of years, they'd wax stronger. The more I reflect on this affair, the more I feel convinced that my brother met Robson when he left Marston's house yesterday morning."

"We shall find that out, Sir Stephen," said Chaney confidently. "By the by, who and what is Mr. Marston? Other than an old friend or acquaintance of yours, I mean."

"Oh," replied Sir Stephen, smiling, "there is nothing much that one could say about Henry Marston. A typical country squire, old bachelor – horses, dogs, hunting, shooting, cricketer once – good company – assiduous in discharge of his duties as magistrate, and so on. That's about all one can say."

"And as far as you are aware, the last man to see the man who announced himself as John Maxtondale," said Chaney. "We must see him first."

"Not the last man," corrected Sir Stephen. "The last man to see my brother – you observe that I am firmly convinced that it is John whose disappearance is in question – was Marston's butler, Moysey."

"We must see Moysey, too. But I want to know what your brother told Mr. Marston on his arrival at Sedbury Manor," said Chaney. "I don't suppose they went to bed there and then – Marston must know something about John Maxtondale's doings during the years that had elapsed since leaving home."

"My car will be in waiting at Monkseaton," observed Sir Stephen. "We will drive out to Sedbury Manor at once."

We were at Sedbury Manor by soon after three o'clock. I took a careful look at the place as we drove up to it: a big, square-built house standing in a wide-stretching, well-treed park, with a great lawn in front, and walled gardens at the side, and having, as far as we could see, no other houses or even farmsteads or cottages near it – a distinctly lonely place. Sir Stephen, as we turned up the carriage drive, pointed across the park.

"If you look straight across there, due south," he said, "you will see the chimneys of Heronswood, above the trees. And there, more to the south-east, you can just see the wheel of the colliery, over the top of the coppices – we can't see that from our windows. And yonder, at the foot of Marston's park, though really, as I said before, in our land, is Home Farm. Robson's place. Anyone going from here to Heronswood, or to the colliery," he added reflectively, "would pass the farm. There is a footpath across this park, running alongside Home Farm buildings."

"Are there no other houses or cottages about here?" asked Chaney. "Is this place of Mr. Marston's absolutely isolated?"

Sir Stephen pointed to a great screen of elms on the east side of the lawn.

"Sedbury village lies there," he replied. "It's quite hidden from here, you see, but there it is. There's a church, a vicarage, two or three farmsteads, a score of cottages. And here and there in these grounds, amongst the trees, are other cottages housing Marston's outdoor servants, gamekeepers and so on. Some fine shooting here – and fishing. There's the lake."

He pointed to a sudden opening in the trees which revealed a sheet of water of evidently considerable size, and so shaded by the overhanging foliage that its surface looked black and dismal. For a second I let myself wonder if the man into whose disappearance we were to inquire was lying beneath those murky waters.

Mr. Marston met us at his front door – a big, broad-shouldered, bluff Englishman. He instantly fired off a question at Sir Stephen.

"Heard anything of him?" he asked.

"Nothing!" replied Sir Stephen.

Mr. Marston turned on his heel, shepherding the four of us into the big, stone-paved, stone-walled hall.

"Umph!" he said. "Neither have I! Come in!"

He led us into a small room, the sort of snug den in which a sportsman delights, and summoning his butler, insisted on giving us all a drink before any business was mentioned. Over our glasses Sir Stephen introduced Chaney and me; Mr. Marston considered us thoughtfully, as if we had been two new specimens of natural history.

"Queer business!" he remarked, setting down his empty glass. "Don't know what to make of it."

"Mr. Chaney wants to ask you a few questions," said Sir Stephen.

Mr. Marston turned to Chaney and stared attentively at him – in silence.

"Nothing very much, sir," said Chaney. "To start with – about identity, now. This man who came to you, the night before last – do you feel positively assured that he was Sir John Maxtondale?"

Mr. Marston nodded his head in a gesture meant to signify unqualified assent and rapped out five words, *staccato*.

"Not a doubt of it!"

"Did he tell you anything of his adventures?"

"Not a word!"

"Didn't he say where he'd been all these years?"

"No!"

"Didn't you ask him?"

"No business of mine!"

"Didn't he even say where he'd come from last?"

"Oh, well, he said that. Waldorf Hotel, London."

"But before that, Mr. Marston? Didn't he mention any place or country – Asia, Africa, America?"

"No – none of 'em."

"Did he say what he intended to do – about the title or estates?"

"No – nothing. Never mentioned 'em."

"Didn't he even mention his family – his brother?"

"Oh, well, he just said that he supposed Stephen was over there at Heronswood."

"No more?"

"No!"

Chaney smiled.

"I suppose you and he, old friends, sat up and talked a bit that night, Mr. Marston? Since he kept off all these subjects, what did you talk about?"

"Old times – hunting, shooting, fishing."

"I see! And next morning, when you went off to sit on the bench at Monkseaton, it was the understood thing that he wasn't to go across to Heronswood until you returned?"

"Well, it was this – I told him that if he'd wait till I came back at one o'clock, we'd have lunch and then I'd go with him to Heronswood."

"And when you'd got back, he'd disappeared? Well, just one more question, Mr. Marston. You're aware of the threats uttered, years ago, by Robson, the farmer? Yes? Did you tell Sir John about that matter?"

"No! Not I! I knew of the threats – long since – but I didn't believe for a moment that Robson would ever have carried them out."

"Not at any time?"

"Oh, well, perhaps at the time. But certainly not now."

"Sir Stephen thinks he would, Mr. Marston."

"Well, I don't!"

"Then you don't suspect Robson?"

"Not for a second!"

"What do you think's happened to Sir John, then?"

But there Mr. Marston shook his head with emphatic decision.

"No!" he replied. "That's your job!"

"Quite so," agreed Chaney. "Then, can we have a word or two with your butler?"

Mr. Marston rang the bell; the footman appeared and at a word from his master led us through the hall and a series of passages to the butler's pantry. Moysey, the butler, was engaged at that moment in polishing some fine old plate; a dish in one hand, a cloth in the other, he looked us over questioningly. He was a good type of the old-fashioned family servant, something over middle age, and of that intense solemnity and respectability which seem to be inseparably connected with his office.

"Well, Mr. Moysey," said Chaney, taking the easiest chair in the room, "we've come to have a little talk with you. You're the last person who saw the gentleman who disappeared yesterday, eh?"

"As far as I'm aware, sir. There may have been others. But – not in this house, sir."

"Do you know who the gentleman was, Mr. Moysey?"

"I do not, sir. I heard my master address him as John, but beyond that, sir, I have no notion whatever of his identity."

"Never seen him before, eh?"

"Not to my knowledge, sir."

"How long have you been here, then?"

"Fifteen years, sir."

"Ah!" said Chaney. "Then it would be before your time."

Moysey looked questioningly at this.

"Yes, sir? Of course I don't know what you refer to."

"Never mind! Well, about yesterday morning, Mr. Marston, after breakfast, went to Monkseaton, didn't he, leaving the gentleman here, alone? What did he do after your master went out?"

"For some time, sir, he was in the morning room, reading *The Times* newspaper. Then – I happening to go into that room, sir – he said to me that he thought he'd have a look round the park. He asked me what time we should have lunch, and when I told him one o'clock, he said he'd be back by then."

"And then, I suppose, he went out?"

Moysey hesitated.

"As far as I'm aware, sir, he went out. He said he was going out."

"But didn't you see him go out?"

"No, sir! And it may seem odd, sir, but there's nobody in the house who saw him go out."

"None of the other servants?"

"None, sir! There was our first footman in the hall, but he says the gentleman didn't go out that way. And there were other servants about – women servants, parlour-maids, housemaids – none of them saw him leave. Of course, there are several doors by which he could have left, but he wasn't seen to leave. And there were men, gardeners, working on the lawn, and in the gardens on either side of the house – no one can remember seeing him."

"Odd thing!" said Chaney. "Why, where did he go after telling you that he was going out? Did you leave him in the morning room?"

"No, sir. He left me in the morning room. He went out into the hall. Possibly he went up to his room. But where he went after that nobody knows. All I know is that he didn't come in for lunch and has never returned."

"Who admitted him when he first came, Mr. Moysey?"

"I did, sir."

"Did he give any name?"

"No, sir. He asked me to tell Mr. Marston that an old friend had called to see him."

"Had he any luggage with him?"

"No, sir, nothing. After Mr. Marston had told me that the gentleman was staying the night, I prepared a room for him, got him some sleeping things, and in the morning took him some toilet articles."

Chaney got up from his chair.

"Just let's have a look at his room," he said. "He may have something there that might give us a clue."

"Nothing there, I think, sir, but what I lent him from the dining room and some papers he brought," said Moysey. "If you will follow me, sir."

We followed Moysey upstairs to a big bedroom, the windows of which looked out over the park. And, as Moysey had said, there was nothing – except, on a table at the bedside, a couple of evening newspapers of the date of two days before and a copy of the *Fortnightly Review*. I dare say I should have taken small notice of these, but Chaney picked up all three and suddenly drew my attention to a pencilled note on the cover of the periodical.

"See that?" he said. "An address! 203A, Hatton Garden, E.C.1."

Chapter 3

MRS. ROBBINS TALKS

HAVING MADE A NOTE of the address and carefully consigned the Fortnightly Review to a capacious pocket in which he carried an accumulation of documents and papers, Chaney turned to the butler.

"Got a telephone in the house?" he asked.

Moysey smiled, shaking his head.

"I regret to say we have not, sir," he replied. "It would be a matter of great convenience to me if we had. But Mr. Marston, sir, is a gentleman of very conservative ideas and habits, and he doesn't favour telephones or electric lighting. There is a telegraph office in the village, sir – close by."

We went downstairs again to the butler's pantry; there, at Chaney's direction, I wrote out a telegram to our faithful Chippendale:

Go at once to 203A, Hatton Garden, find out name or names of occupying firms, and wire them to me at Sedbury Manor, Monkseaton, immediately.

Moysey sent off a messenger with this, and Chaney and I returned to the room in which we had left Marston, Sir Stephen, and Mr. Ellerthorpe. They were still discussing the situation.

"It would have been a great help to me," Mr. Ellerthorpe was saying, "if Sir John had told Mr. Marston anything about his doings in London since he arrived at the Waldorf Hotel. Who, for instance, was

the man who called on him at the Waldorf? That seems to suggest that
he was having business relations with somebody."

"We may have got a bit of light on that upstairs," remarked Chaney.
He pulled out the *Fortnightly Review*. "We found this in his room," he
went on. "Here's an address pencilled on the cover – 203A, Hatton
Garden. What's that suggest to you, Mr. Ellerthorpe?"

"No, but what does it suggest to you?" said Mr. Ellerthorpe. "I
don't boast of the detective mind!"

"It suggests to me – diamonds!" replied Chaney. "Dealing in
diamonds! Perhaps Sir John Maxtondale had come from the diamond-fields. Didn't you say that his luggage bore labels showing that
he'd travelled to Southampton from some South American port?"

"Rio," corrected Mr. Ellerthorpe.

"That's Brazil. There are diamond-fields in Brazil. He may have
some business dealings in diamonds. Anyhow," continued Chaney,
"Hatton Garden, to me, suggests diamonds or something of the sort.
Now, as to this address, pencilled – hurriedly, you see, on a bit of blank
space on the cover of this magazine – I should say that it means that
Sir John, after buying this at the station bookstall – Euston, of course
– when he came down here the day before yesterday, met some man
with whom he had been having dealings, and wrote down this address
for future reference. It is probably the address of some Hatton Garden
dealer in precious stones to whom he was advised to go. But—"

At this point a footman entered the room and approached Mr.
Marston.

"Mrs. Robbins, of the Upper Leys Farm, would like to speak to you,
sir," he announced.

Marston looked surprised.

"What's she want?" he demanded.

"She says, sir," replied the footman, hesitatingly, "that it's – it's
about the missing gentleman. She – she called him Sir John, sir."

Marston looked from one to the other of us in astonishment. We all
knew that no name had been given to the missing gentleman.

"Show her in!" he commanded.

Mrs. Robbins entered – a bright-faced, apple-cheeked old rustic
lady, who bobbed a curtsy to her landlord in particular, and to the
rest of us in general, and smiled all round as if to convey that she was
pleased to see us. Marston stared at her.

"Now, Mother Robbins, what've you come about? Who's this Sir John you've been talking of?"

Mrs. Robbins sank into a chair which Chaney pushed towards her, and began to untie the strings of her bonnet. She gave Marston an arch look.

"Lord bless you, Mr. Marston!" she exclaimed. "What are you talking about? As if I shouldn't know Sir John Maxtondale when I saw him. Why, wasn't I his own nurse till he was growing into a big boy? Know him, indeed!"

"I'll lay anything you've never seen him for five-and-twenty years, anyway, Mother Robbins!" said Marston. "Come, now!"

"Then you'd lose, Mr. Marston, for I saw him scarce more than five-and-twenty hours ago!" retorted Mrs. Robbins. "And talked with him, too!"

"Where?" demanded Marston.

"Where but in my parlour?" declared Mrs. Robbins. "At eleven o'clock in the forenoon of yesterday morning, for a good half-hour. And of that I'm willing to take my Bible oath or swear one o' them affidavies, or anything you or these gentlemen likes, Mr. Marston. Especially," concluded Mrs. Robbins, with a grave shake of her bonnet, "especially as I hear that Sir John is missing."

"Who told you he's missing?" asked Marston.

"It's pretty well known that the gentleman who came here the other night is missing, Mr. Marston," replied Mrs. Robbins. "When there's as many servants, male and female, and especially female, in a house as you've got in yours, it isn't human nature to expect such matters to remain private and confidential – oh, dear, no!"

"But who said it was – who said that the gentleman was Sir John Maxtondale?" demanded Marston.

"Nobody! But I can put two and two together as well as anybody, though no great scholar," replied Mrs. Robbins, with dignified assurance. "And of course it is Sir John!"

Marston glanced at Sir Stephen. Sir Stephen turned to Mrs. Robbins.

"I should like to hear what you can tell us about my brother, Mrs. Robbins," he said. "You say he came to your house yesterday morning?"

"As Sedbury Church clock struck eleven strokes, Sir Stephen," replied Mrs. Robbins. "You see, I was standing in our front garden at that time, when I saw a gentleman coming across the park in our direction. Of course I thought it was the Squire; then I saw it wasn't, because he'd neither dog nor gun with him. He came right close by our garden gate, which opens into the park, and he caught sight of me and stopped and smiled. 'Bless me if that isn't my old nurse!' he says, and opens the gate and comes in. 'Lord save us!' says I, all of a tremble, 'if it isn't Mr. John! Sir John, I should have said.' I says: 'Dear-a-dear! Where ever have you been all this time?' 'All round the world, and in and out of it, my old friend,' he says. 'But here I am again, anyway!' 'Well, come in,' I says, 'and let's hear about it.' And we went into our best parlour and talked – for a good half-hour, Sir Stephen."

"Yes?" said Sir Stephen. "And – what did you talk about, Mrs. Robbins?"

"Oh, well, of course I wanted to know first if Lucy Mills really did run away when he did – that was the gel, you know, gentlemen, that was engaged to Jim Robson and threw him over. Well, Sir John said she did, and, what was more, they were wed at once in London. Then, he said, they travelled in foreign parts – all sorts of queer places they'd been in, till at last they'd settled in South America. But Lucy, he said, was dead, and they'd never had any children, and he was now a lone man – which was the reason, he said, why he'd come home again. 'Why,' I said to him, 'when your father, Sir William, died, they advertised for you all over the world – didn't you see anything in them foreign papers?' 'I did,' he said, 'but I didn't want to come home then.' 'Well,' said I, 'you'll create a nice to-do coming home at this time – there's Sir Stephen got the title and estates, and his one son, Mr. Rupert, who'll look to have 'em when his pa's dead, and now ye'll upset it all!' I said. 'Oh,' he said, 'Stephen can have the estates, and Rupert can succeed to 'em – I don't want 'em,' he said. 'I'm a rich man – made a great fortune in South America – ' "

"Did he say what he'd made it in, ma'am?" interrupted Chaney.

"He didn't, sir – not to me," replied Mrs. Robbins. "All he said was he'd made one, and when he'd done with it, the family could have it. 'But there's the title!' I said. 'You can't throw that away, Sir John.' 'No,' he said, 'but it'll pass from me to Stephen, and so Rupert'll get it in the end.' 'Have you seen Sir Stephen?' I asked him. 'No,' he said, 'Harry

Marston and I are going to see him this afternoon.' 'And where are you going now?' I inquired. 'Oh, nowhere in particular,' he said; 'I was just looking round till lunchtime: Harry Marston's gone to a magistrates' meeting in Monkseaton.' 'Well, Sir John,' I said, 'just let me warn you. You left an enemy here, you know, and, in my opinion, he's as black and bitter as ever! Be careful!' 'Do you mean Robson?' he said. 'That's just the man I do mean!' I said. 'And I says again – mind where you're going!' But he laughed at that. 'Oh, nonsense, Polly' – that was what he always called me when he was a little fellow and I was his nurse – 'I don't believe all that stuff! It would be a very truculent sort of fellow that cherished that feeling for twenty-five years!' 'Sir John,' I said, as serious as I could, gentlemen, 'Sir John, Robson's the sort that would nurse his feelings of revenge for fifty years – keep away from him!' But he only laughed, and when he'd had a glass of my home-brew, he went."

"Where?" asked Chaney.

"Oh, well, master," replied Mrs. Robbins, with a portentous shake of her bonnet, "if you really want to know, he went off in the very direction which I'd warned him against taking. He was always an obstinate one, Sir John, ever since he was that high, gentlemen. Yes, he went right away across the park towards Heronswood. As Sir Stephen there knows very well, there's a footpath at the end of Sedbury Park which leads past Robson's place, Home Farm, to Heronswood, through the coppices and past Dutchman's Cut, which is a piece of water – well, Sir John went that way. Right past – Robson's!"

Silence fell on the room. Sir Stephen broke it.

"Have you mentioned this to anyone, Mrs. Robbins?" he inquired.

"I have not, sir," replied Mrs. Robbins, firmly. "He – Sir John – asked me not to do so until later on. No – not to a soul, sir. But when I heard that a gentleman who had come to stay with Mr. Marston was missing, I put two and two together and decided that that gentleman was and could be no other than Sir John Maxtondale, so I came here."

"Very proper, Mrs. Robbins, very proper!" said Sir Stephen. "Well, keep it to yourself a little longer, if you please. My brother," he added, "may have gone back to London."

Mrs. Robbins murmured something about her ardent regret that Sir John Maxtondale had not taken her advice and kept away from

Heronswood Home Farm, and then, with more curtsies, departed. Ellerthorpe shook his head.

"There you are!" he said, dolefully. "Whether it's so or not, you'll see that local opinion will be that Sir John's been murdered by Robson! What that old party thinks, everybody will be thinking. Anyhow, this will have to be cleared up. There'll have to be a search. I think we should go into Monkseaton and see the Superintendent of Police."

But while we were discussing this, a telegram from Chippendale arrived and was brought in to Chaney, who, after reading it, handed it over to me. It was after Chippendale's style – brief, businesslike:

Seen place mentioned six different tenants their names as follows – Avenser and Goldmark, Smith and Wellstein, Marcus Rosenbaum, Waldo Samman, Cashmore and Morris, Emanuel and Millard. All apparently connected with usual Hatton Garden trade.

"Which, mainly, is diamonds!" said Chaney, when, at his suggestion, I read out the message. "Diamonds! I shan't be surprised, considering what we know about Sir John's coming from South America – Brazil, to be correct – if diamonds are at the back of all this."

"You mean, Mr. Chaney—" asked Sir Stephen. "Exactly – what, now?"

"That he may have had diamonds on him, Sir Stephen, and been followed down here," replied Chaney. "That's got to be considered, anyhow. The Robson theory seems, at the moment, obvious – but I've no faith in the obvious!"

"Do you advise seeing the local police?" inquired Sir Stephen.

"I do! Can't do better. Let us see the Superintendent at Monkseaton," said Chaney. "Tell him everything. Then let the local police take their own line. As for Camberwell and myself, we'll take ours – if you wish it."

"I certainly wish it," said Sir Stephen. "But – you seem to suggest, Mr. Chaney, that your way mayn't be that of the local police?"

"I don't think it will, Sir Stephen," replied Chaney, with a laugh. "I've a pretty good idea of what the local police will do and say when they've heard the story. They'll have hanged, drawn, and quartered Robson within five minutes!"

"And – you?" asked Sir Stephen.

"We," replied Chaney, "are in no hurry. Besides, as I said just now, we distrust the seeming obvious."

Chaney was right about the police. The Superintendent, an elderly man and, as we soon found out, a native of those parts, had no sooner heard all the details of our story, narrated by Mr. Ellerthorpe and brought up to date and embracing Mrs. Robbins's contribution, than he gave Sir Stephen a significant glance.

"That looks like Robson's work, Sir Stephen," he said. "He's never forgotten – nor forgiven!"

"But – all these years!" exclaimed Sir Stephen.

"All very well, Sir Stephen, but he's that sort," replied the Superintendent. "I never told you – never told anyone, in fact – but years since, at the time in question, long before I was Superintendent, I took it on myself to warn Robson. He'd been uttering these wild threats against Sir John – Mr. John as he was then – here in Monkseaton, at a farmer's ordinary, and it had got talked about. Now, I knew Robson, and I warned him against such foolishness. 'There may come a time,' I said, 'when all this could be brought up against you.' Well, it's evidently come! What do you wish me to do, Sir Stephen?"

Sir Stephen was at a loss, but Mr. Ellerthorpe came to the rescue.

"I think there should be a thorough search of the country between Sedbury and Heronswood," he said. "Sir John may have met with an accident. I suggest that you set your men to work, and, to help them, that you see the manager of the colliery and get him to enlist the services of his men. This is certain – Sir John must be found!"

We left the Superintendent making arrangements for a search, to be started at once, and went back to Sir Stephen Maxtondale's car. He had asked Chaney, Ellerthorpe, and me to stay with him at Heronswood during our investigations, and thither we now repaired; it was already evening. Heronswood, a great, gaunt, grey pile of masonry, set in the midst of a thickly wooded park, looked grim and sombre as we drove up to it. But there was a great fire of logs burning bravely in the big hall when we entered; and when dinner was served, half an hour later, Sir Stephen proved himself such a genial and thoughtful host that my first feeling of being overawed and overweighted by the size of the place quickly wore off.

We were halfway through dinner when a young man apparently about twenty-eight or thirty, in riding costume, suddenly burst in on us – a typical specimen of the horse-dog-and-gun variety. His fresh-coloured cheeks were ablaze with haste or excitement; his eyes shone. He made straight for Sir Stephen.

"I say, what's all this I hear?" he demanded abruptly. "I came through Sedbury; I met Dick Ferard there. The whole place is on the go! They say Uncle John has come back from God knows where, and is somewhere about. Is it – is it true?"

"I think it is quite true that your uncle has returned, Rupert," replied Sir Stephen, quietly.

"Then – is he here?" asked Rupert, glancing round the table. "Is—"

"He is not here," said Sir Stephen with some severity of speech. "We'll talk about him later."

Rupert Maxtondale hesitated a moment; then he slipped into a chair and, with no more than a mere nod to Mr. Ellerthorpe, began to eat his dinner. Conversation on our previous topic dropped: Sir Stephen began to talk about the prospects of the coming cricket season.

Dinner over, Chaney drew me aside.

"Say nothing to anyone," he whispered, "but in a few minutes follow me out of this room into the outer hall. We're going out – and if you want to know where, to have a look at James Robson and his surroundings."

Chapter 4

THE UNCURTAINED WINDOW

CHANEY LEFT THE ROOM; I waited; the servants were handing round coffee and cigars. Rupert Maxtondale had already disappeared; he had bolted, rather than eaten, his dinner; it seemed to me that he was badly upset about something. After the obvious check from his father, he had relapsed into silence, and if he looked round at any of us, it was with questioning, if not wholly suspicious, glances. There was something about him to which I took an instinctive dislike; a furtive air, a sullen expression; he was altogether different from Sir Stephen, who was frankness itself.

Waiting a few minutes, until Sir Stephen and Mr. Ellerthorpe had begun to talk, I left the room and in the hall found Chaney, in conversation with one of the footmen. He motioned me to put on my overcoat; together we passed out to the terrace in front of the big house. That was lighted by the gleam from the long range of windows; outside in the far-spreading pleasure-grounds and the park beyond, the night was already dark. Above the woods in the distance we could see in the sombre skies the reflected glow of the lights of Monkseaton; from that direction, too, we heard the rumble of the rising and falling machinery of the colliery shaft; the night shift, doubtless, was going down to its subterranean labours.

"I've found out the way to Robson's place," whispered Chaney, as we walked away from the house. "We take this path at the end of the terrace and follow it across this side of the park till we come to a biggish house on our left; that, so says that flunkey I was talking to, is the steward's place – Mr. Weekes. After that there's a cluster of cottages – labourers' dwellings. And a bit farther on there's a big farmstead – that's Home Farm. Robson's. We call on Robson – privately."

"With what object?" I asked. "The man's already under suspicion!"

"But he doesn't know that," replied Chaney. "At least, if he's gathered that he is or suspects that he is, or if he's really guilty, he'll not let us see that he knows or suspects anything, unless he's a fool. No, we'll call politely and civilly, tell him that at Sir Stephen's request we are searching for his brother, Sir John, and ask if Mr. Robson or any of his household have seen anything of that gentleman. Object? The object, Camberwell, is to get a peep at Robson!"

"You think you'll gain something by a personal inspection?" I suggested.

"Oh, well, I'm not a bad hand at sizing up a man!" chuckled Chaney. "I think I can read a man's face pretty well. Anyway, it's better to be doing something than sitting in there with Sir Stephen and old Ellerthorpe, speculating on this or that theory. By the by, what did you think of the son and heir – young Rupert?"

"Didn't like him at all!" I said.

"Nor did I!" he declared fervently. "Far from it! Mark my words, Camberwell, that youngster's got something on his mind, some secret that he daren't let out. That accounts for his surliness, furtive look, and general restiveness. He's been up to something and daren't let papa know. I shall watch him. Did you see how excited he was about the rumour he'd heard? Well, did you guess what was in his mind? I did! He was thinking: 'If my uncle John has turned up, and if he's married, and if he's got a son or sons, where's my chance of the baronetcy and the Maxtondale properties?' Eh?"

"You think that was it?" I said.

"Bet your life! Natural, too, I suppose. If I were a young fellow of that age, expecting to succeed to an old title and fine estates, I shouldn't welcome anything that threatened to deprive me of my prospects. No, sir! But what's this? Somebody coming along in a hurry!"

We had just reached the end of the long terrace then and were about descending the steps to the path of which Chaney had spoken. This path for a little distance ran parallel with the carriage-drive; along this came a motor car, driven at a fairly fast pace. It slowed down as it came to the foot of the steps, and we then saw that it was driven by a police officer. The door opened and the Superintendent of Police stepped out. Recognising us, he paused.

"Oh," he said, "you're here, eh, Mr. Chaney? Sir Stephen anywhere about?"

"Inside," replied Chaney, nodding at the lighted windows. "Any news?"

"Not from our side," answered the Superintendent. "I just came along to report. I've seen the manager of the Heronswood main colliery and he's going to organise a search-party amongst his men at once. I've also detailed as many of my men as I can spare, so between now and this time tomorrow we'll have combed the district pretty well. But you know, Mr. Chaney, it's struck me – how do we know that Sir John's still in the district? He may have gone back to London."

"He hadn't returned to his hotel in London an hour and a half ago," replied Chaney. "We telephoned there – the Waldorf – just before dinner. We've kept phoning there regularly all day. No, he's somewhere round here. Alive or – dead!"

"Queer business," remarked the Superintendent. "Now, I wonder if he'd anything in the way of valuables on him?"

"May have had," said Chaney, non-committally. "Why?"

"We've a few rather bad characters round here," replied the Superintendent. "Taking us all together, we're a fairly decent and respectable and law-abiding community; still, we have some black sheep. There have been two or three cases of housebreaking lately, and so far I haven't laid hands on the culprit, and in addition to that we've had a good many cases of poaching—"

"A poacher wouldn't be out in the day-time," interrupted Chaney, "and Sir John disappeared about noon."

"Ay, well, but he might have encountered some bad lot or other in those woods," said the Superintendent. "That is," he went on, lowering his voice and glancing round as if he feared to be overheard, "that is, if it isn't Robson! But, between you and me and the post, I fear it is Robson! Robson's the sort of man, Mr. Chaney, who'd never forgive, never!"

"If you think that, then the only thing is to find Sir John's dead body and then – what's that, now, that's coming?"

He broke off to point along the path which we had been about to take when the Superintendent's car arrived. Some hundred and fifty yards away a light was coming along that path, wobbling, jumping, shifting from side to side like a thing possessed, but growing bigger and brighter with every second. Suddenly I saw what it was. Somebody was riding a bicycle down that path, and riding it at such a speed that the lamp in front was swaying about in a fashion that threatened a smash and a crash for the rider. In another minute light and machine dashed up to the foot of the steps, and a bareheaded, almost breathless young rustic, evidently a farm-lad, flung himself at the uniformed figure of the Superintendent.

"Will you come to Robson's?" he gasped out. "Will you come at once to Robson's? The housekeeper sent me – at once, she said. Robson—"

He choked over the name, trying to recover his breath; Chaney laid a hand on his shoulder.

"Steady, my lad, steady!" said Chaney. "Take your time! Now, what about Robson?"

The lad shook himself, making an effort. It was easy to see that in addition to being breathless he was frightened; his face shone white, his eyes were dilated.

"Robson—" he gasped, "Robson, he's dead – lying dead in the parlour! Shot, the housekeeper said. And Mother Kitteridge, sir, she's dead there, as well. Both dead – lying on the parlour floor – I saw 'em! And will you go at once? We saw you pass in your car, Mr. Mallwood, and the housekeeper—"

"Were they dead, then," asked the Superintendent, "when I passed your gate?"

"No, sir – it was just after. There were two shots—"

"Who's Mother Kitteridge?" interrupted the Superintendent.

"Old woman that lived at the cottages. She'd come—"

"Hadn't we better get up there?" suggested Chaney. "Take me up in your car – Camberwell, you go into the house, tell Sir Stephen, and bring him and Ellerthorpe along. Here, boy, you follow Mr. Mallwood and me back to the farm."

In another second or two Chaney and Mallwood were off, and I ran into the house.

Sir Stephen and Mr. Ellerthorpe had left the dining room and gone into the library. The old solicitor was drawing a very easy chair up to the fire. Sir Stephen was looking for some book on one of the crowded shelves. Each turned on me in astonishment as I hurried in; Sir Stephen dropped his book; Ellerthorpe's hands left the chair; I suppose they saw, each of them, that I had news which was likely to be startling.

"Something – happened?" asked Sir Stephen.

I tried to speak as steadily as possible.

"A boy has just hurried down from Home Farm with strange news," I said. "The housekeeper sent him after Superintendent Mallwood; they had seen his car pass. He says that Robson, the farmer, and an old woman named Kitteridge—"

"Good heavens! – Mother Kitteridge!" muttered Sir Stephen. "Yes – yes?"

"Are lying dead in Robson's parlour! Shot!"

"Shot! By whom? But – is it true?"

"The boy's story seemed veracious enough," I replied. "Mallwood and Chaney have gone up to the farm already. They want us to follow."

Sir Stephen tugged at a bell-rope.

"Of course, of course," he muttered. "We'll have a car out at once. Shot? Robson and old Mother Kitteridge? What – whatever can this mean?"

"More than's on the surface," said Ellerthorpe. He turned to me. "Of course the boy didn't know anything beyond the fact that these two were shot?"

"Nothing!" I assented.

"And that they were – positively dead?"

"He said they were dead."

Ellerthorpe gave me a queer, significant look; he and I followed Sir Stephen into the hall. Within a few minutes the three of us were in a car and speeding through the darkness towards Home Farm. There were powerful lamps on that car; in their light, as we sped past, I saw people standing outside the labourers' cottages of which Chaney had spoken to me; there was already a small group of frightened and inquisitive folk at the gate and fence of Robson's farmstead. And there, too, keeping these people back, was the village policeman; the news had spread with amazing quickness. In the light of the car lamps, I got some sort of notion of Home Farm as Sir Stephen, Ellerthorpe, and I hurried across its garden. It was a big, square-built house, set in the middle of apparently well-arranged and carefully kept grounds. On its north side was a thick belt of woodland, coming to the very edge of the gardens; on its south lay an extensive range of outbuildings, barns, stables, granaries, and the like. On the side from which we had approached it lay Heronswood Park; on the other, the park and lands of Sedbury.

The front door was open, but the boy who had hurried to fetch Mallwood from Heronswood and had hastened back behind the Superintendent's car stood guard at it. He jerked a thumb over his shoulder towards an inner door which stood slightly ajar; from behind it came a murmur of subdued voices. I pushed the door wider open and walked in, followed by Sir Stephen and Ellerthorpe. I expected to be at once confronted by the evidences of the tragedy, but I was mistaken. This was a square hall, from which various doors opened. At one of these stood another policeman; Mallwood motioned towards him as my companions and I advanced.

"The doctors are in there," he whispered. "I sent straight to Sedbury for Dr. Bellender; Dr. Monro happened to be dining with him, so they both came. They'll be out presently – you can have a look then."

I had no particular desire to look at the dead man and dead woman; waiting, however, to do so, I looked at the living ones about me. There were several people in that hall. Mallwood, the Superintendent, and Chaney I knew; I made a guess that a middle-aged woman, occasionally wiping a tear from her cheeks, was Robson's housekeeper. But there was another woman there – a woman of between forty-five and fifty years, who attracted my attention: a slenderly-built, sinewy sort of woman, with strong features, sharp eyes, a determined chin, who had fastened upon Sir Stephen as soon as he crossed the threshold, and was now talking volubly to him in a quiet, practical tone.

"I was out seeing to my chickens when I heard the shots," she was saying. "There were two, in quick succession. Of course, Sir Stephen, I knew what they were, having been used to guns all my life."

"Oh, of course, of course, Mrs. Weekes," assented Sir Stephen. "Unmistakable, eh?"

"Exactly! And coming, or seeming to come, from the woods just beyond this house, I thought it must be a poaching affair. Then, in a few minutes, quite a few minutes, a boy came running, and Weekes and I set off here just as we were, to find – well, what we did find!"

"I found them," murmured the tearful woman. "I heard the shots – it was not long after Mrs. Kitteridge had called, and gone in to see Mr. Robson in the parlour – and there they were! And the window was half open at the bottom – Mr. Robson was a great one for fresh air."

"Do you mean to say they'd been shot through the window," exclaimed Sir Stephen, "from outside the house?"

"I don't think there's any doubt of that, Sir Stephen," said Mallwood. "As Miss Holt says, the window's half open at the bottom, and the curtain wasn't drawn nor the blind pulled down. I sized things up at one glance," he went on, turning to me, "and so, I reckon, did Mr. Chaney. They'd been shot dead, both of 'em, by somebody who stuck a gun through the open window from the garden outside."

"Dear, dear!" groaned Sir Stephen. "Sheer, cold-blooded murder. But—"

The door opened. The two doctors came out. Doctor-like, they had little to say, except to confirm Mallwood's opinion.

Sir Stephen, Ellerthorpe, and I went into the parlour. Half the shock had been taken away by what we had heard, but what we saw was sufficient to send my two companions back, hurriedly, to the hall without, pale and trembling. I remained; it was my job. Chaney joined me; for a minute or two we stood silent, looking about us.

It was a good big room, square-shaped, windows on two sides. On the side fronting us, where the old-fashioned fireplace was, a window set in a recess, looked out towards the woods. That was uncurtained, and the blind was not pulled down, either, but the sashes were closed. On the garden side, however, where there were two windows, one had its lower sash thrown well up; we could see the shrubs and flowers in the beds outside. And by that window there was a sort of low fence of laurel; I saw at once that it afforded good cover. Already I began to realise how the affair had been worked; the murderer had crept up to this laurel fence, listened, watched, and finally fired through the open window. And his victims had been within a few feet of his gun.

The doctors had said gunshot wounds – yes. And the effect had been instantaneous, evidently. It seemed to Chaney and me that what had happened was this: Robson had been standing on the hearth-rug; the old woman who had come to see him had, presumably, been sitting in front of him; the middle of that room was clear of all furniture except a chair, now knocked over, set in front of the fire. The first shot had been fired at the old woman; she had sunk or toppled over sideways, the chair going with her. And Robson had made a dart for the window and been instantly shot full in the face; he had spun round and collapsed, and now lay fully spread out, his head bumping the wainscotting at the foot of the windowsill. All over in a few seconds! – and then the murderer had gone quietly through the side garden, to be lost in the woods.

Chaney motioned me out of the room; we could do nothing. He got hold of Mallwood and led him outside to the garden.

"Footprints!" he said. "Let's see exactly what's beneath the window. If it's soft earth—"

But it wasn't earth; it was hard concrete or something of that sort; nothing, at any rate, that would receive an impression. All the paths in that garden were paved in that way. Still, there was soft mould in the flower beds and borders.

We left the local police and the medical men in charge and went back to Heronswood. Whatever this tragedy meant, it was at the moment impossible to guess at. But all of us were asking the same question – had it any connection with the disappearance of Sir John Maxtondale?

It was a long time before I slept that night, but I slept at last. And I was still asleep when Chaney came to my room to shake me awake.

"Get up, Camberwell!" he said "Here's work for us! And this time – Sir John!"

There was only a grey light in the room, but it sufficed to show me the expression on Chaney's face, which told me that Sir John Maxtondale had been found dead.

Chapter 5

DUTCHMAN'S CUT

CHANEY HAD COME INTO my room half-dressed and was hurrying into more clothes as he spoke. I made haste to get out of bed and reach for the nearest garments. And I was so certain of my premonition about Sir John Maxtondale's fate that I took his death for granted.

"How was it?" I asked.

"Same thing as the others," answered Chaney. "Shot through the head! Same gun, same hand, most likely. There's a very bloody and determined murderer somewhere about, Camberwell!"

"Where was the body found?" I inquired. "And who found it?"

"It was found within the last hour, at a place called Dutchman's Cut, which, they tell me, is a sort of ditch, a canal, between the lake in Heronswood Park and a sheet of water at Marston's place, Sedbury Manor. A couple of men from the colliery found him – they'd been searching that part of the district all night."

"We're going there, of course," I said.

"Young Mr. Maxtondale is waiting for us with a car," replied Chaney. "These men came here first – they told the butler, and he roused young Rupert. Queer chap, that; he seems in a devil of a temper about something or other – I can't make him out."

"Does Sir Stephen know?"

"Rupert Maxtondale's gone to tell him and Ellerthorpe. We've phoned Mallwood and sent a man to the police sergeant at Sedbury. It's a queer business, this, Camberwell – three deliberate murders within twenty-four hours! And what it all means is beyond me – at present. Yet there's one thing that seems obvious; I've fixed it up in my own mind already."

"Yes?" I asked.

"Let's call the murderer, whoever he is, X. X comes across Sir John Maxtondale on his way from Mrs. Robbins's house to Heronswood and for some reason or other murders him. Last night X discovers that the old woman, Mother Kitteridge, as they call her hereabouts, knows his secret, and he catches her splitting to Robson. So – he settles both of 'em! How's that?"

"I dare say you're not far wrong," I replied. "Fear of discovery provides a motive for the murders of last night, but what about the murder of Sir John? We know now it wasn't Robson. So – who?"

"That's got to be found out," he said. "But come on – that surly youngster's in a nasty mood already."

We hurried downstairs and to the front of the house; Rupert Maxtondale was already there, seated in a small car; he motioned us to get in.

"Sir Stephen – and Mr. Ellerthorpe?" asked Chaney.

"Coming on later," replied Rupert, gruffly. "Not dressed yet."

He went off along the drive at top speed as soon as we had taken our seats, and from thence onward took no more notice of us than if we had been a couple of suitcases. The car sped along through the park as far as the group of cottages we had noticed the previous night; there it turned off into what was little better than a rough cart-track through the woods. This led to a bridle-path, over the turf of which we ran more smoothly; it opened at last on an irregular-shaped piece of water, fringed and overshadowed on all sides by the woods, then very thick. We skirted this for some little distance until it narrowed to a point where a narrow stream, with evidently artificial banks, ran into it; then Rupert Maxtondale pulled up his car.

"Have to walk the rest," he said gruffly. "Straight ahead, under the trees."

Chaney and I took no more notice of him; he was doing something at the car. There was a narrow path beneath the overhanging branches, close to the edge of the stream; we followed it. The stream itself, some eighteen feet wide, was just a ditch of deep, black water, thickly encrusted with weeds; here and there, however, a waterlily showed itself. Although it connected two sheets of water, it seemed to be sluggish almost to stagnation, and, what with its neglected condition and the thick woods around and above its very banks, it was dark and forbidding and gave one a chilly, eerie feeling.

"Suitable spot for a murder!" muttered Chaney. "Or for hiding a murderer's work! Now, was he murdered here, or was his body brought here? That's got to be found out. There are the men!"

Some twenty yards ahead of us a little group of men stood on the path, at a point where the gloom was greatest; as we drew nearer, we saw that one of them was a gamekeeper, two farm-labourers, the other two, judging by their general appearance and cloth caps, colliers. And as we got still nearer, we saw that they were gathered about something that lay on the bank, covered by a man's greatcoat.

Rupert Maxtondale came running up behind us; together we approached the group. The gamekeeper and the labourers touched their caps; the two colliers, without ceremony, drew aside the greatcoat. Sir John Maxtondale's dead body lay before us. One glance sufficed to show that he had been shot from behind at close quarters, and after that glance Chaney motioned the men to cover up the shattered head and face. But there was something else – one of the colliers was already pointing to it. Attached to the body by stout pieces of clothesline were two weights, of the sort used on farmsteads for weighing produce; weights of twenty-eight pounds each. Four stones. Quite sufficient to keep down, under water, a man whose own weight I set down at something about fourteen.

"Just as we found him, mister," said one of the colliers. "Them weights were there, just as you see 'em! And whoever did it took care to make them knots tight – of course, the water's swelled 'em, but they'd made 'em secure, an' all!"

"Where did you find him?" asked Chaney.

The two men turned and pointed to a black patch in the water from which the weed and scum had been cleared away.

"Right there, mister! Me and Jim here," said the man who had spoken first; "we'd been searching through this wood all night, with lanterns. This morning, when it had come fairly light, we bethought us to take a careful look at this Dutchman's Cut. We got a pole and began sounding. And – well, we found him, just there, as I said. Sunk in four feet of water, close under the bank. With these weights on him, just as you see 'em."

One of the farm-labourers nodded his head.

"Them weights," he said, "is our master's."

"Who's your master?" demanded Chaney.

"Ay, well, mister, I should ha' said him as was!" replied the man. "Mr. Robson. Them weights was with a weighing-machine in a shed just the other side of this wood. Saw 'em there myself only two days ago, let alone I was using 'em in that shed last week. They've been fetched from there, they have!"

"And that piece of clothesline's been cut off a line in one of our cottages, near the steward's house," observed the other labourer. "Lay anything I could soon find out! Some woman or other could tell if her line's been cut."

An interruption came at this stage. We heard hurried, running footsteps on the path behind us and turned – to see a young woman hastening towards us: a handsome, healthy, well-set-up young woman, probably twenty-six or -seven years of age; bright of colour, flushed with running; eager-eyed. She was fully dressed, early as it was, in a smart riding-costume, boots, breeches, short coat, billycock hat, white choker; in one hand she carried a hunting-crop. She made a spot of life and colour in that gloomy, death-haunted place, but Rupert Maxtondale frowned as he saw her, and he strode forward, stifling some expletive.

"Go back, Ettie!" he snarled. "Go back! This is no place—"

The young woman paused, drawing herself up with a questioning look. Rupert Maxtondale went on to her; they exchanged a few words; it seemed to me that she resented his interference, but presently both turned back along the path towards the place where we had left the car, and disappeared.

"Who's the young lady?" asked Chaney.

"Steward's daughter – Miss Weekes," replied the gamekeeper. "Good sport, she is!"

The collier who had given us most of our information suddenly pointed to his legs.

"Me and my mate's about wet through, getting it out of that cut," he said. "I think we'd best to go and change; we were nearly up to our middles in that water. And there's naught we can do at present. The police'll be here before long – we sent another chap to the sergeant at Sedbury as soon as we found it."

"All right," agreed Chaney. "You'll be wanted for the inquest, you know."

"We know that very well, mister," said the collier. "And some nice things we expect to hear come out then! Three on 'em!" he added, as he and his companion turned away. "Never was anything o' that sort in these parts before. You'll be a detective, I reckon, mister?"

"Something of the sort," admitted Chaney. "Why?"

"Nay, I was only thinking you'd got your work cut out," said the collier. "You and the police. And here's the police coming."

Mallwood came in sight, accompanied by several of his men, and in their rear, from another car, appeared Sir Stephen Maxtondale and Mr. Ellerthorpe. The two colliers, at Chaney's suggestion, waited a few minutes, to tell their story once again; then they went off, and the rest of us began in hushed voices to discuss the situation.

A very brief examination of our immediate surroundings convinced us of certain facts. First, Sir John Maxtondale had been shot dead. The shooting had taken place at a point some twenty yards away from that stretch of Dutchman's Cut where the body was found; this was determined by traces of blood on the ground and on the bushes. This point was on the path through the woods followed by Sir John from Mrs. Robbins's house and connecting the Sedbury lands with those of Heronswood. Second, the body had been dragged from this point to a hiding-place in the undergrowth, where, judging from what we saw there, it had been left to remain some little time. Third, it had eventually been drawn from that place to the stream, in which it had been sunk with the two twenty-eight-pound weights securely attached to it. Fourth, there was no doubt that the two weights had been fetched from a shed some forty or fifty yards away, on the side of the wood, or that the piece of clothesline used to attach them to the body had been cut – clean-cut, as with a sharp knife – from a new line then in use in some cottage garden.

But there was a fifth fact – the dead man had been robbed. There was nothing left in the pockets of his clothing. At the place to which the body had first been dragged, there were two or three small matters lying about as if the murderer had tossed them carelessly aside – a handkerchief marked J. M., a box of safety-matches, a bit of lead pencil with a point-protector, a metal ring with two or three keys depending from it. But there was no purse, no watch and chain, no loose money, no pocket-book. Every pocket was empty in coat, waistcoat, trousers; one of the hip pockets in the trousers, the right-hand one, had been turned inside out. Robbery, then, as well as murder, had taken place. But had robbery been the murderer's motive?

Mr. Henry Marston joined us; he came with Mr. and Mrs. Weekes. All three apparently had hurried out of their beds and tumbled into any clothing that was handy; Mrs. Weekes had buttoned herself up in what looked like an old ulster of her husband's. Mallwood at once put a direct question to Mr. Marston.

"Can you remember, sir, if this dead gentleman was wearing a watch and chain when he was with you at Sedbury Manor?" he asked. "It's a matter of importance, if you can."

"Watch and chain?" exclaimed Mr. Marston. "I remember well enough! He was wearing the same watch and chain that he wore when I knew him as a young man – it was one that had belonged to his grandfather. That was one of the things that convinced me that he was John Maxtondale."

"You can't say, Mr. Marston, what money he had in his pockets, of course?" continued Mallwood. "Or – valuables?"

"I'll tell you what he had on him!" replied Mr. Marston, with sudden alacrity. "He'd a fistful of old gold coins – Spanish doubloons, he called 'em – he pulled 'em out of his hip pocket to show me – curiosities, you know."

"Which side hip pocket?" asked Mallwood. "Can you remember?"

Mr. Marston made an effort.

"Left!" he said. "Left – I remember that."

Muttering something to me and Chaney about wondering what was in the right-hand pocket, Mallwood turned to Sir Stephen Maxtondale.

"There's no doubt the body was robbed, Sir Stephen," he said. "It looks as if robbery had been the motive. The question is – who's the murderer?"

Rupert Maxtondale had come up to the group and was listening intently to all this. Miss Weekes had not come back with him – unless she was hovering somewhere, unseen by us, amongst the bushes.

"There's a man you might suspect!" he said suddenly. "Good reason, too, as far as I'm aware. That chap Batty!" He looked significantly at Weekes. Weekes nodded, but hesitatingly. "What do you say, Weekes?"

"Might be, Mr. Rupert," answered the steward. "There's the possibility. Of course, one doesn't like to name – names! But—"

"Who's Batty?" demanded Mallwood. "Don't keep anything back, Mr. Weekes. This is murder! And triple murder!"

"Batty's a man I had to discharge two or three weeks since," replied Weekes. "Workman on the estate – bad lot! I suspected him of poaching, too – I know he'd a gun. I meant him to clear out when I got rid of him, Sir Stephen," he went on, turning to his employer, "but I hear he's been hanging about the neighbourhood—"

"He's been lodging at Mrs. Kitteridge's," interrupted Mrs. Weekes. "I found that out only yesterday."

"Well, he's off now," remarked Rupert. "I've just been round there – it isn't a hundred yards away – to see if I could hear of him, and he's not there. You'd better be after his tracks, Mallwood."

At that point the doctors whom we had seen at Robson's farmstead, the night before, arrived, and they, Ellerthorpe, and Sir Stephen went over to the place where Sir John Maxtondale's dead body lay, still covered by the collier's greatcoat. The rest of us turned aside, talking.

"You see it's robbery?" said Mallwood, turning to Chaney. "This is how I fix it. Supposing it was this man Batty – he'd be down on his luck, of course, Mr. Weekes? Short of money, eh?"

"I should say so," replied the steward. "He'd nothing to draw when he was disengaged, at any rate."

"Well, we'll suppose it was Batty," continued Mallwood. "We'll take it he was out here with that gun Mr. Weekes says he knows he had. He shoots Sir John and robs him. Mrs. Kitteridge finds it out. Batty finds out she's found out. He tracks her to Robson's last night and, getting the idea, or perhaps overhearing their conversation and finding that she's given him away to Robson, shoots both of 'em. How's that for a theory, now?"

"A very likely one!" said Mrs. Weekes.

"What do you say?" asked Mallwood, turning to Chaney. "How does it strike you – as a theory?"

"Granted the premises, it seems a fairly sound one," replied Chaney. "But I think there's a lot of spadework to be done before you can adopt it. I, for instance, should like to hear what Batty's got to say about it. Better ask him!"

Rupert Maxtondale indulged himself with an open sneer.

"Better find him, you mean!" he said. "He's got a good many hours' start!"

Chaney turned and gave Rupert a steady stare that brought a hot flush to his cheeks, and a resentful glare to his eyes.

"I've caught a good many criminals in my time, young man, who had as many days', ay, and weeks' start as you have years on your back!" he said quietly. "I shall catch this one – if I'm asked to!"

A policeman came through the undergrowth, carrying something in his hand, which he held out to Mallwood.

"Picked this up over there, sir, near where you thought the gentleman was shot," he said. "Spent cartridge, sir. One of Wheeley and Chesson's manufacture."

Chapter 6

THE SUSPECT DISAPPEARS

MALLWOOD TURNED THE CARTRIDGE over and passed it to Chaney.

"I shouldn't wonder, considering where it was found, if that is the one," he said. "But the worst of it is that – in this part of the country, anyway – pretty nearly everybody who goes shooting uses Wheeley and Chesson's cartridges! I don't see much prospect of tracing the exact ownership of this particular one."

"Might be done," remarked Chaney. "You might do it by a good deal of patient investigation. But if I were in your shoes, Mallwood, I shouldn't give even one second's thought to it."

"No? Why, now?" asked Mallwood.

"For a simple reason," replied Chaney. "Why should the murderer bother to draw that cartridge – a cartridge, *the cartridge* – at all? And wouldn't he be a bit of a damned fool to throw it away at the actual scene of the murder?"

All that, apparently, had never occurred to Mallwood. But he put the cartridge safely away in one of his inside pockets.

"I dare say you're quite right," he said. "Still, we'll find out if any-body in the neighbourhood ever did sell any Wheeley and Chesson's to Batty. And as I can't do anything more here just now," he added, with a glance at the medical men, who were in conversation with Sir Stephen Maxtondale and Mr. Ellerthorpe, "I'll just step across to the cottages and try to get a bit of information about this man. Somebody'll know something. You'd better come along."

We followed him through the wood and across a corner of the park towards the cluster of cottages which stood near Robson's farmstead and the steward's house. Mr. and Mrs. Weekes had walked away in front of us; at their gate Mrs. Weekes turned.

"I don't suppose you gentlemen have had any breakfast," she said, hospitably. "Would you care to come in and have a cup of coffee?"

Chaney answered, promptly, for the three of us; we followed Mrs. Weekes and her husband through their garden and into the house, where, in a very comfortable and well-appointed dining room, we found Miss Weekes already breakfasting at a lavishly spread table. She showed no sign of surprise at our presence and, remarking to her mother that she'd begun her breakfast because otherwise she'd have been late for her appointment, proceeded to display a very healthy appetite.

Mrs. Weekes's notion of what she called a cup of coffee was a wide-spread one; within a few minutes she was pressing on us a variety of comestibles hot and cold – one must eat and drink, she said, whatever troubles came along. Chaney and Mallwood assented willingly; they were both good trenchermen, and the morning air had been keen. As for me, with a plateful of York ham, carved by Mrs. Weekes in wafer-like slices, and of an extraordinarily fine flavour, I became philosophical and remarked to Miss Weekes, at whose side I sat, that this was a strange world, in which the scenes of life were of such kaleidoscope-like quality that if one stood on one's feet at one moment, one might not unreasonably expect to stand on one's head at the next. I don't think she knew exactly what I meant, but she made a good pretence of doing so.

"You certainly never know what's going to happen next," she said. "Who'd ever have foreseen or expected all this awful business? However, one's got to go on with one's job, whatever happens, and I'm going to be late for mine if I don't hurry up. Mary!" she added, turning to a woman servant who was hanging about the sideboard, "tell Dick to bring the mare round to the garden gate at once – this minute."

"May one ask what the job is?" I inquired. "This isn't the hunting season!"

"The job is teaching a couple of unpromising kids to ride!" she answered. "And as they're both about as active as a couple of sacks of flour, it's a pretty thankless one. But, you see, I'm a professional, so I've got to go through with it."

"Professional – what?" I asked.

"Professional riding-mistress. Not here – London; I'm only here for a holiday. Have you never seen me in the Row? Come and see me, then, any morning – me, with a string of small girls and boys! Now I'm off!"

She hurried off through an open window; a moment later, and she was galloping across the park. I went on with my breakfast, listening to the others. They were discussing Batty, of course. At least, the steward and his wife were informing Mallwood and Chaney about Batty. Batty, it appeared, was a howling bad lot. By trade he was a carpenter and wheelwright and had been employed on the estate. Mr. Weekes had experienced much trouble with him: Batty occasionally drank, and then he absented himself from his employment. Also, Batty had a nasty temper and was not averse to using his fists. Further, he was strongly suspected of poaching, and the gamekeeper regarded him as a highly dangerous man where pheasants, partridges, and their eggs were concerned; he was all the more dangerous because he was so infernally deep and clever that neither gamekeeper, game-watchers, nor village policemen had ever been able to catch him. According to Mr. Weekes, Batty could not have remained six months on the estate but for the fact that he was the cleverest workman they had, and, when he liked, the hardest-working. But in the end Batty had become unmanageable and insolent and altogether impossible, and Mr. Weekes had been obliged to dismiss him. The Heronswood estate wanted Batty no longer – but Batty had not obliged it by going. Instead, he had hung about – that vile old hag (Mrs. Weekes took up the story at this point) Mother Kitteridge, now come to the bad end anyone who knew her would have expected, was Batty's landlady, and Batty had remained under her thatched and dilapidated roof; she and Batty, said Mrs. Weekes, used to drink together. And – there it was.

Fortified by the generous hospitality of the steward and his wife, Mallwood, Chaney, and I went after breakfast to make some inquiry concerning Batty. There were some half-dozen cottages close by, all tenanted by folk employed on the estate, and their occupants were all agog with the current excitement. But not a soul amongst them knew anything about Batty. All that we gained in the way of news of him was that he had not been seen about the neighbourhood for the last few days. No one was able to say, positively, when or where he or she had seen Batty last; Batty, to cut the thing short, was gone – somewhere. But where, or when, nobody knew.

Chaney and I went back to Heronswood after this inquiry; we wanted to know what Sir Stephen Maxtondale wished us to do. Sir John Maxtondale had been found; the local police authorities had begun and were actively pursuing inquiries into the circumstances of his murder and the murders of Robson and Mrs. Kitteridge; we were not sure if our services were further required. But on arriving at the house and seeing Mr. Ellerthorpe, we found that Sir Stephen wished us to remain there for a while; at any rate until the inquest had been opened. That had already been fixed for next day; something might come out then in the elucidation of which our services might be useful. So we hung about the estate, trying to pick up and piece together any scrap of evidence that seemed to bear on the murders. But when Chaney and I retired that night, we were about as wise as when we had arisen the previous morning.

"That Batty theory, Camberwell, is all so much moonshine!" declared Chaney, coming into my room for a final chat. "All rot, my son! Not worth following up for two seconds!"

"No belief in it, eh, Chaney?" I said.

"Belief in it? – bah! Camberwell, if Batty by murdering Sir John Maxtondale for the sake of robbery had come into possession of whatever money and valuables Sir John had on him, however much, however little, he'd have been out of this neighbourhood within the hour! Sure!"

"How do we know he wasn't?" I asked. "Perhaps he was!"

"Then who killed Robson and the old woman?" he demanded. "If Batty killed Sir John, robbed him, and hooked it, it isn't likely he'd return next day to shoot Robson and Mother Kitteridge. No – no! All three murders were the work of the same hand, and that hand wasn't Batty's. The more I think of it, the more I'm convinced, Camberwell, that the thing will work out like this: Whoever shot Sir John Maxtondale, shooting, too, to kill, had some strong motive! What that motive was we can't even guess at, yet. But it was a powerful one. As to the two succeeding murders, they're easily accounted for. Child's play!"

"Well?" I asked, wanting him to put it in plain words. "Say it!"

"Say? Lord! – anybody can see why Robson and the old woman were murdered! You can put it in a few syllables. They knew the murderer's secret! So – they had to be silenced."

"Doesn't all that seem to show that the murderer must be somebody living hereabouts?" I suggested.

"Possibly. Not conclusively. Sir John may have been followed. But it's all guesswork, yet. Of course, there's always this to be remembered, Camberwell: whenever anything of this sort happens, especially in a rural community, you may always be sure that there are people who are in possession of knowledge – sometimes a great deal of knowledge – but who will not speak. Then again, there are always people who have very strong suspicions; people who, if they liked to voice their suspicions, could give most valuable help to the police, and – won't! Just won't! Lots of cases like that, in my experience."

"Have you come across anybody here that you'd place in either of those categories, Chaney?" I asked.

He was silent for a few minutes, pulling thoughtfully at his pipe.

"Well," he said at last, shaking his head, "it wouldn't do to say so to anybody but you, but I have an idea, a feeling, that that surly young dog Mr. Rupert Maxtondale either knows or suspects something. He's damned uneasy in his mind – I'll swear that. I've watched him carefully – and when we get back to town, I'll continue to watch him."

"How do you mean – back to town?" I asked.

"He lives in town," he answered. "At least, most of his time. He's engaged, in some way, at the London offices of the Heronswood colliery – family representative, I suppose. Like that little horse-riding girl, he's only down here on a holiday. I'll have him looked after when I get back."

"Good Lord!" said I. "Sir John was his uncle! You don't suspect—"

"Suspect nothing, my lad! But he may suspect somebody! That's different. If he knows anything, I want to know what he knows. If he suspects somebody, I want to know who it is he suspects."

"He seemed to be pretty thick with the steward's daughter," I remarked.

"Ah, pretty girl!" said Chaney; "very pretty!" He stifled a big yawn. "Well, I'm for bed, Camberwell. Tomorrow – yes, the inquest opens. We may hear something – something."

But up to noon of the following day we had heard nothing. The local police had been very busy; so, too, had the brigade of searchers marshalled by the manager of the Heronswood colliery. The district had been pretty well combed over, and nothing had come to light. As to Batty, no one could tell anything of him – that is, as regarding his whereabouts. Still, Mallwood had secured some slight information about him. An ironmonger at Monkseaton had been unearthed who was prepared to swear that Batty had frequently bought Wheeley and Chesson's cartridges from him, and that the last purchase had been made about a week before the murders. Then there was some information from the Partridge and Pointer inn at Sedbury – an establishment which Batty was in the habit of frequenting. Batty had been there about six o'clock on the very evening on which Sir John Maxtondale arrived at Mr. Marston's house. He was in his best clothes; he was quite sober; he stayed only a quarter of an hour and contented himself with one glass of beer; the best clothes and the unusual abstinence made the host of the Partridge and Pointer incline to the opinion that Batty was going somewhere on business – probably to find a new job. But since then nobody in the neighbourhood of Monkseaton, Sedbury, and Heronswood had seen Batty or heard of him; whether he had returned to his quarters at Mother Kitteridge's after leaving the Partridge and Pointer was a question which nobody could answer. Batty had just disappeared – but, as Mallwood remarked, there was plenty about him in the newspapers, and somebody would unearth him, sooner or later.

As a matter of fact, the newspapers were having a very good time over the Heronswood mystery. On the staff of the Monkseaton Standard, a typical local weekly, there happened to be two youthful reporters whose souls hungered for a chance to rise above the writing-up of football matches and flower-shows; the triple tragedy of Heronswood afforded them an opportunity which was scarcely likely to happen again, and before the London press could hurry representatives to the spot, these two were deluging the press agencies with floods of enthralling copy. In fact, the entire newspaper press of England was full of Heronswood and its problem. There was not only letterpress, set to the best advantage with wide leads and big cover-headings; the picture element came in hot and strong. Pictures of Sedbury Manor and Heronswood Park, Home Farm and Mother Kitteridge's cottage; Dutchman's Cut and Mrs. Robbins's house; the Partridge and Pointer and the ironmonger's shop at Monkseaton. And there were photographs – Sir Stephen Maxtondale; Superintendent Mallwood; Robson's housekeeper; the two miners who found Sir John's body; Mrs. Robbins, as the last person who saw Sir John alive; Mr. Marston – and, last, Batty, from a snapshot taken by one of his mates in the carpenter's shop at Heronswood.

Needless to say, all this widespread publicity brought crowds of people to the opening of the inquest, which was held in the school-room at Sedbury, that being the largest place available. Not a tenth of the assembly could get inside it; those of us who did were most uncomfortable. Mallwood said that the proceedings would be very brief; the Coroner would hear absolutely necessary evidence and then adjourn for a week or ten days. But the Coroner, an elderly and ev- idently very punctilious gentleman, showed, when he had once got to work with his twelve good men and true, that he was avid for information. He was curious to know if it had been really established that the man who called on Mr. Marston was, without doubt, the real and genuine Sir John Maxtondale, ninth baronet, and he bad- gered Mr. Marston with questions until that worthy countryman grew restive and made certain sarcastic remarks which the Coroner did not appreciate. Scarcely less restive and sarcastic was Mrs. Robbins, who retorted to a direct question that she might not be able to tell one pea from another, but wasn't likely not to know a Maxtondale that she'd been a second mother to. And just as the Coroner was becoming convinced about the man found murdered and hidden in the black waters of Dutchman's Cut, a police constable forced his way into the place and whispered to Mallwood, who, on the instant, rose and beckoned Chaney and me to follow him from the room. In a little anteroom, he turned to us.

"There's a man in a car outside who says he's come straight from London to give evidence," he said. "Name of Rosenbaum. Do you know anything of him?"

Chaney plunged a hand into his pocket and from a mass of papers produced Chippendale's telegram. One glance at it and he nodded.

"That's it!" he said. "Rosenbaum. One of the tenants at that place in Hatton Garden. Let's see him."

We went out into the street. There, at the door of the schoolroom, surrounded by an inquisitive crowd, was a very smart and powerful car, at the wheel of which sat a man in a big travelling-coat, out of the fur collar of which protruded a fresh-coloured countenance of the Hebraic cast.

"Mr. Rosenbaum?" said Mallwood.

"Same!" replied Mr. Rosenbaum. "I hurried down here because of what I've read in the papers. I know this Sir John Maxtondale as Mr. Maxton – slight dealings with him. Now, in a word – were any diamonds, cut or uncut, found on him?"

"Diamonds?" exclaimed Mallwood. "No indeed! Had he diamonds?"

Mr. Rosenbaum cast aside a hundred-guinea rug and prepared to alight.

"My good sir!" he said; "I saw Maxton off from Euston. When he left Euston station for Monkseaton, he had thirty thousand pounds' worth of diamonds in his pocket!"

Chapter 7

DIAMONDS!

Mr. Rosenbaum's emphatic assertion produced different effects upon the three of us who had come out to him. As for myself, I seemed to get a sudden light on what had till then been a very puzzling case; the fact – if it was a fact – that Sir John Maxtondale was carrying thirty thousand pounds' worth of precious stones on his person put a very different complexion on the matter. But Chaney showed no surprise and made no comment; his face could not have been more impassive had our new informant told us that he knew nothing. Mallwood, however, started; his astonished exclamation came naturally.

"God bless my soul!" he said. "You don't mean it? Thirty thousand pounds' worth of diamonds? In his pocket? No mistake?"

"Take my oath on it if you like," replied Rosenbaum. "I know! That's why I'm here. For the diamonds are – somewhere."

"Better step inside, see the Coroner, and tell him what Mr. Rosenbaum says," suggested Chaney. "On the ground of motive, his evidence will come in handy. You've no objection to giving evidence?" he continued, turning to Rosenbaum.

Rosenbaum spread his hands – encased in heavily furred driving-gloves.

"My good sir!" he said; "it is what I came for! You can't hear of thirty thousand pounds' worth of diamonds being lost in that way! It's time something was being done to find them."

Mallwood hurried back into the schoolroom; within a few minutes he returned, to usher the newcomer into court and introduce him to the Coroner, after a few whispered words with whom, Rosenbaum entered the witness-box. He took the oath after the fashion of his people and proceeded to tell us who and what he was: Marcus Rosenbaum, dealer in precious stones, of Hatton Garden, London – business address – and Acacia Cottage, Beckenham, Kent – private residence.

"I understand you can give the court some highly important evidence in respect to the deceased Sir John Maxtondale, Mr. Rosenbaum?" said the Coroner. "You have travelled some distance to do so, I believe?"

"All the way, top speed – when permitted – from Beckenham," replied Rosenbaum. "Set off as soon as I saw the papers this morning, before breakfast. As to Sir John Maxtondale, what I can tell is that I believe – from what I have read – that a man I have recently known in London as Mr. John Maxton is identical with the Sir John Maxtondale into the cause of whose death you are inquiring – sure of it!"

One of the legal gentlemen present rose to his feet.

"I should suggest, Mr. Coroner, that the witness be taken to see the body of Sir John," he said. "Positive identification—"

"I have already thought of that," remarked the Coroner, "but that would necessitate a journey to Heronswood and back. I think we had better hear what the witness has to say, and he can be afforded an opportunity of identification later on. What leads you to think, Mr. Rosenbaum, that the man you knew as John Maxton is really Sir John Maxtondale?"

"Several things," replied Rosenbaum. "The description of him in the papers. Similarity in the names. But also because when I parted from him at Euston station a few mornings ago, he told me that he was travelling down to Monkseaton to see an old friend or two."

"Did he give you the names of the friends?"

"He mentioned one, Mr. Henry Marston, of Sedbury Manor. He said they'd been boys together and hadn't met for many years."

The legal gentleman who had spoken before spoke again.

"What made him mention Mr. Marston to you?"

"We'd been talking about hunting in the shires. He said Mr. Marston was a great sportsman."

The Coroner took hold again.

"Tell us what you know of Mr. Maxton – as we'll call him for the present. How did you get to know him?"

"This way: He wrote to me from the Waldorf Hotel, telling me that he had a letter of introduction to me from a client of mine in South America – Mr. Gerharrts, of Rio de Janeiro – and would I please call on him? I did so. He told me that he had recently returned from Brazil and had brought with him a quantity of diamonds which he wished to dispose of in London. He showed them to me. Some were cut; some uncut. I valued the lot at thirty thousand pounds."

"Do you mean that you would have given that amount for them?" asked the Coroner.

"I would have given that amount for them, yes."

"You didn't buy them?"

"We made no arrangement. All I was asked at the time was for an expression of opinion as to the value."

"Was that the only time you saw Mr. Maxton?"

"No; on the morning of May 14th I met him accidentally, in Euston station. He told me where he was going – to see his old friend Mr. Henry Marston at Sedbury Manor, near Monkseaton. He was travelling by the noon train – the twelve o'clock. He had come to the station much too soon – half an hour too soon – and as the train was already drawn up at a platform, I got into the restaurant car with him, to talk a bit."

"About the diamonds?"

"About the diamonds, certainly."

"Did you see them again?"

"Yes; I made another very careful inspection of them."

"Still estimating their value at—"

"At my original figure."

"What did he do with them after your inspection?"

"Put them back where he had taken them from – his right-hand hip pocket. He carried them in an old leather wallet."

"Then, when Mr. Maxton left Euston, he had those diamonds on him?"

"He had them where I have said: in the hip pocket, right-hand side, of his trousers."

"You never heard of or from him again, Mr. Rosenbaum?"

"I never heard from him, nor of him until things began coming out in the papers."

"Well," said the Coroner, "there is just another question. Do you know if Mr. Maxton was negotiating with or showing these diamonds to anyone else?"

"Not that I am aware of," replied Rosenbaum. "He never told me, if he was. You see, I had been recommended to him."

The Coroner seemed to have nothing more to ask, but a local solicitor, who had been commissioned by Mr. Ellerthorpe, on behalf of Sir Stephen Maxtondale, to watch the proceedings, began to question the witness.

"You say, Mr. Rosenbaum, that you valued these diamonds at the sum of thirty thousand pounds, and that you would have given that for them?"

"Yes, that is so."

"Did you tell Mr. Maxton that?"

"I told him I'd give him thirty thousand – yes."

"But you told the Coroner just now that all you were asked to do was to give an opinion as to their value. Is that so?"

"Exactly! But I gave it in that form. I said: 'I'm willing to give thirty thousand pounds for them.' "

"That was an offer. I want to know what Mr. Maxton replied."

"Oh, well – he thought they were worth more."

"That's what I wanted to get at. Now, what did he think they were worth?"

"Well, he thought he ought to get forty thousand for them."

"So that when you say the diamonds were worth thirty thousand pounds, what you really mean is that they were worth thirty thousand to you – to buy and sell again? Is that it?"

"You can put it that way."

"What I'm wanting to get at, Mr. Rosenbaum, is the actual worth of these diamonds. What was it?"

"Put it at something between the two figures," said Rosenbaum.

"Mr. Maxton might have found some other gentleman in your trade to give him forty thousand?"

"He might, but the other fellow wouldn't have made much profit."

"Well, did you renew your offer when you encountered Mr. Maxton at Euston station?"

"Yes, I said I was willing to buy at the price I'd formerly named."

"And – he replied what?"

"Think it over while he was away."

"You are positive about his carrying the diamonds off with him on that journey to Monkseaton?"

Mr. Rosenbaum smiled.

"Unless he threw them out of the window or left them on the carriage floor or on his table in the restaurant car, he had them when he reached Monkseaton," he answered. "The last thing he did while I was there was to put them back in his old leather wallet and place that in his right-hand hip pocket. And," added Rosenbaum, slapping the ledge of the witness-box, "whoever murdered him has got them – of course!"

"Can you give any description of these diamonds, Mr. Rosenbaum?" inquired the Coroner.

"A rough, general one, sir. Some of the stones – most of them – were uncut; a few were cut; I shall be happy to give any information in my power."

"There's just one matter I might refer to," continued the Coroner. "Hatton Garden, I believe, is the centre of the diamond trade in London. Did you ever see Mr. Maxton there?"

"Never, sir. Indeed, he told me he did not know its whereabouts. As I told you, he had a letter of introduction to me, and instead of presenting it in person, he forwarded it by post and asked me to call on him."

"And you don't know if he had any transactions with any other person in London?"

"I do not."

The Coroner turned to the jurymen.

"I think this will be a convenient stage at which to adjourn," he said. "Mr. Rosenbaum's evidence puts a fresh aspect on the case—"

Sir Stephen Maxtondale was whispering to his solicitor; the Coroner paused. The solicitor rose.

"Before Mr. Rosenbaum leaves the box, sir, I should like to ask him another question. Mr. Rosenbaum, during your conversations with him did Mr. Maxton tell you anything about his past? Did he, for instance, say where he had lived?"

"Only that he had lived for some years in South America – Brazil chiefly. He evidently knew Brazil very well – the diamond mines there – Minas Geraes, Paraná, and so on."

"But nothing else – nothing as to his private affairs?"

"No, no, nothing!"

"And – he didn't confide to you that he was really Sir John Maxtondale?"

"He certainly did not tell me that!" replied Rosenbaum. "Oh, no!"

The Coroner formally adjourned the inquiry at this point, and Mr. Rosenbaum presently went away with Mallwood to identify Sir John Maxtondale's dead body, Sir Stephen and Mr. Ellerthorpe following them. Chaney and I, walking back across the park, fell to discussing Rosenbaum's evidence and its value and significance in relation to the murders.

"What do you make of all that, Camberwell?" he asked, as we left the village and its still gaping and wondering crowds – "taking the diamond man's word for it."

"I saw no reason to doubt his word," I answered. "I watched him closely, and I should set him down as a thoroughly reliable witness."

"Very good – all gospel truth," he said. "Then – what's it amount to?"

I had been thinking that question over ever since Rosenbaum stepped out of the box. For what did his evidence amount to? Or, rather, what did it imply?

"I suppose," I replied, "that it really amounts to a suggestion that somebody in London knew that Sir John Maxtondale – Mr. Maxton – carried a pocketful of diamonds, followed him down here, murdered him, and robbed him. Is that about it?"

"That's precisely about it!" agreed Chaney. "Well? I'm wanting to know what you think of that little theory?"

"I can't adopt it," I answered.

"Why?"

"Because of the subsequent murders, Chaney. If some man followed Maxton, as we'll call him, down here and murdered and robbed him, why should that man hang about for more than twenty-four hours to murder Robson and Mrs. Kitteridge? I think the murderer of Maxton would have got away with his booty there and then. What on earth should a man who knew of Maxton's possession of diamonds, and who killed Maxton to get them, know of Robson or the old woman?"

"Sure, I agree with you," he said. "But that doesn't prove that Maxton was not followed from London, watched, tracked next morning to Dutchman's Cut, and there murdered and robbed. That, Camberwell, in view of Rosenbaum's story is quite a good theory."

"What of the other murders, then?" I asked.

"Ah, now we come to the really big question!" he replied. "Just this – had the murders of Robson and Mrs. Kitteridge any relation whatever to the murder of Sir John Maxtondale? See what I'm after?"

"Coincidence, I suppose," I answered. "The long-arm business."

"There's a lot more of coincidence than most people would believe," he said. "I've seen no end of it in my time. It would be a coincidence, of course, that these two murders followed so quickly on the other, in the same neighbourhood. But it is possible that the murders of Robson and Mother Kitteridge have no relation whatsoever to the murder of Sir John Maxtondale."

"Possible, yes," I agreed. "But what do you really think, yourself, Chaney?"

He hesitated a little before replying.

"I should like to know a lot more," he answered at last. "I should like to know about Sir John's doings in London between his arrival there and his visit to Mr. Marston. I should like to know more about Robson, and about Mrs. Kitteridge, and Mrs. Kitteridge's lodger, Batty. I should like—"

Here we turned a corner of the woods and encountered Mallwood's car bringing him and Rosenbaum back from Heronswood. We all stopped.

"Mr. Rosenbaum has positively identified the body," announced Mallwood.

"Oh, no doubt about it!" said Rosenbaum. "That is the man I knew as Mr. Maxton. Not a doubt!"

"What do you make of this, Mallwood?" asked Chaney. "In view of Mr. Rosenbaum's evidence, I mean."

Mallwood had evidently made up his mind. He spoke with decision.

"What I think," he replied, "is that Batty shot Sir John and robbed the dead body; that somehow Mrs. Kitteridge got possession of the secret; that Batty suspected her of splitting to Robson; and that, catching them together, he shot them both and decamped."

"You feel sure of that?" suggested Chaney. "That's your line?"

"That's my line! And," concluded Mallwood, "I shall catch Batty!"

Chaney turned to the diamond merchant.

"You'll be returning to town, Mr. Rosenbaum, at once, I suppose?" he said. "Well, if you'll be so kind, you can help us. Make all the inquiry you can amongst your friends and business acquaintances as to whether Sir John Maxtondale, or Mr. Maxton, showed those diamonds to others. And if you learn anything, let me and my partner know – here's our address in town."

He gave Rosenbaum our professional card; Rosenbaum promised his aid; and he and Mallwood drove off. And Chaney gave me one of his knowing looks.

"Now we know Mallwood's line!" he said, chuckling. "Of course, it's the one and only line Mallwood would take. Well – let's wait a bit."

We had not to wait long. That evening we got a telephone message from Mallwood, informing us that Batty had been arrested at Winckley and was being brought to Monkseaton.

Chapter 8

THE RESTAURANT CAR

CHANEY'S FIRST PROCEDURE ON hearing of Batty's arrest was to inquire as to the whereabouts of Winckley. Winckley, we were told, was a small place about twenty miles away, whereupon Chaney shook his head, and I knew what the gesture meant. Batty, in Chaney's opinion, had he been murderer and thief, would have put more than twenty miles between himself and the scene of his misdeeds in the time available.

We went into Monkseaton next morning as interested spectators of whatever might happen. The court-house, of course, was packed and the magistrates' bench full, but what interested me more than anything else was a group of men, all evidently roughish characters, but dressed in their best clothes, which had arranged itself in a prominent position and was being marshalled and generally superintended by a sharp-looking young fellow who was, we were told, clerk to a certain Monkseaton solicitor of great reputation with the ne'er-do-well portion of the community.

"I've a pretty good idea as to what's going to happen," muttered Chaney, watching this group. "Mallwood has been a bit too previous. If he'd made some quiet inquiry—"

The magistrates came in, packing the bench; Batty's case was called at once. And Batty appeared in the dock. I came to the instant conclusion that Batty, however innocent he might be of this charge, was a particularly bad lot – a low-down, swaggering, defiant, and truculent no-good. He came into view with all the arrogance and conceit of a stage villain and accompanied his plea with a smothered expletive which, luckily, caught nobody's ear. I could see, too, that for two pins the group of men I have already referred to would have burst into cheers on his behalf; it was only the strenuous efforts of the solicitor's clerk in charge of them that kept them quiet.

And now what was there against Batty? Mallwood had raked up some evidence. Batty had been discharged from his employment on the Heronswood estate for bad conduct and drunkenness. There was evidence that instead of going away he had hung about, lodging with Mrs. Kitteridge, and was hard up for funds – two men proved that he had tried to borrow money from them just previous to the date of the first murder. Then there was the fact of the Wheeley and Chesson cartridges – a Monkseaton tradesman dealing in such things said that he had sold Batty a box of such cartridges not very long before.

This was the only witness that Batty's solicitor – the aforesaid practitioner highly popular with local offenders – condescended to question.

"Look at that cartridge!" commanded this gentleman. "Take it in your hand – look at it well! Now, on your oath, is that a cartridge you sold to the accused? On your oath, now!"

The witness turned a somewhat indignant glance in the direction of his peremptory questioner.

"How on earth can I say that?" he demanded, almost angrily. "How can I tell one cartridge from another?"

"Answer my question! Did you sell that cartridge to the man in the dock?"

"I can't say! – you know I can't say. I sold him a box of cartridges. This may have been—"

"Never mind may have been! Can you swear that you sold him that particular cartridge? Yes or no?"

"No, then! I sold him—"

"Attend to me! Do you, in the course of your business, sell a lot of these cartridges – Wheeley and Chessons?"

"Yes – in large quantities."

"Used for sporting guns, aren't they?"

"Of course! That's what they are for."

"Lots of customers in the neighbourhood, then?"

"Yes."

"I'll mention a few names. Lord Winckley? Sir Charles Topdale? Sir William Bivers? Supply all of 'em, eh? And a lot of other people, too, no doubt. Do you supply Sir Stephen Maxtondale?"

"Yes, occasionally."

"And his son, Mr. Rupert Maxtondale?"

"Yes."

"And Sir Stephen's gamekeeper?"

"Yes."

"And Sir Stephen's steward, Mr. Weekes?"

"Yes."

"All with this particular sort – Wheeley and Chesson?"

"Yes, I've said already those cartridges have a big sale round here."

"But these people I've mentioned, Sir Stephen Maxtondale, his son, his steward, his gamekeeper, buy them regularly?"

"Yes, that's so, certainly."

"Then it wouldn't surprise you at all to hear of a Wheeley and Chesson's cartridge being picked up at any time, anywhere, on the Heronswood estate?"

The witness smiled.

"I should think thousands of empty cartridges are picked up there in the course of a year," he replied. "They buy plenty!"

The solicitor held out a hand.

"Give me that cartridge-case back!" he said. The next instant with a contemptuous gesture he had tossed the case across the table and had turned to the bench. "Your Worship," he began, "I am going to show that this is one of the most ridiculous and foolish prosecutions which the obstinacy and stupidity of the police authorities have ever urged them to undertake; in plain language, my defence is an alibi, and of such a nature that it will be absolutely impossible to disregard it. Call Superintendent Mallwood!"

Mallwood obeyed this summons with every appearance of disapproval and surprise, but his ordeal was very brief. All the defending solicitor wanted was to get from him, officially, the exact dates, times, and whereabouts of the murders. And having got what he wanted, he proceeded to prove, in the most unmistakable fashion, that from five o'clock in the afternoon of the day preceding Sir John Maxtondale's arrival at Sedbury Manor until the moment of his arrest at Winckley, Batty was never within so many miles of Dutchman's Cut or Heronswood Home Farm. One by one some eight or ten men were called into the witness-box; the alibi, as its setter-up had said, was not to be challenged. True, the police tried to challenge the credibility of good faith of certain of these witnesses, but there were two or three – of whom one was the landlord of a Winckley inn at which Batty had put himself up – whose testimony was unimpeachable. And in the end Batty was discharged, and he left the dock and the court with his body-guard of friends openly derisive of Mallwood and his satellites.

And now came an episode which, though none of us guessed it at the time, was to have an important influence on the development of these problems – and of their ultimate solution. It was, I suppose, Batty being what he was, only natural that in the first flush of his triumph he and his phalanx of supporters from Winckley (he was a Winckley man, as it turned out, and evidently a popular one amongst his fellow-townsfolk of a sort) should turn into the nearest public-house to celebrate the discomfiture of the police. That, at any rate, was what they did, with the result that an hour later they emerged into the street still more flushed. And then Batty, by ill-luck, came across Weekes, the steward, and, after abusing him, fell upon him. Half an hour later, Batty found himself back in the dock, for the magistrates were still sitting, and the police put their man up at once. And that night Batty did not return to Winckley; instead, he went off to a month's hard labour at the county jail, swearing vengeance on Weekes, Mallwood, and everybody concerned.

We appeared now to be exactly where we were before the arrest of Batty, but on the very next day we got some fresh information. While Chaney and I were consulting with Sir Stephen Maxtondale and Mr. Ellerthorpe as to our next procedure, Mallwood rang us up, asking if we would at once go over to Monkseaton. Arrived at his office, we found him closeted with a smart, alert, well-dressed young fellow whom I thought I recognised and who turned out, on introduction, to be a waiter attached to the restaurant car of the noon train from Euston to Monkseaton.

"This young man has got a day off to come and give some information," said Mallwood. "I thought you'd like to hear it. His name's Albert Strepp, and he's on the first-class restaurant car on that train by which Sir John Maxtondale travelled when he came down to see Mr. Marston. He remembers him – and a good deal else. Tell your tale again, Strepp."

Strepp, who had been making a shrewd-eyed examination of Chaney and me, smiled, as if in depreciation of his powers of narrative.

"Why, I don't know that there's so very much to tell, gentlemen," he said. "Of course, I've read the newspapers about this affair, and as soon as I'd seen the first accounts there, I knew the murdered gentleman was one that came down here to Monkseaton by my train – I remembered him well enough for more than one reason."

"Gave you a good tip, no doubt?" suggested Chaney.

Strepp smiled again – knowingly.

"Well, he certainly did that, sir – he gave me two tips, as a matter of fact – one when he paid his bill for lunch, and the other when I saw him out of the car at Monkseaton. But there were other reasons. He came early to the train – it's always drawn up at Number Fifteen platform some time before it's due to start; he came at about twenty minutes to twelve, which is the scheduled time. And he had a gentleman with him who wasn't travelling—"

"How did you know he wasn't travelling?" asked Chaney.

"Because I asked them if they'd be taking lunch, sir. The first gentleman said he would, but the other said no, he wasn't going on; he'd just got in to talk to his friend till the train was due out. I made a mental note of that because the train was very full that morning, and I knew I should want the seat which the second gentleman had sat down in."

"Well, that second gentleman – can you describe him?" inquired Chaney.

"Yes, sir – he was, I should say, a Jewish gentleman – middle-aged, dark, very well dressed – City man, I should have taken him for."

"Did you notice anything that happened while he remained in the carriage?"

"Just a bit, sir: I was passing up and down, finding seats for people – some of the seats were already engaged. Once, in passing them, I saw the first gentleman showing the other what looked to be diamonds. They had them spread out on the table between them."

"A lot of diamonds?"

"Well, I couldn't say as to a lot, sir. They were diamonds, anyway – sparkled like 'em, at any rate."

"Diamonds such as you see in jewellers' shop-windows, eh?"

"Just that, sir. The gentleman had a queer-looking old pocket book lying on the table, too."

"I suppose you just observed that, in passing along the carriage?"

"That was it, sir. Next time I was along, there wasn't anything on the table – I mean no diamonds."

"When did the Jewish gentleman get out?"

"Just before the train started; a minute or so to twelve o'clock. As he got out, another gentleman came in – at the last minute, so to speak. He wanted a seat and lunch. I'd only that seat left, so I gave it to him."

"The restaurant car was very full, then?"

"Every seat taken, sir, when we started."

"Were there many people in the car when the first gentleman was showing the diamonds to the second?"

"Several, sir. Some had got into their seats, and some were jostling about the gangway."

"Then several people could have seen these diamonds?"

"No reason why they shouldn't, sir. They were in full view."

"Well, about the man who came in at the last minute, Strepp. Did you know him?"

"No, sir, not at all. I've been on that train for three years, and I know a great many travellers by sight, but I didn't know him."

"What did you take him for? I suppose you're a pretty good hand at sizing people up?"

"Pretty fair, sir, I think. I took him for one of the better-class sort of commercial travellers."

"Can you describe him?"

"Fairly well, sir. About thirty to thirty-five; medium height; dark hair and moustache; dark complexion; black morning coat and vest and striped trousers – smart sort of fellow, sir."

"Well, you say he sat at the same table with the first gentleman. Did you notice if they entered into conversation?"

"Oh, yes, sir. They were talking when I began to serve lunch. They continued to talk. When I brought the coffee, the first gentleman offered the other a cigar out of a case he took from his pocket. They went on talking over their coffee – in fact, they were talking all the way. The first gentleman – the one I came to tell about – seemed, if I may put it so, a very sociable sort of gentleman, sir."

"Well, talking all the way, you say – you mean, till the first gentleman got out, at Monkseaton?"

"They both got out at Monkseaton, sir."

"Oh, they did, did they? Both? Um – now look here. Did you see any more of those diamonds after the Jewish gentleman had left – before the train started?"

"No, sir."

"Never saw the first gentleman show them to this man who shared his table?"

"No, sir!"

"Do you think he'd time to do so when you weren't about? You'd be going backward and forward, you know, between the car and the kitchen."

"Yes, sir, but I was never more than a minute or two out of the car. I never saw the diamonds again, after we left Euston."

"Well, just one more question, Strepp. Did you notice anything that made you think these two had met before? I mean what you've been calling the first gentleman and the man you took for a commercial traveller?"

"Oh, no, sir! They were strangers, I'm sure."

"Did you overhear any of their conversation?"

"Scraps, sir. Weather – crops – that sort of thing. Once I heard the elder gentleman saying something about cattle-hunting in South America."

"You haven't seen the commercial-traveller man since on the train?"

"No, sir. And I never remember seeing him before."

"And he got out, with the first gentleman, at Monkseaton? That, of course, was the last you saw of either?"

"The last I saw of them, sir, through the window, as the train went on, was that they were walking along the platform together, with a porter behind, carrying the second gentleman's suitcases."

"Still in conversation?"

"I took them to be so, sir."

That was the end of our interview with Albert Strepp, who was thanked and dismissed with an admonition to keep his eyes open for the gentleman who had shared Mr. Maxton's table. When he was gone, Mallwood looked inquiringly at Chaney.

"Well?" he said. "Make anything of it?"

"Might make a good deal," answered Chaney. "Who's the second man? He got out at Monkseaton."

"Hundreds of people get out at Monkseaton in the course of the day!" remarked Mallwood, lugubriously. "How on earth am I to find any particular one?"

"Ah!" said Chaney. "Stiff question, isn't it?"

He and I left Mallwood and went out into the street. Opposite was the local newspaper office where the two reporters I have already mentioned were employed. Chaney suddenly gripped my arm.

"Camberwell," he said, "the press is a great power! Come across the way!"

Chapter 9

POWER OF THE PRESS

We found the two young reporters in their professional quarters and not particularly engaged, and, it being close upon lunchtime, Chaney, who always had his own way of doing anything, asked them to accompany us to the Maxtondale Arms, supplementing his invitation by a hint that he had something good to put in their way. Having already done very well out of the Heronswood mystery, the young gentlemen were by no means loath to accept this offer of hospitality and were keen enough to get the news. But Chaney said nothing until he had fed them with the best available; then, in a quiet corner, over cigars and coffee, he said his say.

"I've no doubt you boys could do with a bit more stuff for your paper?" he suggested. "Real pie this has been for you, what?"

"We certainly don't get first-class murder mysteries in our weekly bill of fare, Mr. Chaney," replied the senior of the two. "Never remember a murder hereabouts since I came to Monkseaton three years ago."

"Well, you've made the most of it – very good stuff in your paper," continued Chaney. "Intelligent – practical. And the stuff you sent to the press agencies – very good, too. Of course, I suppose they boiled that down a bit?"

"Edited it, Mr. Chaney, edited it!" said the junior reporter, smiling.

"Sub-edited it," said the senior. "Considerably! Still – but what's the new stuff, Mr. Chaney? Fresh development?"

Chaney puffed his cigar a bit.

"Do you think, now, you could get something into the big papers – London morning papers, you know – big provincial dailies and so on – that they wouldn't edit, as you call it? Something that I'd dictate? Of course, I'm no pressman, and I don't know how these things are done, but I want to get an appeal in the papers and not as a cut and dried advertisement, eh?"

"In plain language, Mr. Chaney, you want the London and provincial press to assist you in the solving of this problem?" said the senior reporter. "Well, sir, on behalf of the press, I say – yes, the press will!"

"You can speak for that?" questioned Chaney.

"In a matter of such importance, yes! The press, sir, will do all it can to assist. Consider me as the press, Mr. Chaney."

"And me," added the junior. "Quite right. Matter of duty."

"Good lads!" said Chaney. "Well, now, look here! I'm going to tell you the tale of some recent discoveries. You heard the evidence of Mr. Marcus Rosenbaum at the opening of the inquest? Now we go on from that to something in the way of a supplement—"

"Do you want us to take it down, Mr. Chaney?" interrupted the senior, feeling for a notebook.

"No, no – this isn't for print – it's just to explain matters," replied Chaney. "It'll show you what I want done. Now, this morning, just before we called on you . . ." he went on to retell Strepp's story, emphasising the important points. "Now, this is what I want working through the press, as widely as possible – I want to get hold of the man in the train or to learn something about him – the man, you know, who sat at the table with Sir John Maxtondale, talked with him, got out of the train with him at Monkseaton. That man's got to be found or got to come forward. See?"

The senior reporter produced a notebook and a pencil.

"What you want, Mr. Chaney, is just this," he said; "a paragraph, inserted in a prominent position in the latest reports about the Heronswood murder mystery, embodying the story you've just told us and appealing to the man concerned to come forward. That's it, isn't it?"

"That is it; as strongly worded as possible," assented Chaney. "No flowery stuff – plain fact. Pencil it out a bit."

The senior reporter scribbled; the junior looked over his shoulders.

"How's this?" asked the senior. "Listen!

"*The police authorities earnestly beg the attention of the public to the following appeal. It is known that the late Sir John Maxtondale, recently murdered at Heronswood Park, travelled from Euston station to Monkseaton by the twelve o'clock train on May 14. According to a statement just made to the Monkseaton police, his table in the first-class restaurant car was shared by a gentleman who entered the train just as it was leaving Euston. This gentleman was seen to be in conversation with Sir John during the whole of the journey between Euston and Monkseaton and left the train with him at Monkseaton and was last seen in further conversation with him on the platform. Will the gentleman in question, or anyone who can give any information about him, communicate as soon as possible with—*"

Here the senior reporter paused, pencil in hand. "With whom, Mr. Chaney?" he asked. "You?"

"No, no, we're unofficial, Camberwell and I – we're behind the scenes," replied Chaney. "It'll have to be Mallwood."

"*The Superintendent of Police, Monkseaton*, then," continued the senior. "How will that do?"

"That'll do finely," said Chaney. "You'll get it in everywhere?"

"You'll find it in every principal newspaper in England tomorrow morning, Mr. Chaney! There's an immense amount of public interest being taken in this affair. Triple murder!"

"Never remember anything that excited such interest!" added the junior. "Never!"

"Ah, you wouldn't," assented Chaney, slyly. "Not to be expected. Well, here's another matter. You know, you two, that Sir John, under the name of Mr. Maxton, stayed at the Waldorf Hotel in London for some little time before he came down here to see Mr. Henry Marston at Sedbury Manor? Well, now, I want another paragraph. I want to know if anybody staying at the Waldorf Hotel during the time Mr. Maxton was there can tell anything about him that will assist the police in their inquiries. Can you write that up?"

"Nothing easier," said the senior reporter, and again fell a-scribbling. "How's this?" he asked presently. "Short, straight, plain, Mr. Chaney.

"*The police authorities desire, further, to draw the attention of the public to the fact that the late Sir John Maxtondale for some little time before his death resided at the Waldorf Hotel, London. They would be obliged if any person resident or visiting at that hotel at the time in question, or paying casual visits to it, could give any information as to having seen Sir John there or entered into conversation with him. It has been established that Sir John Maxtondale was a very sociable man, easily approached, and given to talking to strangers, and the police authorities are anxious to acquire any information which would throw light on his doings and movements, recent, and in the past.*

"Communications as in the previous notice, I suppose?" concluded the senior reporter. "Very good! Pleased to do anything to help, Mr. Chaney." He handed his notebook over to his junior. "Get it all off, Jim," he said. "You know what to do with it. Of course, we use it ourselves, in Friday's issue. Well, that's done, Mr. Chaney," he added, as his fellow-worker left the room. "And now – how are you getting on? Any clue?"

"If you want the plain truth, young man, not at all!" replied Chaney. "Not at all, at all!"

"Not a notion who did it?" suggested our guest.

"Not one notion – nor half a one!" admitted Chaney.

"Haven't made any headway, then?"

"I don't see any," said Chaney.

"You aren't going to chuck up the sponge, though, Mr. Chaney?"

Chaney threw away the end of his cigar and rose, stretching his arms.

"Young man," said he, "we never give up, my partner and I! We're like the British Army – we lose many battles, but we never lose a war. We shall continue our campaign until we bring it to a successful issue."

"Good business!" said the senior reporter. "Never say die, eh, Mr. Chaney? But do you know what the folk about here are saying?"

"I do not," replied Chaney.

"They're saying that these murders at Heronswood are the work of a homicidal maniac who's still at large! What do you say to that?"

"What do I say? Why, I say they may be. How do I know?"

"It's struck you, then?" asked the reporter in some surprise.

"I didn't say so, my lad! I only say – they may be. Lots of things may be. But what I want is evidence. Let's hope you're helping us to get some. The press has great power, eh?"

"Most powerful thing in the world, sir!" asserted the representative of the press. "Ah – nobody knows what influence we exert, Mr. Chaney. The press, sir, is the modern pulpit—"

"And, it seems, policeman," laughed Chaney. "Well – we'll see what comes from your kind assistance."

We had not long to wait for results. On the day following the appearance of the inspired paragraphs in the daily press, there walked into Mallwood's office while Chaney and I were there on our now usual morning visit (made, Chaney said, just to see if the police were really doing anything) a smart and smiling man, who carried a folded newspaper. His smile widened to a grin as he laid this before Mallwood and pointed to a marked sentence.

"I think I'm the person to whom this refers, Mr. Superintendent," he said. "I'm the man who had a conversation in the train with the gentleman who's since turned out to be Sir John Maxtondale and who got out with him at Monkseaton."

"And you, sir – ?" inquired Mallwood.

"My name is Heading – Charles Heading," replied the caller, producing a card and laying it on Mallwood's desk. "As you'll see there, I represent Messrs. Trafford and Ruper, wholesale chemists, of Bow, London. I visit Monkseaton once or twice a year – the occasion I'm speaking of was one. I'm in Birmingham just now, and seeing this request of yours in the paper yesterday, I thought I'd run over to see you. Not that I can tell you more than I've already told you in my first few words," he added, smiling. "I don't know anything about Sir John Maxtondale, you know."

"You'd never met him before?" asked Chaney.

"Never. And of course never knew who he was," replied Mr. Heading. "I just chanced to sit at his table in the restaurant car that morning – the train was very full, and that was the last available seat – and we got into conversation, as travelling companions do, nowadays. That's all there is in it. I was getting out at Monkseaton; so was he. We left the train together and presently parted. I never knew who he was, of course."

"What did you talk about?" inquired Chaney.

Mr. Heading smiled; his recollections of Sir John Maxtondale seemed to cause him amusement.

"I think he did most of the talking," he answered. "He was a great talker. A very sociable man, I should say – talked very freely to one. Not the sort of man who cared to sit silent, you know, nor the kind that stands on ceremony. None of your conventional English reserve – I soon saw that he was the sort that had travelled widely and known all sorts of things and people."

"Well, what did he talk about, then?" persisted Chaney.

"Weather first, of course! Then the country we were passing through – he was greatly interested in fields, woods, anything that was green. I made out he'd just returned from abroad, and presently he told me he'd spent years in South America. I have relations out there – the Argentine – so I was interested. He told me a lot about South America – Brazil, the Argentine, Peru, Patagonia – he seemed to have been all over it."

"Did he tell you what he'd been doing there?"

"He didn't."

"Well, here's a very important question, Mr. Heading. Did he tell you he was, or had been, interested in diamonds?"

"No – he never mentioned diamonds."

"Then he didn't show you any?"

"Certainly not! There was nothing more passed between us than what I've told you of."

"And you parted on the platform at Monkseaton?"

"We parted outside the station entrance. I had some luggage to look after – I was staying in the town overnight. He walked away towards the centre of the town, and of course I never saw him again."

So that was all there was in that, and we had got no further. But when Mr. Heading had gone, Chaney raised a point which he had never previously mentioned – to me, at any rate.

"I'll tell you what, Mallwood," he said suddenly. "There's something just occurred to me that you people ought to inquire into. What time does that twelve o'clock noon from Euston get in here?"

"About two-thirty. Two-thirty or two-thirty-five," replied Mallwood.

"Well, Sir John Maxtondale didn't present himself at Sedbury Manor until late in the evening," continued Chaney. "Mr. Marston had dined, anyway. Say it was between eight and nine. Where had Sir John been during the six hours that had elapsed between arriving at Monkseaton and calling at Sedbury?"

"Ah!" exclaimed Mallwood. "Worth following up, eh?"

"You'd better follow it up," said Chaney. "He must have been somewhere. How far is it from Monkseaton to Sedbury Manor?"

"Short of three miles," replied Mallwood.

"Well, it wouldn't take him six hours to cover that bit," said Chaney. "Get on to it."

But when we looked in next morning, Mallwood had got no information on the point. He had, however, acquired some on another – the newspaper appeal had borne more fruit.

"Here's a letter here – came in this morning – from somebody who met Sir John at the Waldorf Hotel," he said. "You'd better read it – there's something about diamonds in it, right enough."

He handed the letter over to Chaney, who glanced at the signature and let out an exclamation.

"Somebody?" he said. "This is from Sir Basil Windover, the famous traveller and mountaineer. Written from the Travellers' Club, d'ye see, Camberwell? Well, we can depend on what he's got to say!"

We read the letter – not a very long one, but of considerable importance. It was addressed to the Superintendent of Police, Monkseaton, and ran as follows:

Dear Sir:

I have just read your appeal for information, and I think I can give you some. About a fortnight ago, being in its neighbourhood, I dropped into the Waldorf Hotel for lunch, and after lunch got into conversation with a (somewhat elderly) gentleman who was sitting near me in the lounge. I found that he had recently arrived in England from South America, and as I have travelled extensively in those regions, we exchanged experiences and reminiscences. I gathered that he was, or had been, interested in the diamond trade, and he produced from his pocket and showed me some very fine stones, some cut, others uncut. He displayed them rather openly, and I warned him against making any show of them in a public place. I gave him my card; he had none, but gave me his name as Mr. John Maxton. From what I have read in the newspapers, I feel sure this gentleman was the Sir John Maxtondale who has come to such an unfortunate end.

Yours truly,

Basil Windover

Chaney folded the letter and gave it back.

"Well," he said, "all I say as to that is that if Sir John would show thirty or forty thousand pounds' worth of diamonds to one chance acquaintance, he'd show 'em to another. The fact that he had 'em on him may have been known to half a dozen people. Mallwood, your people will have to find out where Sir John was between the time he left Monkseaton station and the time of his arrival at Sedbury Manor."

Chapter 10

THE PANAMA HAT

ACCORDING TO THE NOTES and memoranda in my case book, several days elapsed at this stage of the proceedings before anything further happened. No additional information came our way. We ourselves discovered nothing. Chaney began to chafe; I myself wondered what good we were doing by hanging about Heronswood, going into Monkseaton to discuss things with Mallwood, thinking, speculating, practically idling our time away. The affair, startling as it had been to the neighbourhood, seemed to be following the process associated with the proverbial nine days' wonder. Sir John Maxtondale had been buried with his ancestors in the family burial ground in Sedbury churchyard; Robson and Mother Kitteridge lay in their respective places not far away from him. Rupert Maxtondale had left Heronswood and gone back to town; so, too, had the pretty Miss Weekes, to whom, I frankly confess, I had taken something of a fancy. Chaney asked Sir Stephen Maxtondale to let us go, too; we seemed to be at a dead end there at Heronswood. But Sir Stephen begged us to remain a little longer and to renew our attempt. We were not to be discouraged, he said; the case was a more difficult one than any of us had imagined it would be. And we were not to be afraid of spending money; it was absolutely necessary to clear up the mystery of Sir John Maxtondale's murder; moreover, there was another feature of the case which was causing Sir Stephen great anxiety – how was he to know that his elder brother, after all, had not left a successor in South America? We could solve that question only by inquiries, and we spent a great deal in cabling to various South American centres – Rio de Janeiro, Buenos Aires, Bahia, Pernambuco. The result was practically nothing. But such information as we did get amounted to this – that Sir John Maxtondale was known to certain officials in Rio as Mr. Maxton, a private resident who lived as a single man and had no family. And no one seemed to know anything of him as one who had any connection with the diamond trade.

About this time, however, there came to light another piece of information which simplified matters to a certain degree. We discovered by exchange of cablegrams that when Sir John (as Mr. Maxton) left South America, he transferred from a bank in Rio de Janeiro to its London branch a sum of something over fifty-five thousand pounds. This sum lay practically untouched in the hands of the London branch. We found that Mr. Maxton had called there once – not long before his visit to Mr. Marston – to establish his identity and had at the same time drawn three hundred pounds in notes. Out of this sum he had paid his hotel bills for a fortnight; the balance he probably had in his pockets at the time of the murder. The bankers were able to furnish us with the numbers of the notes, but although we disseminated this piece of intelligence as widely as possible, nobody came forward to say that any such notes had passed through his or her hand since Sir John's death. They, with the diamonds and the personal valuables, seemed to have completely disappeared – the murderer, no doubt, had hidden them as carefully as he appeared to have hidden himself.

So there we were – with our noses pressed against a brick wall, said Chaney. Then one day – the afternoon of a delightful spring day, as I remember very well, when Heronswood and its beautiful park and gardens were looking at their very best – Mallwood phoned us. Would we go into Monkseaton at once; he had news for us. Sir Stephen had placed one of his cars at our disposal; it and a chauffeur were always in readiness; we went off to Monkseaton at once. And there was Mallwood wearing an expression which seemed to betoken mystery of the first order.

"You know what you said to me after we'd had that letter from the famous traveller?" said Mallwood. "About finding out where Sir John was, or where he went, between his arrival at Monkseaton station and his turning up at Mr. Marston's at Sedbury Manor? Well, I've had some information!"

Chaney vouchsafed one word: "Dependable?"

"Oh, quite so!" replied Mallwood. "Thoroughly reliable, my informant. In strict secrecy, of course. Now, as you've come in here from Heronswood, have you ever noticed, on the Sedbury road, just before you get into the town, a nice old house that stands in a walled garden, with a fine old cedar-tree on the lawn – Cedar Tree House, in fact?"

Chaney nodded, silently.

"Well, that's Mr. Portinscale's. Mr. Portinscale is an old – oldish – gentleman who used to be senior clerk in the office of Matthewman and Burder, solicitors, of this town. I don't think he was ever engaged in any other office in his life – I've heard that he went to Matthewman and Burder's as office-boy and worked his way up to the senior clerk-ship—"

"Qualified solicitor?" asked Chaney. "Did they give him his articles?"

"No, he was never a qualified solicitor," replied Mallwood. "He remained just what he'd begun as – a clerk, unarticled. But it used to be said that he knew a damned sight more law than either of his principals, and that this practice was really run by him. Very cute, clever old chap, Mr. Portinscale, I can assure you!"

"Well?" demanded Chaney.

"Well, last night a man came to see me, privately," continued Mallwood, who was evidently enjoying the telling of his story. "Said man was one Cooper, known to me as a respectable, hardworking fellow, a jobbing gardener. After pledging me to secrecy, Cooper told me that on a certain afternoon, which by careful comparison of dates I soon ascertained to be that on which Sir John Maxtondale arrived in Monkseaton, he was working in Mr. Portinscale's garden (Mr. P., I should tell you, retired some five years ago and now amuses himself with his garden) when a gentleman – fine-looking man, said Cooper, middle-aged – walked in. Knocked at Mr. P.'s door and was admitted. This was a little after three o'clock. When Cooper left, at six o'clock, the gentleman was still there – Cooper saw him and Mr. P., sitting in the parlour. Now, from careful comparison of the description and photographs given in the papers with his recollection of the caller, Cooper is certain that the man he's referring to was Sir John Maxton-dale!"

"What's kept Mr. Portinscale silent, then?" asked Chaney.

"Um!" replied Mallwood. "Mr. Portinscale is a bit of an eccentric! He has the reputation in the town of only doing things in Mr. Portin-scale's way. If he wants to speak, he speaks. If he doesn't want to speak, he doesn't speak."

"How do you propose to make him speak, then?" asked Chaney.

"This is a case of murder," replied Mallwood. "If the caller was Sir John Maxtondale, Mr. P. must speak! We could put him on oath. But I suggest we call on him, tell him what we've heard – no mention of Cooper – and ask him a few plain questions."

"Such as – what?" inquired Chaney.

"I think I shall leave that to you," answered Mallwood. "You're better at that game than I am. But let's go, now – it's only five minutes' walk."

We set out on foot, leaving our car at the police station. Cedar Tree House stood alone, with no other house very near it, on the roadside, at the extreme edge of the town, a low-roofed, old-fashioned place, covered with creeper and ivy and overshadowed by the great tree from which it took its name. It was surrounded by a high wall of time-mellowed old red brick, but in one side of this there was a gate of wrought iron, and through that you could see into the grounds. Mallwood took a cautious peep through the bars.

"There's Mr. Portinscale!" he said. "See?"

What I first saw was an enormous Panama hat – a hat of quite extraordinary size. It appeared above the top of a rustic seat – what there might be beneath it I could only guess at.

"Reading the newspaper," remarked Mallwood. "Come on! But be careful – he's a queer old customer to deal with."

He opened the gate and we advanced into the garden, Mallwood leading. Pursuing a flank movement, we eventually obtained a front view of Mr. Portinscale; at least, we obtained one when, hearing our footsteps on his gravelled walk, he dropped the outspread *Times* on his knee, and sternly regarded us over the top of a very large pair of sil-ver-mounted spectacles. Sizing him up, I began to realise Mallwood's dread of him. Mr. Portinscale was a little, slightly-built person of apparently sixty-five to seventy years of age, chiefly remarkable for an apple-cheeked, clean-shaven face, a long upper lip, an aggressive chin, a pair of unusually bright brown eyes, and a very alert, watchful look. Somehow, sitting there immovable and silent in his garden (for, after catching sight of us, he neither rose nor, indeed, stirred in his seat), he reminded me of a vigilant fox-terrier, on the lookout for whatever is going to happen.

"Good afternoon, Mr. Portinscale," said Mallwood, nervously. "Fine weather we're having just now, sir. Allow me, Mr. Portinscale – Mr. Chaney, Mr. Portinscale, Mr. Camberwell, Mr. Portinscale. We – er—"

Then he came to a full stop; Mr. Portinscale, still gripping the *Times*, looked Chaney over, looked me over. Then he looked Mallwood over.

"Um!" he said. "Well?"

"Mr. Chaney and Mr. Camberwell, Mr. Portinscale," continued Mallwood, "are employed by Sir Stephen Maxtondale to inquire into the mystery of his late brother's death."

"Murder!" said Mr. Portinscale.

"Beg pardon, sir – I should have said murder," replied Mallwood, humbly. "I chose the – the less ugly word, sir."

"Murder," remarked Mr. Portinscale, "is murder."

"I agree with you, sir – so it is," assented Mallwood. "Well, sir, I am doing what I can to assist these two gentlemen in the elucidation of this mystery—"

"Not done much so far!" remarked Mr. Portinscale.

"We haven't, sir – I'm bound to admit it," replied Mallwood. "A very difficult business, Mr. Portinscale – I never had a stiffer job in my time. But we're doing our best—"

"The question," interrupted Mr. Portinscale, acidly, "is – what are you doing here?"

"Oh, well, Mr. Portinscale, we're – er, wanting a bit of information—"

"None to give you!" said Mr. Portinscale. "Haven't any!"

"But, Mr. Portinscale, we've heard something! We've heard that Sir John Maxtondale, on the day of his arrival in Monkseaton, called to see you! And—"

"How did you hear that?" demanded Mr. Portinscale.

"Oh, well, Mr. Portinscale, you don't live in the middle of a desert, you know," said Mallwood, trying to be humorous. "High road outside your gate, you know, sir."

Mr. Portinscale glared at his questioner.

"Well, what if he did?" he asked with asperity.

"He did, then, did he, Mr. Portinscale?" asked Mallwood, eagerly.

"Why shouldn't he?" demanded Mr. Portinscale. "Who knows more about the neighbourhood than I do?"

"Very true indeed, Mr. Portinscale," agreed Mallwood. "Greatly relieved to hear what you say, sir. Might – might one ask what time Sir John left you, now?"

"You might," replied Mr. Portinscale. "You may! Seven o'clock. And he'd been here since three. Now, then!"

"Deeply obliged, Mr. Portinscale. And – and might one ask, further, what – what was the object of his visit?" asked Mallwood.

"You might," again responded Mr. Portinscale. "To see me!"

"Exactly, sir. And – might one ask what – what you talked about?"

"No, you mightn't!" snapped Mr. Portinscale. "Anything else? Because if there is, I shan't tell you."

"Oh, well, in that case, sir – I suppose we shall have to be satisfied, Mr. Portinscale. We only want to get more light on the murder."

"Can't throw any!" declared Mr. Portinscale. "Should have come forward long since if I could. Don't know anything. Visit here nothing to do with murder. Nothing more to say."

He picked up the *Times* again, as if to intimate that the interview was over, and Mallwood began to murmur something about our obligations and to show signs of sheering off, defeated. But Chaney found his tongue.

"Beautiful garden you have here, sir," he remarked. "Beau – ti – ful!"

Mr. Portinscale dropped the *Times* and gave Chaney another and closer look. Chaney was rapt in admiration of something in the floral line, close by.

"Fond of flowers?" demanded Mr. Portinscale, softening.

"Ah!" sighed Chaney. "Worship 'em!"

Mr. Portinscale laid down the *Times* and rose. Erect, he looked like a mushroom; the Panama hat acted as umbrella to his shoulders.

"Show you round if you like," said Mr. Portinscale.

"Greatly honoured, sir," replied Chaney.

Mallwood moved off.

"I must go," he said. "An appointment. Much obliged, Mr. Portinscale."

"Um!" said Mr. Portinscale. He motioned Chaney to follow him. "Better show in a week or two," he said. "Still—"

For over an hour I followed Mr. Portinscale and Chaney round the grounds and gardens of Cedar Tree House. Whether Chaney really loved flowers, or whether he really understood all that Mr. Portinscale talked about, I have never known from that day to this – Chaney always preserved a strict reticence on the subject – but what I do know is that at the end of the perambulations Mr. Portinscale had become the most friendly creature in the world, and asked us into his house to partake of – much needed – refreshment.

"And how are you getting on with your investigations, now?" he inquired, when we were all snugly bestowed, glasses in hand. "Poorly, eh?"

"Very, sir!" replied Chaney, frankly. "No appreciable headway. If somebody could give us even a hint—"

He looked knowingly at Mr. Portinscale. I had a faint suspicion that Mr. Portinscale winked.

"Just so!" said Mr. Portinscale. "Exactly! Ah, well – I cannot give any direct hint. It is true Sir John Maxtondale called on me, on arrival. It was just to ask me – he knew me in the old days – how things were; how the land lay, you know. But he told me no more than he told Mr. Henry Marston. I have no idea as to who murdered him – murdered he certainly was. But I'll tell you two gentlemen something, on condition that you do not tell Mallwood – Mallwood is a thickhead!"

"Rely on our discretion, sir," said Chaney.

"Well," continued Mr. Portinscale, "I think it will be found that the murder of Sir John has something to do with the relations between Sir Stephen Maxtondale and his son, Rupert—"

"Ah!" exclaimed Chaney. "Ah!"

"Don't misunderstand me," said Mr. Portinscale; "I'm not saying a word against Rupert. But the position is this, and you should know it. Rupert Maxtondale as a very young man gave his father a great deal of trouble. He was sent down from Oxford. He had accumulated a load of debt – really serious load. Not at Oxford, in particular, you understand – in various quarters. The Turf – other ways. Well, Sir Stephen paid it all off. But – there was a fine 'but' to the transaction. Rupert was then just twenty-one. Sir Stephen told him that henceforth he'd have to earn his own living! Not one penny would he give or allow him. But he put him in the way of earning his living. The family interest in the coal mine had just been turned over to a limited liability company – chief shareholder, Sir Stephen; head offices, London. Master Rupert was packed off to London as a clerk, with a commencing salary of two hundred and fifty pounds. It will have been increased by now – but there you are! That's all he has to live on – he, the heir to a baronetcy and a fine estate worth fifty thousand pounds a year! Fact, sirs!"

"Couldn't he raise money on his expectations?" suggested Chaney. "I suppose the estate's entailed."

"The estate is not entailed," replied Mr. Portinscale. "Rupert Maxtondale is absolutely dependent on his father's goodwill. He has to keep himself on whatever his present salary may be. Well, he lives in London. How, only he knows. And, gentlemen, I am firmly of opinion that the murder of Sir John Maxtondale has some connection with Rupert's affairs, though not to his knowledge. There may have been – there may be people whose interest it was to get rid of Sir John once and for all. Money interests – money!"

Chapter 11

THE SERVANTS' HALL

I KNEW CHANEY SO well by this time that it was easy for me to see that Mr. Portinscale's talk was giving him a new interest in the case, which up to then had presented so many baffling features. He settled down in his chair and began to ask questions.

"You'll understand me, sir," he said, "when I ask you how you come to know all this? For you speak as with absolute knowledge!"

"Mine is absolute knowledge," replied Mr. Portinscale. "You see, I was for a great many years chief clerk to a leading firm of solicitors here in the town. Now, the Maxtondale family solicitor is one Ellerthorpe, a London man—"

"We know Mr. Ellerthorpe – well," observed Chaney.

"Ay, well, although Ellerthorpe is the family solicitor, for what you might call business matters – conveyancing and so on – he hasn't, and never had, all the business," continued Mr. Portinscale. "My principal, the late Mr. Matthewman, had a great deal of it, being on the spot – he was always consulted about anything very confidential. It was through us, for instance, that all the inquiries about John Maxtondale were made when he disappeared. Now, when the business about Rupert and his debts came out, Sir Stephen put the whole matter in Mr. Matthewman's hands. He was so angry with Rupert that he wouldn't see him – he even forbade him the house; it's only quite recently that Rupert's been allowed to come home now and then for a short visit. What really happened was this – Sir Stephen, the debt business having come to his knowledge, put the whole thing in our hands. He issued a sort of ultimatum. We were to ascertain the entire amount of Rupert's debts – he'd been going the pace at a pretty hot rate – and to pay off every penny. As to Rupert himself, he was to be given a post in the London offices of the Heronswood Colliery Company, under supervision of the manager, Mr. Collinghurst, and for ten years was to earn and depend upon a certain salary, which was to rise in stated amounts each year; during that period of ten years his father was not to give him or find him one penny. In other words, he was on probation and had to make good. Whether—"

"Excuse me, Mr. Portinscale, but how long since is this?" asked Chaney. "How many years have elapsed?"

"Nine! Rupert Maxtondale is now thirty – he was twenty-one when all this happened. It's understood – at least as far as I know – that he's kept his part of the bargain. Anyway, during the last year or two he's been allowed to come home now and then."

"Have you any idea what he gets in the way of salary now?" inquired Chaney.

Mr. Portinscale reflected awhile.

"I can reckon things up," he said. "I drew up the document which Rupert was made to sign. He was to begin at a salary of two hundred and fifty pounds a year, and – if he behaved himself – it was to rise by annual increases of fifty pounds. So he will now be getting—"

"Seven hundred a year," said Chaney. "And his father, I understand, is worth fifty thousand a year! Um!"

"Sir Stephen paid over twenty-five thousand pounds on Rupert's account," remarked Mr. Portinscale. "Fair lot of debt, gentlemen, for a lad who'd only just attained his majority when the smash came!"

"I was wondering, considering how extravagant he must have been, how he managed to exist on even seven hundred a year," said Chaney. "Especially if, as you tell us, he lived in London, by himself, with nobody to look after him."

"Collinghurst has been supposed to look after him," said Mr. Portinscale. "But of course he could only do so to a certain extent. And what I'm wondering about is – has Rupert again got himself into the hands of moneylenders, as he did before? It's true that it's quite

well known that the Heronswood estates are not entailed, and that
Rupert's future is entirely dependent upon Sir Stephen's goodwill
towards him – he could cut him off if he liked, and Sir Stephen's a hard
man if crossed or disobeyed – but there's always the sporting chance
that Rupert will come into everything, and – you see what I mean?"

"I see!" agreed Chaney. "There may be somebody in the back-
ground who has a financial interest in Rupert and who, if Sir John
Maxtondale had claimed and insisted on his right, would have been a
loser? That it, sir?"

"That is it," replied Mr. Portinscale. "That is exactly my idea. But
as to who such a person or persons may be, I know nothing."

"Do you know Mr. Rupert Maxtondale's address in town?" asked
Chaney.

But Mr. Portinscale did not know that, and after thanking him and
assuring him that we should regard as strictly confidential all that he
had said to us, we took our leave and went back to Heronswood.

Chaney was full of what we had just heard. There was an idea in it,
he said, an idea that was worth following up.

"Let's suppose a bit, Camberwell," he said, as we walked back
across Heronswood Park. "Supposing, now, that, as the old gentleman
suggested, there is somebody who has a financial interest in Rupert
Maxtondale? Supposing there's someone who's lent him money on
his chances, prospects? Supposing that someone discovered that Sir
John Maxtondale had returned and, in order to safeguard himself,
removed him – and, knowing that Robson and Mother Kitteridge
knew of his doings and were about to reveal them, removed them, too?
What about that, now?"

"Wouldn't all that mean that the someone lived hereabouts?" I
suggested.

"It needn't," he answered. "John Maxtondale might have been followed from London. But then, of course, it might have been some
local person – how do we know what Rupert Maxtondale's private
affairs are? There may be some person about here who has a financial
interest in him. The fact is, Camberwell, we know nothing! Still,
there's something in the old gentleman's theory, and we ought to do a
bit of work at it. What I'm wondering about at present is: should we
tell Sir Stephen of this notion?"

I was thinking about that myself, and I said so, adding that the question needed a good deal of consideration.

"Well, we can't hang about here," said Chaney. "We're doing precious little good. My idea is that we ought to get back to town and do some investigating with Rupert as an objective – find out what sort of life he really leads, what company he keeps, if he's really carrying out his share of the pact between him and his father, and so on. That, I feel sure, is our line – all other lines seem to be leading nowhere."

He was referring, I knew, to the fact that we had not been able to trace anything through Sir John Maxtondale's missing valuables. The numbers of the banknotes known to be in his possession when he left London had been circulated and broadcast, but nothing had been heard of a single one of them. As for the diamonds, it was almost beyond the bounds of possibility that they would ever be traced.

"I think we ought to speak to Sir Stephen, frankly," concluded Chaney, "and then – get away!"

"Yes, but what are we to speak to him about?" I asked. "We've no real evidence against Rupert! We can't go to Sir Stephen and ask him if he thinks his son has any connection with all this! He'd immediately ask us if we've any grounds for such a suggestion. And – we haven't. It's all mere surmise."

However, that very evening we were brought face to face with something that was not mere surmise. Sir Stephen Maxtondale's domestic staff was headed by a butler, Rabbage, a grave and solemn person of whom all his fellow-servants stood in much awe. Rabbage, I gathered, had been in the employ of the Maxtondale family for at least thirty years. When Sir Stephen insisted on housing us during our investigations, he placed us in charge of Rabbage, and Rabbage, after a careful inspection and estimation of us, evidently considered it his duty to show us every attention and make us extremely comfortable. He was a man of reserved speech, very discreet, and of precise manners, and certainly not given to gossip, and I was accordingly very much surprised when, on the evening of our return from seeing Mr. Portinscale, he drew me aside and said that if convenient and agreeable to us, he begged the favour of a little private conversation with Mr. Chaney and me. There was that in his manner which convinced me that Rabbage had something of importance to communicate.

"Certainly, Rabbage," I replied. "When? Where?"

"Any time after dinner is over would suit me, sir," he said. "I can wait on you and Mr. Chaney in your own room, sir" (he had given us a sitting room, near our bedrooms, in which we could enjoy whatever privacy we desired), "or perhaps you would prefer to come to my pantry? Whichever you please, sir."

"Come to our room, Rabbage," I answered. "What time, now. Nine o'clock?"

"Nine o'clock will be very convenient to me, sir," he said. "My duties are over then – until it is time to close the house."

I made Chaney acquainted with Rabbage's desire, and Chaney immediately became alertly inquisitive.

"The old chap's got something to tell!" he exclaimed. "Heaven send it's something worth listening to! If we could only get hold of any direct clue! Well, Rabbage is a likely man. One thing's certain, Camberwell – Rabbage won't say anything unless he's convinced that there's something in it."

Rabbage came to our sitting room exactly as the clock in the old turret above our heads struck its nine strokes. His first action was to see that the door through which he had entered was closed behind him; his next to glance at the window; seeing that it was open, he asked permission to shut it.

"When one has a confidential communication to make, gentlemen, it is as well to ensure complete privacy," he remarked. "I don't want anything I may say to you to be overheard."

"Perfectly safe here, Rabbage," said Chaney. "You know the quarters better than we do. Well? Something confidential, eh?"

"And serious, sir," replied Rabbage. He took the chair between us which I had placed for him, and dropped his voice to a low murmur. "The fact is, gentlemen, I have been wanting to talk to you for some days. At first I thought I would say what I have to say to Sir Stephen himself, but on reflection I think I had better say it to you – Sir Stephen is upset enough already."

"You can trust us, Rabbage," said Chaney.

"I am sure of it, sir – Mr. Ellerthorpe told me before he left that if I ever wished to speak to you about – well, about these recent affairs – I could do so with perfect confidence. But until quite recently, gentlemen, I had nothing to speak about."

"And now," said Chaney, "you have?"

"Now I have, sir. The fact is, gentlemen, there is a good deal of talk going on in our servants' hall. I have done my best to check and suppress it, but in a big house like this, with a staff of nearly twenty servants, many of them females, it is difficult to stop gossip."

"And the gossip is about – what?" asked Chaney.

Rabbage looked round again, at doors and window. His voice dropped to a whisper.

"About Mr. Rupert!" he said. "Just that, sir, Mr. Rupert!"

"What about him?" inquired Chaney.

"It's difficult to explain, sir. It is not what our servants are saying themselves – I hope they're too well trained for that! – but what they're repeating as coming from outside. From the people who live hereabouts, you understand – labouring people, the people over at the colliery, and so on. They talk, those people, and what they say spreads, gentlemen."

"And what are they saying, Rabbage?" asked Chaney. "Out with it!"

Rabbage shook his head regretfully.

"They're saying, sir, that Mr. Rupert knows more about these – these dreadful occurrences than he's ever admitted," he replied. "Just that, sir!"

"But on what grounds?" asked Chaney.

"Well, sir, there are two – I don't know if you'd call them grounds or reasons or what," replied Rabbage. "And in both cases the information must have sprung from somebody in this house – by somebody, I mean one or other of our servants, but I haven't the remotest idea which. People are saying, sir, that there are two suspicious features as regards Mr. Rupert. First, it's known that he was out with his gun, unaccompanied by any keeper or anybody, on the day on which Sir John Maxtondale was shot. Second, it's known (and that can certainly only have filtered out from this house) that on the evening on which Mr. Robson and old Mrs. Kitteridge were shot, Mr. Rupert left the dinner-table before dinner was really over, making some excuse to his father, and left the house, to which he didn't return till very late. These two facts are known, sir, and people are saying they're very suspicious."

"Are they – these people – suggesting that Mr. Rupert Maxtondale shot his uncle, Robson, and Mrs. Kitteridge?" asked Chaney.

"Not quite that, I think, sir, but that Mr. Rupert knows something about it," replied Rabbage. "The fact is, gentlemen, there are people about here – I grieve to say, most people about here – who are inclined to believe anything about Mr. Rupert Maxtondale. Mr. Rupert, sir, is not and never has been liked. He is unpopular."

"Why?" asked Chaney.

"He was unpopular as a boy, sir. His manner, you understand. Overbearing and, if I may put it so strongly, rude and even insolent to the tenants. Not at all like his father, gentlemen," added Rabbage. "Sir Stephen is the most considerate landlord you could imagine. Everybody likes Sir Stephen."

Chaney considered all this during a few moments of silence.

"Of course, that's all mere gossip?" he said, suddenly. "Eh, Rabbage?"

"Oh, mere gossip, of course, sir," assented Rabbage. "Country people, gentlemen, will talk – you can't stop them from talking."

"You don't attach any importance to it yourself?" asked Chaney.

"Not to the mere gossip," replied Rabbage. "But – if I'm to speak frankly, gentlemen, I've been upset in my own mind about something that happened when Mr. Rupert was down here this last time. You see, gentlemen, I'm an old servant. I've been here many years; naturally, I know many family secrets. I know, for instance, that Mr. Rupert was a bit – a good bit! – wild and extravagant in his youth – when he was little more than a boy in fact – and that though his father put things right for him, it led to Sir Stephen's taking very stern measures about him and practically banishing him to London to earn his own living. It's only of recent years – the last two or three years, gentlemen – that Mr. Rupert has been allowed to come here – a matter of which I didn't approve, though I'm bound to say that Sir Stephen used to go up to town periodically to visit him—"

"Why wasn't he allowed to come down here?" asked Chaney.

"I think Sir Stephen got the idea that he knew people in this neighbourhood whom it wasn't desirable he should know," replied Rabbage. "He wanted to break off all that sort of thing. But," he continued, after a pause, "I've been wondering, gentlemen, if all those old associations have been discontinued? Which brings me back to what I was going to say to you."

"Yes – what was that?" inquired Chaney.

"Well, sir, just this. A few days after Mr. Rupert came down last time – it was, as a matter of fact, two days before the affair of Sir John's death took place – a man came to the front door one morning and asked for Mr. Rupert. He was a sporting-looking sort of man – loud clothes, rakish – and a complete stranger to me. I fetched Mr. Rupert to him – the man wouldn't give any name or enter the hall. Fortunately Sir Stephen was away. Mr. Rupert and the man walked away across the terrace, talking; it seemed to me that Mr. Rupert was vexed. I saw them leave the terrace for the park, where they disappeared. Mr. Rupert was out until lunchtime; I thought he looked worried when he came back. Well, gentlemen, next morning very early I had to go into Monkseaton, and there I saw this man again. And – Mr. Rupert was with him. He, I knew, had ridden off just after breakfast. They didn't see me, and of course I took care to keep on the other side of the street. There may be nothing in it, gentlemen," concluded Rabbage, "but – well, I didn't like the look of that man."

That was all the butler had to say. But when he had said it, Chaney and I made up our minds to leave Heronswood at once. Our work, evidently, awaited us in London.

Chapter 12

WARRINER'S WHARF

AFTER RABBAGE HAD LEFT us, Chaney and I sat up some time, talking. As usual, most of the talking was done by Chaney; I still considered myself a disciple, sitting at the feet of a master.

"Get back to town, Camberwell! – that's what we've got to do," said Chaney. "Old Panama hat was right – this affair has something to do with Rupert Maxtondale. How, in what way, Heaven knows! We've got to find that out."

"How do you propose to do it?" I asked.

"Find out all about him! What his life is. Where he lives. Whom he associates with. If he's living within his income or has got into debt again. All that can be done without much difficulty."

"Starting out from – what?" I inquired. "We must have a base."

"Our base will be the London offices of the Heronswood Colliery Company," he replied. "I know where they are – Warriner's Wharf."

"Where's Warriner's Wharf?" I asked.

"On that stretch of the river called the Pool. Where the Custom House is. And near the Coal Exchange, if you know where that is."

"Never knew there was such a place," I said.

"Very likely – but it's one of the principal buildings in that region. Opposite Billingsgate, at the corner of St. Mary-at-Hill. That's where they do the coal business – millions upon millions of tons in a year, my boy!"

"How would you start out from the Heronswood offices?" I asked.

"That's easy enough. We know that Rupert puts in his day there. Ought to, at any rate. Perhaps he does, perhaps he doesn't – anyhow, we can be certain he'll be there at some time or other. Well, that's all right – when he leaves the offices, we follow."

"He knows both of us," I objected.

"When I say we, I speak in – what do you call it – metaphor, eh? I mean we put somebody on to watch him, on our behalf. We have the cleverest chap in London for that job."

"Chippendale?"

"Chippendale, of course. Show Chippendale his man, and Chippendale will follow wherever his man goes!"

"And how are we to show Chippendale this particular man? As I said just now, Rupert Maxtondale knows me and he knows you, and if he sees either of us hanging about Warriner's Wharf or the Coal Exchange—"

"Leave it to me," said Chaney; "I'll fix it. But that's our line – now let's get to bed and be off to town as soon as we've had breakfast tomorrow morning."

"And – Sir Stephen?" I suggested.

"That's easy, too. We want to follow up some investigations about the diamonds. Oh, quite easy! And look here – we'll have to be polite and say farewell (for the time being) to Mallwood. But not a word to Mallwood of what we're really after! Let Mallwood pursue his own little game here."

Sir Stephen made no demur, this time, about our leaving Heronswood. He was bewildered by the whole thing. As for his own personal belief, he was inclined to adopt the first theory started by the local wiseacres – that somewhere in this Arcadian community there was a homicidal maniac, cunning and clever to the last degree, in whose keeping the diamonds were safe enough, perhaps for ever, and who, for all we knew, might break out again and shoot somebody else.

"Let me know of anything you discover," he said at parting with us. "It seems a hopeless quest, but do what you can. It would be a great relief to me to get at the truth, whatever it may be, a great relief!"

He turned away into the house, waving a hand, and we drove off, Chaney shaking his head.

"Not so sure about that, Camberwell," he remarked. "Instead of being a great relief, it might – may – be an overwhelming blow. However . . ."

Then we said goodbye to Mallwood. Mallwood pointed despairingly to a pile of papers on his desk.

"I don't know how many signed statements relating to this affair I haven't got there!" he groaned. "There are scores there, anyway. I'm about settled by it – we're no nearer to a conclusion than we were at starting. Well, I suppose you're after those diamonds, eh?"

"Might as well be," replied Chaney.

"How do you tell one diamond from another?" asked Mallwood. "Still, I reckon they're bound to come to the market at some time, eh? Well, let me know how you get on. I'll keep you informed from this end. But I don't expect anything."

"No – and he won't find anything either!" remarked Chaney, when we had got away. "The end of the line is in London, my lad. And if we once get our fingers on it, Camberwell – eh?"

Chaney, as I knew by that time, was a confirmed optimist. If one thing failed, he immediately took to another, always with renewed enthusiasm and confidence. And now, as soon as we reached our office, he had Chippendale into our private room and was deep in his subject.

Chippendale took in everything as readily as a sponge sucks up water. He had already absorbed all the information that had been appearing in the newspapers; now he turned his attention to Chaney's new ideas. Chaney finished up his explanations with a question which showed his faith in our sharp-witted clerk.

"Now you know all about it, Chippendale," he said. "So – what do you suggest? What's to be done first?"

"That's easily answered, Mr. Chaney," replied Chippendale. "I'll go along to Warriner's Wharf and make a careful inspection. I shall find a place from which the offices of the Heronswood Colliery Company can be watched in safety. When I've found it, perhaps Mr. Camberwell will go down with me – say, tomorrow afternoon – wait with me until the staff leaves, and then point out our man? After that, you can leave the rest to me."

"Good!" assented Chaney. "Go this afternoon. You know where Warriner's Wharf is?"

Chippendale evidently thought it beneath him to answer this question in words; his look signified that there wasn't anything in the geography of London that he didn't know. He turned from this subject to give us an account of all that had gone on at the office in our absence, and when this was over, put on his hat and, remarking that he shouldn't return that day, departed Citywards.

Next morning Chippendale made his first report. He had been to Warriner's Wharf and made a critical examination of its position in relation to what we desired. The offices of the Heronswood Colliery Company occupied a central place in a block of buildings facing the river, and there was no point of vantage immediately in front of them from which the entrance could be watched unobserved. But a little to the side, on the wharf itself, there was an old tavern, the Admiral Hawke, from the upper windows of which one could see everybody who went in and everybody who went out of the colliery offices. And Chippendale, with his usual readiness and thoroughness, had already seen the landlord of the Admiral Hawke, and, for a consideration, had the use of a window at any time desirable to his purposes.

"So if Mr. Camberwell will go down there with me this afternoon?" suggested Chippendale. "Four thirty, eh, Mr. Camberwell? Then—"

"Then you can get to work, I suppose?" said Chaney. "Good lad! Sooner the better."

I accompanied Chippendale Citywards at the time he suggested. I left myself entirely in his hands. First he thrust me into a tube train, and here and there lugged me out of it into other trains; finally he led me into fresh air at the Monument. I did not know that part of London very well; indeed, scarcely at all; but I recognised Billingsgate by the smell of fish. And after manœuvring round various corners and dodging through sundry passages and courts, he suddenly turned the angle of a warehouse and revealed Warriner's Wharf.

Warriner's Wharf, in comparison with the streets behind it, was comparatively quiet. It was a sort of parallelogram, having the river on one side, a façade of somewhat dingy-looking offices and warehouses on the other, a warehouse closing up one end, and a public-house, the Admiral Hawke, already reported by Chippendale, the other. The front door of the Admiral Hawke faced us, but Chippendale had no intention of using the front door. Once more we dodged through a passage or two, a court or two, and came out at the back of the tavern. There was a door there which Chippendale boldly opened and entered. It was not yet time to open the house to would-be customers, but a fat man who sat in a snuggery just within, smoking a rank cigar and reading the newspaper, showed no surprise at our unceremonious entry. He cocked a fishy eye at Chippendale, a mere inquiring one at me, and then nodded affably.

"You can go up, guv'nor," he said, addressing our enterprising clerk; "you and your friend can go up. All serene, guv'nor!"

He resumed his literary studies, and Chippendale motioned me to follow him up some very dirty stairs. Two flights – then he opened a door and admitted me to an atmosphere of stale beer and bad tobacco. There was a bare floor, some hard chairs, a table, a few sporting prints on the walls, and over the fireplace the printed and varnished rules, set in a worm-eaten frame, of the Order of Ancient Dolphins.

"Club room," explained Chippendale. "Stuffy! Better open the window, I think, Mr. Camberwell. Not very grand quarters, sir – but, you see?"

He pointed out of one of the two windows, and I saw that from where we stood we commanded a full, uninterrupted view of the front entrance of the Heronswood Colliery Company, Limited. The colliery offices faced the river; there was nothing of any note about them, except that they were not quite so dingy or dirty as those on either side, and that the big brass plate at the door shone as if it were cleaned every day. The door itself was in the middle of the building and was approached by half a dozen stone steps over which hung a big lamp. Everything about the place seemed very lifeless, and I began to wonder how I myself, had I been brought up at Heronswood, amidst woods, parks, pleasure-grounds, and gardens, should have liked to be ordered to a dismal hole like this, and for the moment I pitied Rupert Maxtondale.

"Now, Mr. Camberwell," said Chippendale, "you keep behind this curtain and watch the door across there. Five o'clock, sir, is the – what do they call it? – psychological moment. At least, it is if we go by what I saw yesterday afternoon."

"And what did you see yesterday afternoon?" I inquired.

"This, Mr. Camberwell. At five o'clock – you can hear St. Paul's from here when the wind's right – at five o'clock, sir, to the minute, I saw two men leave that door. Bosses, both of 'em. Youngish men, smartly dressed. What we used to call toffs. One of 'em dark; the other light."

"The light one would be Mr. Rupert Maxtondale," I said.

"So I guessed, sir, from your previous description, but I wanted to make sure," replied Chippendale. "The other chap, however, is just about the same age. Well, as I say, out they went at five o'clock, and I formed the opinion from their movements that they do that every day."

"What were their movements, then?" I asked.

"Well, sir, they were as follows," answered Chippendale, in his best style of precision. "Just before five a car, driven by a chauffeur in a plain dark livery, came round that corner to the right. It pulled up in front of the colliery offices. Then the two men I've spoken of came out. They entered the car; the car was driven away, leaving the wharf at the opposite end. So—"

"Car!" I exclaimed. "But we want to track Rupert Maxtondale!"

"I purpose to do so, sir," he said, quite unperturbed. "I shall do so. We do nothing this afternoon – all that's necessary today is that you should show me the man. But tomorrow, with the help I shall enlist—"

"What help?" I asked. "We don't want—"

"Outsiders? No, sir, there'll be no outsider. Miss Platt, sir, will give me her assistance."

That made me smile. Miss Platt was Chippendale's sweetheart. She was just about as smart, alert, knowing, painstaking as he was. We had employed her services before – in the Murder in the Squire's Pew case, in which she had tracked and watched the good-for-nothing parson – and we knew her abilities.

"Oh?" I said. "So Miss Platt's going to help, eh, Chippendale? And in what particular way, now?"

"When the car containing these two young gentlemen goes off, sir," replied Chippendale, "it will pass, at the farther entrance to the wharf, a certain taxi-cab, the driver of which will have received his orders from me. Miss Platt will be in that cab, sir. Though unseen, Miss Platt, and the driver aforesaid, will keep that car in sight wherever it goes! And the result will be communicated to me by Miss Platt, and by me to you."

"All right, Chippendale," I said. "But – why shouldn't we be in the cab?"

"No, sir – I shall be otherwise engaged," he replied. "I must do this my own way, Mr. Camberwell. There's five o'clock, sir!"

The deep boom of St. Paul's sounded suddenly over the City. One – two – three – four – five. On the fourth stroke a smart-looking car came round the corner and drew up at the door we were watching; on the fifth the door opened, and two men came out and descended the steps. One was Rupert Maxtondale. But who was the other? Whoever he was, I made a careful inspection of him through a pair of field-glasses which I had taken care to bring with me. He was apparently about Rupert Maxtondale's own age, which I had previously taken to be thirty or thereabouts, a tallish, active-looking fellow, well set up, well dressed, even to a fashionable smartness; dark complexion, dark hair, almost black moustache, carefully brushed upwards from the corners of his lips. He wore his black bowler hat a little to one side; this gave him something of a rakish appearance; altogether his was not the figure one expected to see emerging from the office of a coal company. Nor, for the matter of that, was Rupert Maxtondale, either. Rupert was very smartly dressed, too. At Heronswood I had only seen him in shooting or riding kit; he had always looked untidy. But here he was in a perfectly fitting dark suit, crowned by a soft hat of pearl-grey; obviously dealing in coal did not necessitate the wearing of sombre attire.

"Which is which, Mr. Camberwell?" asked Chippendale. "But I scarcely need ask, sir. It'll be the one in the grey hat."

"Right, Chippendale!" I assented. "That's Mr. Rupert Maxtondale. But I wonder who the other is?"

"One of the bosses there, I should say, sir. But I'll find out. Now they're off, Mr. Camberwell. You see my bit of a plot, sir? When they're off tomorrow afternoon, we follow."

The two men had by this time entered the car. We heard the door slammed to; the car drove off by the entrance at the other end of the wharf.

"I should like you to find out who that other man is, Chippendale," I said. "Can you manage that?"

"Leave it to me, Mr. Camberwell," he replied. "Before I've done, sir, I'll know everything about the inside of that office as intimately as if I worked there."

We left the stuffy room and went downstairs. The fat gentleman still sat in his little snuggery, reading his paper. Chippendale motioned me to go outside; he himself joined the fat gentleman. A few minutes later he came out to me and we walked away through the alleys and courts.

"The other man, Mr. Camberwell," said Chippendale, "is Mr. Collinghurst, manager of that office: Mr. Leonard Collinghurst."

I was surprised to hear that. Although he had not said so in so many words, I had gathered from Mr. Portinscale that Collinghurst was – well, at any rate, a middle-aged man. Portinscale had said that Rupert Maxtondale had been placed in charge of Collinghurst on being sent to his probation in London. Now it turned out – unless appearances were very deceptive – that he and Collinghurst were pretty much of an age.

"We may want to get some information about him, Chippendale," I said; "that's got to be considered."

"Anything you like, sir," he replied. "You and Mr. Chaney have only to give it a name, and the thing shall be done. Self and partner, Mr. Camberwell – meaning me and Fanny. Fanny, sir, Fanny is a bit of all there!"

Next day, about four o'clock in the afternoon, Chippendale made his excuses and disappeared from the office. We did not see him again until ten o'clock next morning. When he walked in then, Miss Fanny Platt walked in with him.

Chapter 13

MALMESBURY MANSIONS

I HAVE ALREADY SAID that Miss Fanny Platt had been employed by us on a previous occasion. At Chippendale's instance she had been commissioned to watch and track a certain ne'er-do-well parson whom we suspected of complicity in a murder, and she had done her work very well. Consequently when we knew that Chippendale had once more enlisted her services, we anticipated some good results and on her entrance became at once curious to know what she had to tell us.

"Well," demanded Chaney, after complimenting our ally on her increasing good looks and undoubted charms, "any luck last night? Find out anything worth reporting?"

Chippendale signed to Miss Platt to proceed. Miss Platt plunged straight into detailed narrative:

"Lots, Mr. Chaney!" she replied. "At least, considering the short time we were at work. I'll begin at the beginning – my beginning, anyway. I was down at the entrance at Warriner's Wharf at five minutes to five, sharp, yesterday afternoon, with the taxi-cab which Chippendale had commissioned and the driver to whom he'd already given special and particular instructions. Of course, I was lying low – there's plenty of cover about there. At five o'clock a private car came in at the other end of the wharf and pulled up at the offices of the Heronswood Colliery Company. A minute or two later, two gentlemen came out of the front door. From what Chip had told me, I knew which of these was Mr. Maxtondale and which Mr. Collinghurst. They got into the car. The car passed my taxi-cab. I came out of my hiding-place, got into the cab, and we followed, cautiously – of course both the driver and I had taken care to note the private car's number. We followed by way of Monument Street, King William Street, Cheapside, Newgate Street, Holborn, as far as the Holborn Restaurant. The two gentlemen got out there and went into a bar, but they weren't in there more than a few minutes – I suppose they called for a drink."

"Correct supposition, no doubt, my dear," remarked Chaney.

"Then they came out and resumed their journey," continued Miss Platt. "So did we. It was easy, Oxford Street, Portman Street, two or three turns through those small streets between Portman Square and Edgware Road to that big block of new flats called Malmesbury Mansions. There the chase came to an end. At Malmesbury Mansions – the front entrance – both gentlemen got out."

"And entered?" asked Chaney.

"And entered," assented Miss Platt. "Both. The car drove away and went to a garage close by."

"Oh, you made sure of that!"

"Certainly I did, Mr. Chaney. The two gentlemen were safe for the time being."

"Well – and afterwards?"

"Having ascertained that, I went to meet Chip at the spot we'd arranged on—"

"Minerva Café, Oxford Street," interrupted Chippendale, softly.

" – and there," continued Miss Platt, "I reported to him what I'd discovered. That finished my share in the job – up to then. He came in where I left off."

Chaney turned to Chippendale.

"Anything more, Chip?" he asked. "That all?"

"Not by a long chalk, Mr. Chaney!" replied Chippendale, cheerfully. "That's only the beginning, sir. We did a good deal and found out a good deal after that. But as the evenings are now beginning to be long, we took our time – it was no good going prospecting round Malmesbury Mansions until after dark had set in. So we enjoyed ourselves for an hour or two – tea first, then the pictures. Then about nine o'clock we strolled along to Malmesbury Mansions. Now, I wanted to get inside there – into the front entrance anyhow. I guessed there'd be a hall-porter there, and probably a board inside giving the names of the tenants. So while we were having tea at the Minerva, I made up a dummy letter and addressed it to Alfred Manvers, Esq., and wrote beneath the name: "Try Malmesbury Mansions first – if not – Marlborough Mansions."

"Good idea!" chuckled Chaney; "I see the dodge."

"We walked round to Malmesbury Mansions and after prospecting a bit I left Fanny outside and went in. There is a good big entrance hall there, and I saw at once that, just as I expected, there was a hall-porter there and also a board with names on it. I went up to the hall porter's box and, showing him the letter, said that the sender wasn't certain whether Mr. Manvers lived at Malmesbury Mansions or Marlborough Mansions. No Mr. Manvers there, the hall-porter said, and he pointed to the board on the wall. Now, that was just what I wanted, and I took a jolly good look at it – there were about twenty to twenty-five names. There was no Rupert Maxtondale amongst them. But there is a Leonard Collinghurst. He's got Flat Nineteen."

"You're sure there was no Maxtondale?" asked Chaney. "Positive?"

"Dead certain; I took particular care," replied Chippendale. "Of course, having applied to the hall-porter first, I didn't dare to linger over the name-board, but I saw all I wanted to see. Then I cleared out – and it was a good job I did, for if I'd been in that hall a minute longer, Mr. Maxtondale and Mr. Collinghurst would have spotted me! Then they'd have known me again, which would have been highly inconvenient, probably."

"How would they have come to spot you?" asked Chaney. "Came in?"

"No, they came out! A minute after I'd rejoined Fanny at the other side of the street, the hall-porter came out and whistled for a cab. Then two men came out and I recognised Maxtondale and Collinghurst. They were both in evening dress – regular swells; everything tip-top from shining shoes to opera-hats. And they'd a lady with 'em – togged up to the nines! Diamonds! Or what looked like 'em. She – but I'm no hand at describing that sort of thing – Fanny can tell you."

"She was very beautifully dressed," said Miss Platt. "Of course, being across the street, and it being dark and all that, I can't give you details, Mr. Chaney and Mr. Camberwell, but you can take it from me that she looked uncommonly handsome – and she was a handsome girl, too! I was near enough to see that."

"Girl, eh?" said Chaney. "How old, now?"

"Oh, well, I say girl," replied Miss Platt, "but it would be more correct to say young woman. Anything between twenty-five and thirty, I should say."

"You say you were near enough to see that much," I said; "can you describe this young woman?"

"Well, fairly well, Mr. Camberwell. Tallish – very good figure – bright complexion and very bright eyes – I could see her eyes sparkle in the lamplight. Brownish hair, I think – with a bit of gold in it. Laughed very merrily – she was laughing when they came out of the door and while they stood waiting for the cab. A jolly sort of young lady, I should say. And she certainly was beautifully dressed – no doubt about that. I wish," concluded Miss Platt, regretfully, "I wish I'd been closer – her gown and her cloak were worth seeing, I'll bet."

I glanced at Chaney – Chaney saw that some idea had occurred.

"Well?" he said. "You're wondering – ?"

"Miss Platt's very good description made me think of a certain young lady we encountered at Heronswood, Chaney," I answered. "Do you think—"

Chaney smote his desk with a thump.

"By George!" he exclaimed. "Exactly! I wonder if that's so? Might be – Well," he went on, turning to our assistants, "what next?"

"Next, Mr. Chaney," replied Chippendale, "they all got into the cab and went off. I followed – on foot, of course as hard as I could, after telling Fanny to go home. Fortunately, at the next turning there was a block in the traffic; fortunately, too, I saw an empty taxi close by. I got into it and told the man to keep the other in sight. After that it was plain sailing – I tracked 'em till their cab stopped and they got out."

"And where did they get out?" asked Chaney.

"Hyacanthus Club," replied Chippendale, tersely.

"And where and what is the Hyacanthus Club?" demanded Chaney. "Never heard of it! And I know most of 'em."

"Nobody ever heard of it – till lately," said Chippendale. "It's in Steek Street, off Oxford Street. Same premises used to be the Miraflora Club. That was raided and suppressed. As to this, well, the policeman on duty, close by, told me that there was nothing known against it, so far – dancing-club, frequented by apparently quite respectable people. Started about six months ago."

"And you saw 'em go in there?"

"All three. There I left 'em, Mr. Chaney. Didn't see any use in hanging about all night. But," continued Chippendale, hopefully, "I can find out everything there is to be known about the place in a day or two, if you wish."

"Go ahead!" said Chaney. "Full report. I suppose you couldn't get inside, Chip?"

"I could," replied Chippendale, "I know a chap who is a regular frequenter of these places – he'll know all the ropes. Only necessary for me to stick on a swell outfit – and I can do that, easy."

"Good boy!" said Chaney. "Try that, too, and keep your eyes open – and your ears." He turned to me. "Anything else?" he asked.

"Yes," I answered. I looked at Miss Platt. "Do you think you could come here early tomorrow morning?" I inquired.

"I can come here any time tomorrow morning, Mr. Camberwell," she replied. "What do you call early? Five? – six? – seven? – eight?"

"Nine o'clock will do," I answered. "Be here at nine o'clock."

"Smart? – or otherwise?" she asked.

"Smart!" I said, smiling. "We're going into a smart region."

Chaney turned on me when Chippendale and his sweetheart had withdrawn.

"What's the game?" he asked.

"Miss Weekes is the game, Chaney," I replied. "She told me when we were breakfasting at her father's that she was a riding-mistress in London, and that she could be seen any morning in the Row with a string of small girls and boys. Very well – I propose to escort Miss Fanny Platt to the Row tomorrow morning, with the object of ascertaining if Miss Ettie Weekes is the young lady whom Miss Platt and Mr. Chippendale saw in the company of Mr. Rupert Maxtondale and Mr. Leonard Collinghurst last night – see?"

"I see!" he said. "Good business! Um! I wonder, now—"

But he left that unfinished, and I didn't ask him to finish. I had a lot of vague wonders myself, chasing each other here and there in my brain. This – that – the other –

Miss Platt, very smart and up to date, turned in at the office as the clocks struck nine next morning, and by five minutes past that hour she and I were in a taxi-cab, going westward.

"What's the job, Mr. Camberwell?" she inquired as we moved off. "Anything similar to last night's?"

"Something of the same sort," I replied. "The fact is, I want to point out to you – if we're successful in finding her there – a young lady whom I hope to see in the Row this morning—"

"Riding?" she asked.

"Riding, I expect. Well, if we see her, I want you to take a very good look at her and then—"

"Tell you if she's the young lady we saw last night outside Malmesbury Mansions, I suppose! Is that it, Mr. Camberwell?"

"You've hit it!" I answered. "That's exactly it."

"And what then?" she asked.

"Then I want you to follow her and to see where she goes. That – for the present – is all."

"Bit difficult if she's on horseback," she remarked. "But I can come again tomorrow morning – on a horse."

"Oh, you ride, do you?" I asked, somewhat surprised. For Miss Platt, if she was anything, was a genuine Cockney.

"Ride anything – barebacked, if you like," she answered coolly. "I've got an uncle who's a farmer down in the country – Buckinghamshire. He's some good horses – goes hunting himself – and I've ridden ever since I was a kid. I can easily hire a mount tomorrow morning – if this young lady is in the habit of coming to the Park every day."

"I don't think there'll be any necessity for that," I said. "The young lady I'm hoping to see is a riding mistress. I expect to see her in charge of a string of children. You'd follow that lot on foot – or in a taxi?"

"Well, let's see her first," replied Miss Platt. "If I've once seen her, the rest can be left to me."

"Safely, I'm sure," I hastened to say. "You and Chippendale are very clever."

"So – so!" she said. "We can learn."

However, arrived in Hyde Park, Miss Platt assumed the role of teacher rather than that of taught. Taking arrangements into her own hands, she instructed me as to what we were to do. We were to walk, in presumably rapt conversation, under the trees at the side of the Row, paying no particular attention to the riders, and certainly not stopping to look at any of them. If I saw the lady of whom I was in search, I was merely to say so to my companion and then keep my eyes on anything but the object of our attention – everything else could be left to Miss Platt.

The Row was already pretty full. We took one turn up and another down without result. But at our second turn Miss Ettie Weekes, very fetching in her dark habit, white stock, and bowler hat, hove in sight, shepherding a string of small girls and boys, variously mounted. And with this lot, as Miss Weekes's assistant, was a smart groom.

"Here we are!" I said. "You look – and I don't."

Miss Platt looked.

"That's easy enough," she said a second later. "I know the lot. At least, I know the groom. He's from Litterton's."

"And what's Litterton's?" I asked.

"Swell West End place – just off Edgware Road," she answered. "Teach riding – let park hacks out and so on. Quite easy, this."

"But – the young lady?" I demanded, anxiously. "Is she—"

"I can't be sure. I believe she is the one I saw last night. But you see I only saw her by the light of the street-lamps, and there was the width of the street between us. Still, I'm very strongly of opinion that she is. Now, Mr. Camberwell, you leave this to me – you go away. Does she know you?"

"Yes – she knows me," I admitted. "That is, I've met her."

"Then go away just now – go across the grass there and clear out. I'll call round at your office later. Bye-bye."

I went. Miss Platt had a way with her. Also, I knew that it was best to leave things to her and await results.

The results came in two hours later. Miss Platt entered my room, seated herself, and nodded.

"Came off all right," she announced. "I followed her quite easily. First of all to Litterton's, where she left her horse and took a taxi. And then – to Malmesbury Mansions!"

Chapter 14

THE NIGHTCLUB

I HAD BEEN EXPECTING to hear that. Something – I don't know what – had already prompted me to the conclusion that the handsome young lady seen in company with Rupert Maxtondale and Collinghurst was Ettie Weekes. Therefore I showed no surprise at Miss Platt's statement.

"You actually traced her there?" I asked.

"Watched her enter," replied Miss Platt. "And subsequently I saw still more. After she'd gone in, I thought that, being on the spot, I'd just hang round a bit, inspecting the neighbourhood – such knowledge once acquired, Mr. Camberwell, always comes in useful. So I scouted round here and there, and, coming back to the front of Malmesbury Mansions, I saw my lady emerge from the front door. She'd changed her riding habit for a smart walking costume, and she had a kiddie with her."

"A – what?" I exclaimed.

"Kiddie – kid – youngster – small child," answered Miss Platt. "In plainer language, a little boy, Mr. Camberwell. Fine little chap, too – about five years old, I should say. And with them a smart nurse – looked like a French girl."

I don't know whether this news caused me to open my mouth and stare at Miss Platt in blank astonishment, but I certainly was surprised, and for the moment could scarcely think of anything to say. What I did say sounded, no doubt, extremely foolish.

"Was – was it hers?" I asked.

"Now, come, Mr. Camberwell, how on earth should I be able to answer that?" demanded Miss Platt archly. "But what do you mean or which do you mean? The young lady's or the French nurse's?"

"The young lady's, of course," I said. "Who else?"

"Well, it might have been somebody else's, you know, after all, Mr. Camberwell – a friend's, for instance. All I can say is that the young lady held the boy by the hand, and the nurse walked behind. I should say the young lady, from what I saw, was the proud and doting mamma."

This was, indeed, the sort of information that made me sit up and think. Ettie Weekes a young and devoted matron! In that case —

"See anything more?" I inquired.

"I followed them a bit," continued Miss Platt; "followed them, in fact, as far as Park Lane. When I saw that they were going to cross into the Park, I turned back, for I'd got an idea. I went back to Malmesbury Mansions, Mr. Camberwell, walked straight in, and inspected the board in the hall on which there's the names of the people who have flats there. See?"

"Excellent idea!" I said, admiringly. "And you found—"

"I found that there's only one couple living there," replied Miss Platt. "Anyway, there's only one couple with its names on the board. And that's Mr. and Mrs. Ronald Morton."

I made a note of that.

"You didn't see the name of Maxtondale?" I asked.

"No such name there, Mr. Camberwell. But there's Collinghurst. Chip saw that, though. Mr. and Mrs. Ronald Morton have Flat Number Eighteen; Mr. Collinghurst has Flat Nineteen – next to theirs. All the other people in Malmesbury Mansions appeared to be of the single persuasion."

"Could you recall any particular name there if one were suggested to you?" I asked.

"I think so – yes, I'm sure I could. I studied the board very carefully."

"Did you see the name Weekes? Miss Weekes? Miss E. Weekes?"

"No, that I'm sure I didn't. No such name there, Mr. Camberwell. And, as I say, I read all the names carefully. There was no one about in the hall when I entered, so I took my time. Then the hall-porter stuck his head out of the office. 'Wanting somebody, miss?' he asked. 'No,' I said, 'I'm looking to see if you've any flats to let here.' 'For a single person, miss?' he inquired. 'Self,' I said. 'There's two or three on the top floor,' he answered. 'Like to look at them, miss?' 'What do they run to – a year?' I inquired. 'Oh, from a hundred and fifty pounds onwards,' he answered. 'And upwards, I suppose,' I said. 'Far too much for me – good morning,' I said. And cleared out, of course."

Chaney came in just then. I summarised Miss Platt's discoveries to him. He sent her away presently and turned to me with a very serious face.

"I say, Camberwell, this is getting what they call a bit thick!" he exclaimed. "I told you from the beginning that that chap Rupert Maxtondale had something on his mind! Well, here it is! – double-life business."

"Looks like it, Chaney," I agreed. "But, to my mind, the question is: how is all this relative to the affairs at Heronswood?"

"Ay, but that's what we've got to find out!" he answered. "That it's some relation I'll bet my bottom dollar! What I would like to know is – who knows of these things?"

"In particular – what things?" I asked.

"Well it looks to me as if Rupert and the steward's daughter were secretly married," he said. "Now, then, who knows of that? Not Sir Stephen Maxtondale, you may be sure. But do her people? I doubt that, too. I should say nobody knows – unless it's that manager fellow, Collinghurst.

"Well, don't you see, whoever knows must, of course, have a big hold on Rupert!" he went on. "A word to Sir Stephen and who knows what might happen? Sir Stephen Maxtondale, if my judgment of him's correct, is a very proud man and wouldn't be at all pleased to know that his son and heir had married the daughter of the steward. Remember, from all we've heard, that Sir Stephen can cut Rupert off with a shilling, as the saying goes. The estates are not entailed – Rupert's absolutely dependent upon his father."

"What're you working up to, Chaney?" I asked.

"Well, now, supposing that Rupert has had, or, rather, has, some financial backer in London – or elsewhere? Rupert, if he's married to the girl, and lives in an expensive flat, and keeps servants, and the French nursemaid, and all that, and goes out o' nights, dressed up, with his wife, to nightclubs, isn't going to do it all on the allowance we've heard of. Somebody's finding him in money, on the chance of being well rewarded when he succeeds to the title and estates. Now, supposing that the somebody was somewhere about when Sir John Maxtondale turned up so unexpectedly and inconveniently – eh?"

"But – who can we think of?" I asked.

"What about that man that Rabbage told me of? The sporting-looking individual who called at Heronswood when Rupert was last down there and whom Rabbage afterwards saw in Monkseaton. Who's he? We ought to know."

"There's a lot we ought to know," I remarked. "No end! What do you propose?"

He thought this over for a while; then he rose from his chair and, opening the door, called for Chippendale.

Chippendale was invaluable at times like this – a past master in the arts of listening and sizing things up. In ten minutes he had heard all there was to hear and was ready with a suggestion.

"The thing to do, Mr. Chaney and Mr. Camberwell," he said, "is to visit the Hyacanthus Club. I can do that – I know a chap who's keen on all those places and knows all the ropes; he'll get me in."

"Who is he?" asked Chaney. "Dependable?"

"Safe as houses, sir! Chap that's in the office I used to be in. But," continued Chippendale, "I was just an ordinary clerk – he's an articled clerk. Bit of a swell and has money. Name of Mossman – Albert Mossman."

"You'll have to tog up," said Chaney.

"That's all right, Mr. Chaney. I'm prepared – new dress clothes not so long since, sir. We shall do it proper, me and Mossman. Of course, it'll cost a bit."

"Take what you want out of the cash, then. Don't stint yourselves, either," added Chaney. "No use sticking at an extra shilling or two in a case of this sort – and I think we've got carte blanche, as the French say, eh, Camberwell?"

"Chippendale may lay out whatever is strictly necessary," I said, cautiously. "He's not given to extravagance."

"There's just another thing, gentlemen," remarked Chippendale. "I should wish, considering everything, that Fanny should accompany me. Fanny, gentlemen, can come in uncommonly useful on occasion."

"You'll be nominating Fanny for a partnership with us before long, my lad!" said Chaney. "Take her!"

After that came a few days' waiting. It appeared, from Chippendale's reports of his conversations with his friend Mr. Albert Mossman, that a little time was required for the necessary arrangements. Then one morning Chippendale informed me that all was settled.

"We're going tonight, Mr. Camberwell," said Chippendale. "Fanny, sir, has got a new frock. She's not one to do things by half, Fanny. And Albert, Mr. Camberwell, he's taking a girl, too. Of course, she doesn't know what we're going for – she's just a makeweight, so that there'll be two couples of us."

"Well, keep your eyes open, Chippendale," I said. "And if those three people are there, watch them!"

"Eyes will be open, all right, Mr. Camberwell," he answered, reassuringly. "And also ears. Of course, it may be necessary to go more than once. But I hope to have something to report tomorrow."

He was halfway out of the door when he turned back.

"There's just one little matter you might give me a tip about, Mr. Camberwell," he said. "You know more about these things than I do. Now, I've been in the habit of wearing a made-up tie, sir – you know, you can get those made-up dress ties to look as if you'd tied 'em yourself. But Albert, he says no gentleman should ever wear a tie in evening dress that he hasn't tied himself. What do you say, sir?"

"I think there's a prejudice against made-up ties, Chippendale," I said. "Your friend is probably well up in the latest fashions. I'm not. Better agree with him."

Chippendale sighed.

"I never could make a bow tie," he said, sadly. "They slither round to the side. But I dare say Fanny can fix things. You mightn't believe it, Mr. Camberwell, but Fanny—"

He gave me a half-sentimental look which was clearly intended to convey an overwhelming sense of Miss Platt's abilities. And of those abilities – in certain directions – I certainly entertained no doubt.

Chippendale did not turn up at the office until, for him, an unusually late hour next morning. He looked somewhat pale, and a little fishy about the eyes, but he had a story for us.

"We didn't do badly last night, for a short cut, Mr. Chaney and Mr. Camberwell," he said. "In fact, I think I may say we did very well. First of all, about that club, gentlemen. From all I saw, I should say it's quite an ultra-respectable place and not at all likely to attract the attention of the police authorities. We were there from about ten o'clock till between two or three in the morning, and I saw nothing that evaded the law. Dance-club, pure and simple; very nice class of person, too. I danced with some uncommon nice ladies, and Fanny, gentlemen, was in great request amongst the gentlemen – real swells, too, they were; one or two of them, Fanny said, were real lords. But about the business side of it – I can tell you exactly all about that club now. The entrance fee is a guinea, or introduction by somebody who's already been there. Bert Mossman, he arranged all that. Then you pay half a guinea each, every time you go. Supper's seven and sixpence, not including wines. They don't charge exorbitant prices for the wines, either, nor for drinks. And you can't get a drink anyway after regulation hours – only soft drinks – coffee and so on. Very strictly regulated place, I should say, which means, of course, as far as I could see. And I talked to several fellows there, and Fanny, she got a good deal out of the ladies. Quite proper ladies, as far as I could judge, gentlemen. No rowdyism anywhere. But now you want to know if I discovered anything. I did! I discovered a good deal. To begin with, the place belongs to the two gentlemen at Malmesbury Mansions, Mr. Collinghurst and Mr. Ronald Morton."

"Is that a positive fact?" asked Chaney.

"That's what I was told by a man who talked to me a good bit and who seemed to know," replied Chippendale. "And the two were there and so was the young lady that I saw the other night coming out of Malmesbury Mansions with them. They were all there dancing, like all the rest of us, but there was an air of proprietorship about the two men that didn't escape my notice, gentlemen. However, they've a man there as manager – known openly as manager – who's very much in evidence. He was in evening dress, of course, but I should have said that he'd have looked much more his real self if he'd been in a suit of loud clothes, making a book on the racecourse! That sort, you understand – sporty."

Chaney pricked up his ears. I knew what he was thinking of. He was recalling Rabbage's account of the man who had called on Rupert Maxtondale at Heronswood.

"Oh!" he said. "Can you describe him, Chip?"

"Certainly, Mr. Chaney – I took particular notice of him when I found out who and what he was – and I soon discovered that, for he was here and there, all over the place, seeing after things, and frequently in talk with the two men from Malmesbury Mansions. Big, fleshy chap – fourteen or fifteen stone – round, clean-shaven face, fresh complexion, light hair, rather bulbous nose, small eyes, bit overdressed – flash jewellery and that sort of thing. Wore a made-up tie, Mr. Camberwell."

"Did you get his name?" asked Chaney.

"I did – I heard a lady address him soon after we got in," replied Chippendale. "She called him Mr. Mason."

Chaney asked Chippendale a few unimportant questions; then he and I settled down to consider what we should do. There was no doubt whatever – could be no possible doubt – that Rupert Maxtondale was living a double life in London, a life that his father knew nothing about. It was quite evident that Sir Stephen exercised no supervision over his son's doings; quite evident, too, that Sir Stephen was, in all probability, grossly deceived in his London manager, Collinghurst. And the question before us was – should we put Sir Stephen in possession of the facts which had come to our notice? Or should we pursue our investigations still further in the hope of even more important discoveries?

When Chaney had a question to answer or a discussion to make, he always slept on it, and he slept on this. But next morning he had made up his mind.

"Camberwell," he said as soon as he came to business, "I've thought everything over. We must see old Ellerthorpe."

"And tell him – all we know?" I asked.

"Every blessed thing!" he answered. "Ellerthorpe is the family solicitor and he employed us. We must put him wise – and at once. Stick your hat on."

Chapter 15

CONSULTATION AND REVELATION

MR. ELLERTHORPE, FOUND SEATED at his desk in his private office, received us with an apathetic glance.

"Any news?" he asked in a tone which matched his glance. "Something to tell me?"

Chaney seated himself at the side of the desk before he replied.

"We've no definite news, Mr. Ellerthorpe," he said; "that is, as regards the murder business. Have you heard anything from Heronswood?"

"Nothing!" replied Mr. Ellerthorpe. He looked speculatively from one to the other of us.

"Want to see me about something?"

"We want to ask you a few questions, Mr. Ellerthorpe, on a subject which, it seems to us, may be relative to the murder of Sir John Maxtondale," announced Chaney. "I may as well go straight to the point. Do you know anything of the exact relations between Sir Stephen Maxtondale and his son, Mr. Rupert?"

Mr. Ellerthorpe looked sharply at Chaney. His tone and manner changed.

"What do you mean?" he asked, a little snappily. "Father and son, of course!"

"I mean exactly what I say, Mr. Ellerthorpe," replied Chaney. "That they are father and son we are quite aware. But do you know – more?"

"Do you?" asked Mr. Ellerthorpe, suspiciously. "You – seem to!"

"In strict confidence – you employed us, you know, Mr. Ellerthorpe – we do!" said Chaney. "But we want to know what you know – and if you know what we know. It's – necessary."

"What do you know?" demanded Ellerthorpe.

"I'll tell you, in strict confidence," responded Chaney. "Before we left Monkseaton we were placed in possession of what we consider very important, and, possibly, very significant, information as to the past and present relations of Sir Stephen Maxtondale and his son. I'm not going to tell you how or where or from whom we got our information, but we believe it to be absolutely correct. And we want to know – in view of our wish to supplement it with further information which we ourselves have acquired in the course of our investigations which you commissioned us to make, if you are in possession of this knowledge—"

"How on earth can I tell if I know unless I know what it is that you know?" interrupted Mr. Ellerthorpe with some show of irritation. "What is it?"

Chaney drew his chair nearer to the desk.

"We were told certain things – as facts," he said. "I should like to know, from you, as family solicitor, if they are facts. First, Mr. Ellerthorpe, is it a fact that Mr. Rupert Maxtondale as a very young man got heavily into debt?"

Mr. Ellerthorpe began to push about the papers with which he had been occupying himself at our entrance.

"Is this – necessary to your purpose?" he asked.

"Absolutely!" replied Chaney. "I won't pursue investigations in any case, Mr. Ellerthorpe, if anything is kept from me!"

"Well, yes, then," said Mr. Ellerthorpe. "That is a fact. He did!"

"Is it a fact that Sir Stephen paid off the debts – a big sum?"

"Yes – that's correct."

"On certain conditions?"

"There were conditions."

"Were the conditions that Mr. Rupert Maxtondale, free from his debts, should enter the London office of the Heronswood Colliery Company at a certain salary, which was to be subject to an annual increase; that he was to remain in that employment a certain number of years and to be absolutely dependent on his salary; that he was not to incur any further debts, and that he was, in short, to make good? Is that all correct?"

"Yes, that's all correct. Your informant—"

"Never mind our informant, Mr. Ellerthorpe! The important thing is to know if what he told me is true. Evidently it is. But another question or two. Was Mr. Rupert practically entrusted to the London manager of the Heronswood Colliery Company, Mr. Collinghurst?"

"Yes, that's true. Collinghurst is a steady, reliable—"

"We'll drop Mr. Collinghurst for the moment. Is it a fact, Mr. Ellerthorpe, that Mr. Rupert Maxtondale is entirely dependent on his father, and that, though he is, of course, heir to the title, he need not necessarily inherit the estates? In other words, the estates are not entailed?"

"Yes, that's also true. But—"

"A moment, Mr. Ellerthorpe, and I've done. It comes to this – Mr. Rupert is entirely dependent upon his father's goodwill, and his father's goodwill is dependent on Mr. Rupert's adherence to the conditions? Am I right?"

"Yes, you're quite right. But," added Mr. Ellerthorpe, "as far as I'm aware, Mr. Rupert Maxtondale has kept and is keeping the conditions. He lives on his salary, in a very quiet way, and the period of probation—"

Chaney waved a hand; he never encouraged purposeless talk.

"Mr. Ellerthorpe – I'm afraid we shall shock you. Mr. Rupert Maxtondale is not doing anything of the sort. Mr. Camberwell and I are in a position to prove to you – and mind, Mr. Ellerthorpe, that we've come to you in strict confidence – that Mr. Rupert Maxtondale is living a double life here in London. It is true that he attends the office of the Heronswood Colliery Company at Warriner's Wharf regularly and punctually. But that is only one side of things. The other is this – Mr. Rupert Maxtondale is a partner in a West End nightclub, a dancing-club, the Hyacanthus. The other partner is the Mr. Collinghurst just mentioned. Mr. Rupert Maxtondale, under the name of Ronald

Morton, lives in an expensive flat at Malmesbury Mansions, and we believe that he is married to Miss Ettie Weekes, the daughter of Weekes the steward at Heronswood. We believe they have been married some time, Mr. Ellerthorpe, for there is a boy, who appears to be about five or six years of age. And," concluded Chaney, "we're informed that he's a fine little chap, too!"

I was watching Mr. Ellerthorpe closely while Chaney was talking; never in all my – limited – experience had I seen a man's face change as his did! In a few minutes he went through many moods: he was doubtful, he was incredulous, he was surprised, eventually he was amazed. Speech seemed to fail him; he rose from his desk, walked about the room; finally, bringing himself to a halt, he plunged his hands in his pockets and confronted Chaney.

"Do you mean to tell me that all that is true?" he asked. "True?"

"We've no doubt of it!" replied Chaney.

"And – and – that Rupert is married to – to the steward's daughter?"

"He's either married to her or she's living with him," said Chaney, bluntly. "And," he added, "from what I saw of the young lady at her father's house, that morning when her mother gave us some breakfast, I should say they're married."

"Good God!" exclaimed Mr. Ellerthorpe. "Sir Stephen would – would—"

"Yes?" asked Chaney.

"Oh, I don't know what he'd do! Sir Stephen is a proud man, and that his son – only son, too! – should marry his steward's daughter—"

"Damn fine girl, anyway," muttered Chaney. "Might have done worse – much worse!"

"That's not the point," said Mr. Ellerthorpe, severely. "The Maxtondales are a very old family. But this nightclub business! You're sure?"

"Certain! And, personally, I'm not surprised at anything I've told you, Mr. Ellerthorpe," replied Chaney. "Sir Stephen Maxtondale has only himself to blame. He sends this lad – heir to fifty thousand pounds a year! – up here to live on a miserable salary, leaves him alone, only asks him down to the parental roof now and then, and, in a word, neglects him. What do you expect? A young fellow who's accumulated twenty-five thousand pounds' worth of debts at twenty-one isn't going to settle down readily to a screw of three hundred or even five hundred pounds a year – he'll look about for some means of supplementing his income. Well, he and Collinghurst have hit on one – nightclubs, Mr. Ellerthorpe, are very profitable. As to his marriage – for I'll lay any odds you like that they are married – I see nothing improbable in that. I understand that the young lady came up to Litterton's some years ago as riding-mistress – well, she and Rupert came from the same district, met, had, no doubt, tastes in common; and each wanted companionship. Natural thing they should marry. Nothing at all improbable or to be wondered at in what I've told you, Mr. Ellerthorpe."

"What I want to know," said Mr. Ellerthorpe, "is – what has all this to do with the murder of Sir John Maxtondale?"

"Ah, now we come to it," replied Chaney. "Supposing – we've got to suppose, now and then – supposing that somebody has been financing Mr. Rupert Maxtondale on the strength of his expectations? We know what his expectations are – that, in due course, he'll succeed his father and come into possession of the family property and estates. Well, although Mr. Rupert is dependent on his father, and although the estates are not entailed, there are plenty of people who would take a sporting chance that Mr. Rupert will eventually get everything, and would cheerfully advance him money. Now, supposing that such a person suddenly became aware of the existence of Sir John Maxtondale? What would that mean? Nothing less – you'll correct me if I'm wrong, Mr. Ellerthorpe – nothing less than that the Heronswood property and estates were not Sir Stephen's at all and therefore could not come to Rupert – or if they ever did come to him, not for a long time. What then? I think it's obvious. There are people who, seeing their money in danger, wouldn't stick for one second at clearing Sir John out of the way!"

"As a barrier between them and their chances of getting this money from Rupert, you mean?" said Mr. Ellerthorpe.

"Exactly! I say there are people who wouldn't scruple about removing Sir John – as a barrier. Not for a minute!"

"But – are you suggesting that – if there are such people or such a person – the fact of Sir John's return was discovered in London and that he was followed down to Heronswood and murdered?" asked Mr. Ellerthorpe.

"I don't say it was discovered in London," replied Chaney. "It may have been discovered locally. For anything you or we know, there may be somebody in the neighbourhood of Heronswood who's acted as financial backer to Rupert. Tell me this, Mr. Ellerthorpe, if you can. When the settlement of the young fellow's debts was made some years ago, had he any local claims on him? Had he been borrowing money anywhere round about Heronswood?"

Mr. Ellerthorpe reflected awhile.

"It is some years since all that happened," he said at last; "Sir Stephen employed a local firm of solicitors, Matthewman and Burder, of Monkseaton, to wind up and settle matters. But as family solicitor I had a good deal to do with it – chiefly as adviser as to what should be done. I remember that there was a man in that neighbourhood who gave me some trouble – I had to have him here and talk very seriously to him before we got a settlement with him – he held a good deal of Rupert Maxtondale's paper, bills, promissory notes – that sort of thing."

"Moneylender, I suppose," said Chaney.

"No, he wasn't – had he been a professional moneylender, it would have been easier to deal with him," replied Mr. Ellerthorpe. "He'd some connection with the Turf – was, or had been, a bookmaker, I think. But these weren't racing debts – bets or anything of that sort. He'd advanced Rupert money privately. His name, I recollect, was Mason. He lived – then – at Birmingham."

Chaney started at mention of the name and turned to me.

"Mason!" he exclaimed. "Mason? Isn't that the name Chippendale spoke of?" he asked. "Manager at the Hyacanthus?"

"Same name," I assented.

"Do you remember this man Mason, Mr. Ellerthorpe?" continued Chaney, turning to the solicitor. "His general appearance, anyway?"

"As I said just now, it's some years ago," replied Mr. Ellerthorpe. "But yes, I do remember something of the man – I took an instinctive dislike to him. Just the type you expect to see on a racecourse, loud-voiced, flashily dressed, assertive – a common sort of person. I think," he continued, smiling, "I think, or seem to recollect, that as regards his actual personal appearance he was very red-faced and had an unusually big nose. A – oh, nasty sort of person altogether. Still, he had the whip hand of us, and I had to settle with him. Mason – yes, that was the name. But why do you inquire?"

"Because the present manager of – and perhaps partner in – the Hyacanthus Club is a man named Mason, and from what you say about his appearance, I should say he's the man you're talking about," replied Chaney. "And on this follows what seems a highly important matter. We heard, just before leaving Heronswood, that one morning during Mr. Rupert Maxtondale's recent stay there, a man corresponding to the description of this Mason called at Heronswood Park and asked for Mr. Rupert, who at once went out with him and was away from the house – presumably with him – for some time."

"Who told you that?" asked Mr. Ellerthorpe.

"Rabbage, the butler. And Rabbage told me more – that he himself, being in Monkseaton next morning, saw this man again – in company with Mr. Rupert Maxtondale."

Mr. Ellerthorpe began to shake his head in a very significant fashion.

"Dear, dear, dear, dear!" he said. "I wonder if this is – is all that you seem to suggest? If it is, there will be no end of trouble. I dread to think what Sir Stephen may say and do. He is a good landlord, a generous man, a man of nice feeling, but he has very strict and unbendable notions, and when he discovered the truth about his son's affairs at the time you have mentioned, he was very angry – terribly angry. Of course, he made matters right, but it was on conditions. And if he finds that these conditions have not been adhered to – dear, dear, I'm afraid there'll be trouble. And then – this marriage. You really think there is a marriage?"

"Hope so, for the girl's sake, anyway," replied Chaney. "There's a youngster, too, Mr. Ellerthorpe. Don't forget that."

"I'm not forgetting anything," sighed Mr. Ellerthorpe. "The child is, of course – if it is a marriage – in the direct line of succession to the title. Well, I see no way of keeping all these things from Sir Stephen. They're bound to come out sooner or later. I think, however, I had better see Mr. Rupert Maxtondale first."

"So do I!" asserted Chaney. "Just what I should suggest. Have it out with him before approaching his father."

"Yes, yes," said Mr. Ellerthorpe, "but – would you mind being present, as informants? Rather awkward and delicate situation, I know, but you could say, without giving names, that the information had been given to you by people who knew that you were employed on the case, eh? We must really get at the truth, the plain undoubted truth, you know."

"We've no objections to anything you propose in that way, Mr. Ellerthorpe," replied Chaney. "It's the plain truth that we want."

Mr. Ellerthorpe turned to a telephone directory and then to his telephone. In a few minutes he replaced the receiver and looked round at us.

"Mr. Rupert Maxtondale is coming along at once," he said.

Chapter 16

THE TWO
TELEGRAMS

THE WINDOWS OF MR. Ellerthorpe's private room looked out on the gardens and roadway of Lincoln's Inn Fields, and as I stood in one of them, watching whatever it was that was just then going on, I saw a car come up to the entrance and Rupert Maxtondale get out of it. It seemed to me from the hurried glance which he gave at the front of Mr. Ellerthorpe's offices that he was anxious and even perturbed; there was undoubted anxiety on his face when, a moment later, he was shown in. But that expression changed on the instant. At the first sight of Chaney and me he pulled himself up, scowling.

"Hello, Ellerthorpe!—" he had already begun as the door opened. "What—" But there he stopped. "What did you send for me for?" he demanded, sharply.

"Take a seat, Mr. Rupert," said Ellerthorpe. "I think you know these gentlemen? Mr. Chaney, Mr. Camberwell?"

Rupert Maxtondale paid no attention to this. He did not so much as vouchsafe a single glance in our direction after that first look of dislike and – was I wrong in surmising it? – fear. And we, on our part, offered no salutation to him, but we continued to watch him, steadily.

"What do you want, Ellerthorpe?" he asked again. "And why, if you wish to see me, don't you see me in private?"

"Because I don't wish to see you in private!" retorted Mr. Ellerthorpe, with a sudden show of spirit which made Rupert start and glance suspiciously at him. "And I have a reason, of course, for desiring the attendance and presence of Mr. Chaney and Mr. Camberwell. I want to ask you some questions."

"What about?" growled Rupert.

"But before doing so," continued Mr. Ellerthorpe, "I want to remind you that I am fully acquainted with the terms and conditions of the agreement which you made with your father some years ago: I know every condition, every term. Now, my first question is – are you keeping to the conditions laid down?"

"Who's been saying I'm not?" asked Rupert angrily.

"Mr. Chaney and Mr. Camberwell, in pursuing the inquiry with which I, at your father's request, entrusted them," continued Mr. Ellerthorpe, "have received certain information which inclines me to think you are not. That information—"

"So you've set spies to work!" interrupted Rupert, furiously, and with a dark scowl in our direction. "Professional spies."

I thought that would rouse Chaney to speech. It did. He stepped forward.

"Look here, young man!" he said quietly. "Just let me remind you that whatever it is that we have been able to tell Mr. Ellerthorpe we could have told your father! We have not told your father. We came to Mr. Ellerthorpe, bringing him information which has come in our way."

Rupert scowled more blackly than ever, glancing at Chaney out of his eye-corners as if at some animal that he longed to kill.

"Pack of lies, no doubt!" he sneered. "Who—"

"In that case, you can no doubt tell us the truth," said Mr. Ellerthorpe. "So we will go straight to the point – to the various points. Is it or is it not true that you have an interest, a financial interest, in a certain nightclub, known as the Hyacanthus?"

Rupert's face flushed. But he assumed an air of bravado.

"Well, what if I have?" he retorted. "What's that to do—"

"We will take it – from that answer – that you have," continued Mr. Ellerthorpe. "Is it also true that your father's manager, Mr. Collinghurst, has a like interest?"

"Well, and what if he has?" demanded Rupert. "He's—"

"We will take it that he has," said Mr. Ellerthorpe. "Now, Mr. Rupert, we come to a much more important question. Is it true that you are married to the daughter of your father's steward – to Miss Ettie Weekes?"

I thought that would produce an effect. Rupert Maxtondale rose from his chair, not violently, but quietly and faced round on Chaney with a look that was not at all good to see.

"Damn you and your spies' tricks!" he said. "This is your work, you damned spy! I knew as soon as I saw you and your precious—"

"You had better answer my question," interrupted Mr. Ellerthorpe. "As Mr. Chaney has pointed out to you, all this could have been put before your father without your knowledge. You are being treated considerately – but I want a plain answer to my question. Are you married to Miss Weekes?"

Rupert turned on him with a strange look which I failed to understand. Then he spoke one word.

"Yes!"

"May I ask since when?"

"Oh, it's about – about six years since. When – soon after she first came to town. Damn it! – can't I marry whom I like, Ellerthorpe? What—"

"You can do anything you like, as far as I'm concerned," said Mr. Ellerthorpe. "I merely want, as your father's solicitor, to know—"

Rupert suddenly turned towards the door.

"And now I suppose you and your damned spies will go and split to him!" he exclaimed. "All right – go, and be damned to you! Let him cut me off with a shilling – I dare say I can scrape a living, somehow. Quite as good, anyhow, as the miserable screw he condemned me to for years. Fifty thousand a year for the father – and three hundred for the son – only son, too!"

"You've recently had a great deal more than three hundred," said Mr. Ellerthorpe, "and I think you'd better sit down again and restrain yourself. Whether you think it or not, these gentlemen and I are trying to help you."

"Rot!" sneered Rupert. "Tell that to—"

"We're not going to tell it to anybody," said Mr. Ellerthorpe. "Be reasonable! Mr. Chaney and his partner have been charged by your father with a certain commission, but your private affairs don't come

into it, unless these affairs have any connection with a certain most
serious matter – the murder of your uncle, Sir John Maxtondale."

Rupert suddenly stared from one to the other of us.

"Good God!" he exclaimed. "You don't think I had anything to do
with that!"

Chaney came forward again. For him, his tone and manner in dealing with this angry young man were immensely mild.

"We don't think anything of the sort, Mr. Maxtondale," he said.
"Put that clean out of your mind! But there are one or two matters
you might help to clear up – in your own interests. No doubt," he
went on, suavely, "no doubt you're feeling a bit nettled—"

"What do you want?" interrupted Rupert impatiently. "What is it
I can clear up?"

"Well, a good deal of information has been put before us," replied
Chaney. "I want to get the clear truth about it. You had dealings some
years ago with a man named Mason?"

"Well – I had," admitted Rupert.

"Is that the same man who is now your manager at the Hyacanthus
Club?"

"It is!"

"I want to ask you a plain question – again in your own interests.
Has Mason any hold on you – financial or otherwise?"

Rupert hesitated in answering this. He turned in his chair – which
he had resumed at a second request from Mr. Ellerthorpe – and for a
moment looked Chaney up and down, carefully, as if trying to arrive
at some idea of him.

"Is that straight?" he asked suddenly. "I mean – about my own
interests?"

"Straight as a dart, sir!" said Chaney. "No lies!"

"Then I take back what I said just now," continued Rupert. "No
offence meant! I've had reason to be suspicious. Badly treated, in my
opinion – by more than one, and especially by my own father. No,
then – Mason has no hold on me – none!"

"Is Mason the man who called on you at Heronswood one morning
when you were last there?" asked Chaney.

"He did call there, yes."

"May we know why?"

"No mystery about it. Mason's a native of those parts. He happened to be in the neighbourhood for a day or two, and, knowing that I was at Heronswood, he called to consult with me about some alterations which were then being carried out at the Hyacanthus Club – structural alterations."

"Thank you," said Chaney. "That settles that point! Another, now – is there anybody that you know of who'd lose money – who would have lost money – if Sir John Maxtondale had stepped into his place and taken title and estates? I mean, if you'd lost – through his sudden turning up – the next chance to them?"

But Rupert Maxtondale shook his head.

"I don't know of anybody," he said, "I don't owe money to anyone. Nobody's advanced me anything. I've lived on the allowance," he added, turning to Mr. Ellerthorpe. "Whatever you may think, I've lived on it. My wife earns something, too – at Litterton's. Indeed, we'd saved enough to go shares with Collinghurst in starting that club. And the club's paying, and it will pay, because Mason is very particular not to cross any borderline. We shan't have any trouble with the police, and we're attracting a good class of customers. But – I want to know what all this is for? Are you going to tell my father?" he concluded, turning to Mr. Ellerthorpe. "After all, he as good as turned me out, and—"

"It would be far better if you told him everything yourself," said Mr. Ellerthorpe. "But before we discuss that, there's a highly important question – two or three questions, really – I should like you to answer. You say your marriage to Miss Weekes was secret?"

"Secret, yes – had to be."

"Who witnessed it?"

"Oh, well, Collinghurst for one. And some friend – girl here in town – for another."

"Then there are two people know of it. Does Mason know?"

"Mason knows. At least he sees me and my wife together as Mr. and Mrs. Maxtondale – though we call ourselves Morton here in town."

"And you're not afraid of any of these people giving away the secret?"

"I'm quite sure that not one of them would give it away. Collinghurst and Mason are absolutely safe, and my wife's friend wouldn't, according to her."

"Well, one more still more important question. Do your wife's people know of the marriage? Does anyone at Heronswood or in the neighbourhood know of it? I want to know that particularly," concluded Mr. Ellerthorpe. "Because—"

Before he could say any more, a clerk entered the room with a telegram. Mr. Ellerthorpe, interrupting himself, took it and at once opened it. I saw his face change in expression and it was obvious that the message was one of serious import.

"No answer, at present, Wilson," he said.

The clerk retired; Mr. Ellerthorpe re-read the telegram. Suddenly he rose from his desk and passed through an open doorway into another room; a second later he called to Chaney and me to join him there. And as soon as we had crossed the threshold, he closed the door on us.

"Here's some startling news from Heronswood!" he said. "Read this!"

He thrust the telegram into Chaney's hands; I leaned over to read it.

Very serious accident to Sir Stephen this morning fear the worst please break news to Mr. Rupert and come down with him at once. Weekes.

Chaney handed the telegram back.

"Fortunate that the son's here, Mr. Ellerthorpe," he said. "You can catch that twelve o'clock train."

"Yes, yes!" responded Mr. Ellerthorpe. "I wasn't thinking of that. What – what can this accident have been? I hope – however, it's no use speculating. We'd better tell Rupert the news at once. You see that Weekes says – the worst! I suppose that means – but let us go back."

We went back to the other room. Rupert Maxtondale glanced questioningly, almost suspiciously, at us.

"Something wrong?" he asked. "You look—"

"This wire is from Weekes, the steward," said Mr. Ellerthorpe. "Your father has had an accident. Weekes doesn't say what accident – you'd better read this."

He handed Rupert the telegram. Rupert read it without show of haste. Watching him closely, I saw no change in his expression. He passed the telegram back to Mr. Ellerthorpe and plunging a hand in his pocket, drew out a fistful of loose silver.

"All I've got on me," he said. "I suppose you can supply—"

"That is all right," interrupted Mr. Ellerthorpe. "We had better catch the twelve o'clock from Euston." He glanced at his watch. "Eleven, now," he continued. "Do you want to call at – where is it? – Malmesbury Mansions?"

"May as well," replied Rupert. "Plenty of time. Why couldn't Weekes give more information?" He paused, thinking. "Couldn't we wire him asking for further news to be sent to Rugby? The train stops there."

Chaney and I went away then, leaving Rupert and Mr. Ellerthorpe settling their arrangements. Outside, Chaney shook his head.

"I hope that's the truth that Weekes has given, Camberwell," he said. "That it really is an accident. I've half a mind to go down. But we shall hear – we can phone Mallwood. He'll have heard the latest by this."

"If the worst happens, it will settle a good many things satisfactorily for Rupert Maxtondale," I remarked. "His father will have died knowing nothing of the secret marriage nor of the Hyacanthus Club nor that Rupert has been living a double life. And I suppose Rupert will come in for everything."

"Fifty thousand pounds a year!" said Chaney. "That is – if his father's left all to him. Well, well! – you never know what's going to happen next."

What happened next to us was that Chippendale, as soon as we entered the office, handed us a telegram.

"Came in five minutes since," he said.

Chaney tore open the envelope, glanced at its contents, and nodded.

"Just what I expected," he muttered. "It's from Mallwood. Sir Stephen's dead. Read that."

I took the telegram and read it carefully.

Sir Stephen Maxtondale met with strange accident this morning and has since died certain of foul play probably murder glad of your assistance at once. Mallwood.

I glanced at Chaney. He nodded again.

"We can catch the twelve o'clock," he said. "Go down with those other two, of course. But – I'm wondering, Camberwell."

"What about?" I asked.

"If we'll tell them about that," he answered, pointing to the telegram, "or if we'll keep it to ourselves. Most likely they'll get a wire handed in at Rugby. 'Foul play – probably murder'! says Mallwood. Good Lord! – I wonder what's happened. No, we won't show the wire to those two; we'll keep the news to ourselves – for the present."

Chapter 17

LADY SYBIL'S BRIDGE

THERE WAS NO TIME to lose if we were to catch the twelve o'clock train from Euston to Monkseaton, and I began to make the necessary preparations. Chaney was already making his. Presently he came into my room.

"Camberwell," he said, "we'll take Chip with us."

"Why?" I asked. "And – who's to remain in charge here?"

"Chip may be uncommonly useful," he answered, "and we can get that girl of his to come and look after things. I'll see to it – I want Chip to be there; you don't know what we may need in the way of help."

He went out to Chippendale and I heard him get on the phone to Miss Platt. A moment later he poked his head in at my door again and informed me that she was coming. And within twenty minutes Miss Platt, businesslike as ever, arrived and took everything over as calmly and collectedly as if she had been running our office all her life; and Chaney, Chippendale, and I set out for Euston.

Sir Rupert Maxtondale – as we now knew him to be – and Mr. Ellerthorpe were already in the restaurant car when we boarded the train, and as they appeared to be deep in consultation, we three took seats at some little distance from them. Neither had shown any surprise at our presence, but when the train had started, Mr. Ellerthorpe came along to us.

"I'm not surprised to see you here," he said, "but I should like to know if anyone sent for you, Chaney."

"Yes," replied Chaney, promptly; "Mallwood. We found a wire from him when we got back to our office."

"And—" began Mr. Ellerthorpe.

"Pretty much like yours from Weekes," said Chaney. "Serious accident." He glanced along the car. "Probably fatal," he added. "And – he wanted us."

"I wonder why," said Mr. Ellerthorpe. "But we must wait. I expect another wire at Rugby."

He left us then and went back to Sir Rupert. Lunch was being served; we ate and drank and looked out of the windows. Rugby came: Mr. Ellerthorpe went to the door of the car. A wire was handed to him. He came back into the car opening it. I saw his face change. He showed the wire to his companion. Sir Rupert looked, nodded, said nothing, turned to the window again. Mr. Ellerthorpe came along to us.

"Sir Stephen is dead!" he said. "Died at nine o'clock this morning."

"From Weekes?" inquired Chaney.

"From Weekes."

"Does he say what time the accident happened?"

"He says no more than this: 'Sir Stephen died at nine o'clock, never having regained consciousness,' " replied Mr. Ellerthorpe. "Of course, we haven't a notion as to the nature of the accident."

"Sit down a minute," said Chaney, making room on his own seat. "Don't tell Sir Rupert, Mr. Ellerthorpe," he went on in a low voice, "but, as a matter of fact, we knew that Sir Stephen was dead when we came to the train."

"You did! How?" exclaimed Mr. Ellerthorpe.

"Mallwood told us in his wire. Here it is," continued Chaney, producing the telegram from his pocket. "Now, notice two or three things. Mallwood first refers to the accident as 'strange.' Then he suggests 'foul play.' And then he hints at 'murder.' "

Mr. Ellerthorpe groaned.

"Good heavens!" he muttered. "When are we going to get to the bottom of this? What does it all mean? When is it going to end if this last affair is murder?"

"We shall have to redouble our efforts, sir – that's all," said Chaney. "And this time we must stick at nothing. I suppose," he went on, with a glance along the car, "I suppose, sir, you know how things are left? The title, of course, is settled – nothing can interfere with that. But – the estates and the personalty."

Mr. Ellerthorpe glanced at Chippendale. Chaney hastened to speak.

"Our clerk, sir, is as secret as we are," he said, reassuringly. "Only – more so!"

"Excellent tribute to his character!" remarked Mr. Ellerthorpe, smiling. "Well, there's no reason for secrecy. Sir Stephen Maxtondale has died intestate!"

"You don't say so!" exclaimed Chaney. "And all that money – and lands and all the rest of it. Fifty thousand a year, I've heard."

"It is a fact, though," replied Mr. Ellerthorpe. "I have never been able to persuade him to make a will. He – the fact is, he wanted to wait until the end of what he considered his son's probation. And now – it's too late."

"Then – Sir Rupert comes in for – what?" asked Chaney.

"Everything!" said Mr. Ellerthorpe. "Everything!"

He went away at that, and Chaney turned to Chippendale and me, sitting side by side, opposite him.

"Queer life, this!" he said. "Two hours or so ago our friend at the other end of the car was – well, we know how he stood, approximately, in this world's goods! Now a baronet and in command of fifty thousand a year!"

"Millionaire!" observed Chippendale, laconically.

"Quite right, my lad!" agreed Chaney. "A millionaire! Well – what shall we hear next? What'll happen next?"

What happened next was that when we all got out of the train at Monkseaton, a policeman in plain clothes met us. Superintendent Mallwood's compliments and there was one of the cars from Heronswood outside and would we all drive straight to the Weekes's house in Heronswood Park? The Superintendent was waiting for us there.

We followed the man outside the station to the car – its chauffeur greeted his new master with the recognition of his sudden access to fortune. Chaney drew the plainclothes man aside, motioning me to follow.

"Have you been over there?" he asked.

"Yes, sir. Just come from there. The Superintendent felt sure you'd come by this train, so he sent me in to meet you."

"What was the accident to Sir Stephen?" inquired Chaney.

"Fell through a bridge, sir – a drop of sixty feet. It's a bridge in the park, near the steward's lodge, which, I understand, Sir Stephen used to cross every morning, regularly. He didn't live many minutes after he was found. Never regained consciousness, I understand."

"Superintendent Mallwood, in his wire to me, said something about foul play – suspected foul play," said Chaney. "Do you know anything about that?"

The man gave us a significant look and dropped his voice to a whisper.

"They're saying," he answered, "they're saying, thereabouts, that the bridge had been interfered with! I didn't quite catch how, exactly, but that's what I gathered. They'll be able to tell you more when you get there, Mr. Chaney."

We went back to the car. Chaney and I got in with Mr. Ellerthorpe and Sir Rupert; Chippendale sat in front, by the chauffeur. We moved off in silence, but once clear of the town, Mr. Ellerthorpe turned on Chaney.

"Learn anything from that man?" he asked.

"Next to nothing," replied Chaney. "He says that Sir Stephen met with a serious fall from some bridge near Weekes's house—"

Sir Rupert let out a sudden exclamation.

"Good God!" he said. "That must be Lady Sybil's Bridge! – I've told him more than once that it was rotten and ought to be replaced. Did – did he fall from it?"

"I gathered that," replied Chaney.

"A drop of sixty feet, at least!" muttered Sir Rupert. "The last time I crossed it, I said it wasn't safe – it's been there a hundred years, I'll bet, without ever being touched."

"What bridge is it?" asked Mr. Ellerthorpe. "I can't place it from my memory."

"You may never have seen it," said Sir Rupert. "It's a narrow foot-bridge in the woods, spanning a very deep ravine through which one of the park roads runs. It's on a path which runs from the house, through the woods, to the steward's lodge and about fifty yards from Weekes's orchard. My father used to take that path every morning, you know," he went on, turning to Mr. Ellerthorpe; "he was a very early riser and always breakfasted at eight o'clock, winter and summer, and as soon as he'd breakfasted, set off to the estate office at Weekes's place – never knew him miss doing that in all my experience of him. And he always took the path I'm telling you of, and of course always crossed the bridge."

"I suppose that habit of his was well known?" asked Chaney.

"Everybody knew of it," said Sir Rupert. "Everybody! Regular as clockwork, he was, about that walk to the estate office. He'd fixed habits. And he'd one about that bridge. My great-grandmother, Lady Sybil, who had it made – and the path cut, too – stuck the bridge where it is because from it there's a wonderful view of the park. When my father crossed the bridge every morning, he used to stop to admire that view. He never missed doing that. And I see now how it happened, Ellerthorpe. The rotten old railings must have given way! And – a drop of sixty feet! I told him, last time I was at home, the whole thing should be mended – what was really needed was a new bridge. But he'd such a fancy for keeping old things untouched."

We were in Heronswood Park by that, and presently we pulled up at the gateway of the steward's lodge. Weekes came out to us; behind him came Mallwood. And while Weekes went into the house with the new baronet and Mr. Ellerthorpe, Mallwood remained with us in the garden.

Mallwood looked graver than I had ever seen him look. After assuring himself of Chippendale's identity, he motioned us to follow him towards a gate which gave access from Weekes's garden to the estate office, a building that stood on the edge of the park.

"My man tell you anything when he met you at the station?" he asked as we walked along. "Any details?"

"He merely told us that Sir Stephen had fallen from a bridge, and that there was some idea that the bridge had been interfered with," replied Chaney. "Coming along in the car, Sir Rupert, having heard that much, told us more – about his father's habit of crossing the bridge every morning on his way to the estate office, and so on. Sir Rupert also said that when he was here last, he formed the opinion that the bridge was rotten and should be repaired."

"Rotten, eh?" muttered Mallwood. "Humph! Well – you shall see something for yourselves!"

Entering the estate office and leading us along its main passage, he paused at a door at its farther end and, producing a key from his pocket, unlocked the door and admitted us to an unfurnished room in which there was but one object. That – set up against a wall – was what appeared to be a length of what is called rustic railing, such as would be used for the sides of a short footbridge. It was some nine or ten feet in length and, save for signs of some slight damage through a fall, intact.

"Look at this!" said Mallwood. "This is a piece of the railings which formed the left-hand side of the bridge you've heard of. That bridge carries a certain footpath over a ravine or cutting which is a good sixty feet below. Sir Stephen crossed the bridge every morning of his life when he was at Heronswood, on his way to the estate office. And when he crossed it, he always did the same thing – there's scarcely a man or woman about here, or child either, that hasn't seen him doing it! When he got to the centre of the bridge, he used to lean both hands on the railing on the left-hand side and stand, sometimes for a good five minutes, admiring the view – there's a wonderful view from that bridge, as you'll presently see. Well, this morning, at a little after half past eight, his usual hour, he was seen—"

"Ah!" exclaimed Chaney, starting. "He was seen – actually seen – was he?"

"He was actually seen – by two workmen, whose evidence you'll hear," continued Mallwood. "Oh, yes, the affair was witnessed, right enough. He was seen to walk on to the bridge and halfway across to stop, as usual, and place his hands on the top rail of the left-hand side. And the next instant he and the railing on which he was leaning his full weight crashed to the road beneath – a sixty-foot drop! And – why?"

He paused, staring at us for a minute; then he suddenly pointed a finger to the length of railing set up against the wall.

"That railing had been sawn through in four separate places!" he whispered. "When Sir Stephen put his hands on it, it was hanging by what you might call four threads. Look for yourselves!"

We all three went closer and looked at the railing. What Mallwood had said was true enough. The top rail had been sawn through at both ends of the length before us; the connections at the bottom had been similarly treated. Nothing could be more certain than that a sudden and fearful death awaited the man who leaned on that rail above a drop of sixty feet.

Chaney examined the signs of severance with great care.

"Freshly done," he muttered. "Small-toothed saw. I suppose," he went on, turning to Mallwood, "I suppose you examined the bridge as soon as you got to it? Did you notice any traces of sawdust?"

"I thought of that," replied Mallwood. "No, there were none. But there was a high wind blowing this morning, and it blew pretty hard up that valley."

"Well, there's no doubt about what's happened," said Chaney. "And no doubt, either, that this is murder! Just that – murder!"

"Murder, right enough!" agreed Mallwood. "I should just think so. Just as much as the other affairs were murder. Cool, deliberate murder!"

"Any suspicions – clues – anything?" asked Chaney.

Mallwood hesitated in answering.

"I've ideas of my own," he said after a pause, "but I'm not going to say anything about them yet."

"Found anything helpful?" inquired Chaney.

"We've discovered that a saw, such as would do this job, is missing from the estate carpenter's shop since yesterday," replied Mallwood.

"Estate carpenter's shop, eh?" said Chaney. "Ah! Isn't that where that fellow Batty was employed till Weekes fired him?"

"It is!" answered Mallwood.

"Is Batty out of prison – he got a month for assaulting Weekes, didn't he?" asked Chaney.

"He did – and I think the month was up a few days ago," replied Mallwood.

Chaney gave Mallwood a searching look.

"Thinking of him, I reckon?" he said.

"Something of the sort," admitted Mallwood. "He vowed vengeance on Weekes in the dock, and he may have thought that Weekes, living close to it, would step on the bridge. Weekes often walked out along that path to meet Sir Stephen of a morning. But I've set inquiries on foot as to whether Batty's been seen about."

The door opened just then. Sir Rupert Maxtondale came in, with Mr. Ellerthorpe and Weekes in attendance. Once again Mallwood had to tell the tale he had told us.

Chapter 18

BATTY ONCE MORE

Presently we all left the estate office and walked out to Lady Sybil's Bridge. As Chaney and I had never been in that part of the Heronswood properties before, I made careful note of our surroundings and of the relation of the bridge to, first, Heronswood itself and, second, to the steward's house and the estate office. Just behind the office a path led across a corner of Weekes's grounds and then passed through a wicket-gate with a thick coppice, which it traversed for some fifty or sixty yards. At the farther extremity of this coppice we came out on a terrace of green turf, and from this projected the footbridge made by the Lady Sybil of long ago. Spanning a ravine or cutting of some sixty to seventy feet in depth, the bridge, at its other end, communicated with another level of turf, beyond which was the edge of the deep woods of Heronswood Park.

Mallwood had caused both ends of the bridge to be roped off, and a constable in uniform to be posted at that end of it which we now approached. Passing through the ropes, we went close to the bridge and made a careful inspection of its shattered timbers. It was easy to comprehend what had happened; where the piece of rail-fencing which we had just seen at the estate office should have been, there was now a wide gap. It was not a pleasant thing to think of a man plunging through that gap to the depths below. And one could not fail to notice that the road at the foot of the ravine, on which anyone so plunging would fall, was of a hard, granite-stoned surface. We stood looking at all this for some time, in silence. Then Chaney spoke, addressing Weekes.

"I understand that somebody witnessed the accident?" he said.

Weekes, who was obviously much upset by the death of his employer, nodded, pointing towards the road on the other side of the cutting.

"There were two of our estate workmen doing a job over there," he answered. "Mending a fence. They saw Sir Stephen come out of the wood and walk on to the bridge. They saw him – it was his usual habit – put his hands on the railings, on that side, looking up the valley, as he always did. And they say that the instant he leaned his weight on it, the rail gave way, and – down he went!"

"Yes?" said Chaney. "And—"

Weekes looked at Sir Rupert, as if doubtful whether these details should be gone into.

"Go on!" said Sir Rupert. "He wants to know."

"One of the men made his way down the cutting," continued Weekes. "The other ran for me. I got some help and came here and we carried Sir Stephen up to the office."

"He was alive?" asked Chaney.

"Only just. He died soon after we got him in."

"Did he say anything before he died?"

"Oh, no! Not a word."

There was a brief silence. Then Weekes spoke again, in a low voice.

"It's the biggest wonder in the world that I wasn't killed with him!" he said. "I should have been if it hadn't been for what you might call an interposing of Providence – I should indeed!"

"How so?" inquired Chaney.

"Well," replied Weekes, "as often as not I used to walk out to meet Sir Stephen of a morning. He liked me to meet him. And nine times out of ten I used to be first and to meet him on the other side of this bridge – generally in the wood across yonder. Then we'd come back together. And we both used to lean on the railings there and talk. We should have done that this morning – we always did it. And then—"

He broke off, shaking his head.

"And how was it you didn't meet him this morning?" asked Chaney. "What was the interposing of Providence you spoke of?"

"I'd set out to meet him," replied Weekes. "I set off as soon as I got up from breakfast. I was crossing our lawn on my way here when my wife called me back to look at some repairs she was having done in our front kitchen. That kept me a bit – and the man came running with the news of the accident while I was still in the house. But for that, I should have been with Sir Stephen."

No one offered any comment on this, and we left the bridge and went back to the estate office. There Sir Rupert and Mr. Ellerthorpe left the rest of us and went on to Heronswood; Weekes turned to Mallwood and to Chaney and me.

"Will you come in and have a drink?" he said. "It's more than a bit upsetting, all this."

We followed him into his house and to the room in which we had once breakfasted with him. Mrs. Weekes was there, placidly sewing. At sight of us she laid aside her work and, evidently anticipating her husband's wishes, picked up a bunch of keys from her basket.

"You know all these gentlemen already, my lass," said Weekes, "and their business. Get us a drop of whisky – we can do with it."

Mrs. Weekes shook hands with all three of us, addressing each by name. We introduced Chippendale. She bustled to the big sideboard.

"I wish you were here on pleasanter business, gentlemen," she said. "Nothing but sorrow and trouble, I declare. I suppose Mr. Ellerthorpe will have come, too?"

"Yes," replied Chaney, "he's here, ma'am."

"Well, there's your work set for all of you, I think," continued Mrs. Weekes, as she set out decanter and glasses. "We seem to live in mystery hereabouts. Please help yourselves, gentlemen."

Weekes helped us all; when he had got his own glass in hand, he took a good drink, at the end of which he sighed deeply.

"Ay, well!" he remarked, "mystery or no mystery, me and my wife have our ideas – and some foundation for them, too! We have!"

"What are they, sir?" inquired Chaney.

"Well, to start with," replied Weekes, "there's no doubt the railings of that bridge were sawn through, on purpose. Some time last night; they were safe enough yesterday. The fellow who did that meant to kill somebody! But – it wasn't Sir Stephen he had in mind – not it! It was – me!"

He set his glass down with a thump and looked round at us as if to challenge denial. Mrs. Weekes, who had quietly resumed her sewing, sighed.

"The wickedness of some people," she murmured, "is incredible!"

There was a brief silence – until Mallwood spoke.

"You've somebody in mind, Mr. Weekes?" he said.

Weekes shook his head, with a good deal of meaning in the gesture.

"Ah, I should think I have," he answered.

"Strange if he hadn't!" murmured Mrs. Weekes. "Considering – everything!"

"Give it a name, sir," said Mallwood. "All friends here, I think."

Weekes took another pull at his whisky and soda and set down the glass with an emphatic gesture.

"Name?" he said. "Batty! That's the name. Batty!"

"You think Batty's responsible for this – and that he meant it for you?" suggested Mallwood.

"Look you here, Superintendent and gentlemen," replied Weekes. "Put it to yourselves. Ever since I discharged him for drunkenness and slackness, Batty has sworn he'd have his revenge. He assaulted me in Monkseaton market-place after the magistrate – foolishly, in my opinion – had discharged him on that first affair. He got a month for that, and he swore in the dock and, they tell me, again in the cells that he'd make it hot for me when he got out. Well, he is out! He came out last week. And I'll lay anything that Batty's is the hand that sawed the rails of that bridge through, hoping that I should be the victim. He knew my habits. Batty – that's the man. A scoundrel!"

"Has anything been seen of him round here since last week, Mr. Weekes?" asked Chaney. "Have you heard anything?"

"I have not, sir! But I can tell you something," replied Weekes. "Our foreman carpenter tells me that since yesterday afternoon there's a saw missing from our carpenter's shop. Now, that shop is locked up every night at six o'clock, and the foreman has the key. But that fellow Batty had a key, too, and when I discharged him, his key wasn't forthcoming; he said, on being asked for it, that he'd lost it."

"Damaging evidence," said Mallwood. "We shall have to go into it. But – if Batty's responsible for this, what about the previous crimes? You said just now, Mr. Weekes, that in your opinion the magistrate acted foolishly in discharging Batty. Why, now – in face of that alibi?"

"Because I didn't believe in the alibi!" replied Weekes. "Who were the fellows that supported it? Chaps like himself – scum!"

"Not all," said Mallwood. "There were two or three respectable men. However, in this case, bearing Batty's threats against you in mind, we must make inquiries about him."

"Batty! That's what I think!" repeated Weekes. "He meant me!"

"And," said Mrs. Weekes, softly, "he'd have had my husband if it hadn't happened – quite accidentally – that I called him back just as he was setting out to meet Sir Stephen. A moment later. . ."

We went away presently and, once clear of the steward's house discussed Weekes's suggestion. Mallwood was inclined to see a good deal in it.

"Of course, Weekes is all wrong in condemning the magistrates about that alibi," he said. "Their worships couldn't do otherwise than adopt it, in view of the evidence. But there's no doubt that Batty did threaten to have his revenge out of Weekes when he left prison. Let's go across to the cottages and see if we can find anyone who's seen him about here."

The cottages on the Heronswood estate, tenanted by workmen employed by the steward, were situated near the estate office and had all been built during recent years, under the direction of Sir Stephen Maxtondale. They were more or less model dwellings; Sir Stephen had prided himself on them. And, as Chaney remarked when we drew near them, their occupants, chiefly gamekeepers, game-watchers, carpenters, estate labourers, woodmen, were not likely to give us any information; Batty, had he revisited the scenes of his former labours, intent on thoughts of vengeance, would not have gone near any of these people. But beyond Home Farm and on the confines of the park, there was a cluster of old dwellings, half timbered and mostly thatched, occupied by farmworkers in the employ of the late tenant, Robson. Some of these cottages lay half or wholly hidden in the surrounding woods; it was much more probable that we should hear of Batty from their occupants than from the workpeople of the estate. Accordingly we went over to these first and began a house-to-house inquiry of the women, who came to their doors, full of curiosity, as soon as our presence was known in the little settlement.

Nobody had seen Batty – of late. Of course, everybody knew him; hadn't he lodged with old Mother Kitteridge? But since the time of

Mother Kitteridge's tragic end Batty hadn't been seen thereabouts. Indeed, most of the women were under the impression that Batty was still in durance vile.

"Who's got Mother Kitteridge's cottage now?" asked Mallwood of the last woman we spoke to. "And where is it?"

The woman pointed to a path, close by her own garden gate, which wound away into the woods.

"It's up there, mister," she replied. "A hundred yards or so. Nobody's got it; it's been empty ever since Mrs. Kitteridge was put an end to that night, along of poor Mr. Robson. There's all her furniture still left there – I don't know what they're going to do about it. There's some of 'em say that Batty had stuff of his own in that cottage – furniture that he fetched there when he came to lodge with Mrs. Kitteridge. Anyway, mister, if you want to look in, there's nothing to stop you, for the place has never been locked up since the old lady's death – it's open for anybody to walk into."

"Oh," said Mallwood, "that's queer, isn't it? Why hasn't it been locked up?"

"Why, you see, mister," replied the woman, "it's nobody's business. I don't understand the rights and wrongs of it, but they say that that cottage and the piece of wood and the land it stands on doesn't belong to either Sir Stephen as was, poor gentleman, on the one hand, or to Mr. Marston of Sedbury, on the other. It's a bit of property that neither of 'em had a right to."

"Why, whose property is it, then?" asked Mallwood. "That's a queer tale!"

"Well, they say it belonged to Mother Kitteridge herself, mister. I've heard say that both Mr. Marston and Sir Stephen used to try to buy it from her, regular, and that she always made the same answer to them, and that was that they could have it if they liked to cover it with gold sovereigns, which, of course, neither of 'em cared to do, for it's a good piece of land!"

"Never heard a word of this before!" exclaimed Mallwood. "How much land had the old witch?"

The woman came out of her garden into the road and pointed towards Sedbury Park.

"It's a three-cornered piece," she answered. "It goes from the corner of our garden here up to where Mr. Marston's property begins. Then it runs along the edge of his park for about a hundred and fifty yards to a point where the cottage, Mrs. Kitteridge's cottage, stands, and from there it comes across, cornerways like, to our garden again. That," she added, pointing to a tall elm near which we were standing, "that tree's in Mrs. Kitteridge's property; this" – pointing to a hollybush at the corner of her own garden – "is on the Maxtondale estate."

"Well, well!" muttered Mallwood. "And has nobody come forward to claim this property of Mother Kitteridge's? Hadn't she any relations?"

"There's nobody been that I know of," said the woman. "Mr. Marston, he was riding past here one day, and he was talking to me about it, and he said it would go to the King."

"Did he, now?" said Mallwood. "And you say the cottage is open?"

"Never been locked up since she was buried, mister. You can walk straight in."

Mallwood signalled to us to follow him; we went along the woodland path to the cottage, a queer old half-timbered place, standing in a little clearing. As our informant had said, the door was unlocked, and we opened it and walked into a sort of half-kitchen, half-living room. There was a lot of very old and very quaint furniture there, and it seemed to me that nothing had been touched since its late owner's death. Indeed, on the dust-covered table in the centre of the room lay Mother Kitteridge's knitting, her spectacles, and a local newspaper, just, I imagined, as she had laid them aside when she set out on her fatal visit to Robson at Home Farm.

Chaney was examining the old furniture, and I was making a note of the date of the newspaper when Mallwood called us from an inner room to which he had penetrated. Going in there, we found him in a sort of scullery, looking at certain objects set out on a side-table.

"Look here!" he said. "See these things? Somebody's been here – and not so very long ago, either! Those bits of food are still fresh and soft."

The bits of food he alluded to were a half-loaf of bread and a piece of cheese; each, as he said, quite soft. Near them was a glass from which somebody had been drinking beer, and close by were two empty beer-bottles. Also on the table stood an unopened bottle, and a jar of pickled onions, a fork still resting in its uncorked neck.

"Somebody's been having a supper here – last night," said Mallwood. "Was it – Batty? Come on upstairs – let's see if anybody's slept here."

We tramped up the queer old stairs to the rooms in the high-sloping thatched roof. One room was evidently that once sacred to the person of Mother Kitteridge; it was as she had left it, neat, tidy, though in need of a dusting. The bed was made there. But in a room at the rear the bed-clothes were flung back, and the pillows were disarranged, as if somebody had just left the bed, throwing the things carelessly aside.

"Lay anything Batty's been here!" muttered Mallwood. "He knew the place. We'll have to find Batty."

We went back to Monkseaton in Mallwood's car, late that evening. As we neared the edge of the town, a closed car, driven by a chauffeur in the Maxtondale livery, passed us at a swift pace, going in the direction of Heronswood. In it sat the new Lady Maxtondale, a small boy, and an obviously French nurse.

Chapter 19

THE CORONER TAKES OVER

MALLWOOD, WHO WAS DRIVING us back to Monkseaton in his own car, turned sharply on me, seated at his side, as the Heronswood limousine flashed past us.

"That was the steward's daughter – Ettie Weekes!" he exclaimed.

"Yes," I said, in, I believe, a matter-of-fact tone. "It was."

"In a Heronswood Park car! With a boy! And – was it a nurse?" he demanded.

"French nurse," said I.

"What's that mean?" he asked. "Heronswood car – and Heronswood liveries? The steward's daughter!"

I glanced over my shoulder at Chaney, sitting behind us.

"Better tell him," said Chaney. "It'll all be out in an hour or two. She's on the spot now. Lost no time, either!"

I turned to Mallwood, who was endeavouring to look at me, his steering-wheel, and the road in front all at once.

"It means, Mallwood, if you want the plain truth, that the steward's daughter, once Miss Ettie Weekes, is now Lady Maxtondale of Heronswood," I answered, laughing a little at his amazed face. "That's all! Quite simple."

Mallwood nearly ran us into the off-side hedgerow.

"Good Lord!" he exclaimed, as he righted the car. "You don't mean it. Married! – to Rupert?"

"Sir Rupert," I said. "Though, to be sure, he wasn't Sir Rupert when she married him. They've been married – secretly – some years; that boy is five or six, I forget which."

"Lord! Does anybody know?" he asked. "Did – did his father know?"

"Sir Stephen did not know," I replied. "That is certain!"

"Did her people know?"

I couldn't answer that, straight off. I remembered that Rupert Maxtondale had left a general, covering question unanswered in Mr. Ellerthorpe's office.

"I don't know," I answered. "They may have known – and they mayn't. Perhaps they didn't. I think it was perhaps a secret – all round. I can't say, definitely. But there's the fact. He's now Sir Rupert and she's his wife, and, consequently, Lady Maxtondale."

"How long have you known?" asked Mallwood.

"Since this morning – definitely," I replied. "We guessed it before, but this morning we heard it from his own lips."

"Where?" he asked. He was growing more and more inquisitive. "In London – or coming down? – you came down with him."

"In London, Mallwood. At Mr. Ellerthorpe's, if you want to know."

"I want to know a lot," he muttered. "How do I know this hasn't something to do with all these murders? Was it before or after you heard of Sir Stephen's death that you learnt this?" he went on. "I'd like to know that."

"Before," I answered. "Definitely before."

"Wait till we get in and you shall hear all about it, Mallwood," said Chaney. "As you say, this secret marriage may have some relation to recent events. We'll tell you all we know."

We went into Mallwood's private room at the police station when we reached Monkseaton, and there I put him in possession of everything that we knew ourselves. But at the end he shook his head.

"I could have understood that having something to do with the first lot of murders," he said, "but I don't see how it can have anything to do with this last affair. The more I think over that, the more I'm inclined to believe in Weekes's theory."

"That he was meant to be the victim?" said Chaney.

"Exactly! He – not Sir Stephen. And, in that case, it's Batty!"

"Then get after Batty," rejoined Chaney. "Batty must be some-where about. Find him!"

"What are you going to do?" asked Mallwood.

"At the moment we are going to the Maxtondale Arms," replied Chaney. "To dine and sleep – and do a bit of talking between ourselves. After that – well, we don't know. We're not sure as to our further commission, you see, Mallwood. But tomorrow morning we'll run out to Heronswood again and see our employer, Mr. Ellerthorpe; then we shall get our orders. See you there, no doubt. And in the mean time you get busy about Batty."

We left Mallwood at that, walked on to the Maxtondale Arms, booked rooms, and in due course dined together. Afterwards, over our pipes, we talked things over. And the question, of course, was: Did Batty do it?

"May have been Batty's method of revenging himself, this bit of business," said Chaney. "Batty was fully acquainted with what you may call the daily routine there and knew Weekes's habit of going to meet his master. If Batty did this, though, it by no means settles the problem of the previous murders. In other words, the murder of Sir Stephen has nothing to do with the murder of Sir John and the murders of Robson and the old woman."

We discussed these various points from several angles for some time; then Chaney, as was his wont, suddenly refused to consider them any longer and went to bed, having first borrowed what he called a love-story from the young lady in the office, wherewith, he said, to compose his thoughts to a sweet and gentle placidity before sleeping. Chippendale presently followed his example. As for me, I remained a little longer in a quiet corner of the lounge. Some townsfolk had come in and were discussing the tragedy of the morning; I wanted to hear their opinions. But there was only one opinion amongst them. Batty – that was the man! Hadn't Batty vowed vengeance, black, red, and purple, on Weekes when he turned to leave the dock five weeks ago? Oh, of course it was Batty! And a damned diabolical piece of work too, and they hoped Batty would swing for it.

Next morning Chaney and I chartered a car and, with Chippendale in attendance, drove over to Heronswood. The butler received us and took us into his pantry.

"Extraordinary changes of fortune here, gentlemen!" he said. "I scarcely know if I stand on my head or my heels! Sir Stephen – a good master, gentlemen! – lying dead in the house. Sir Rupert lord of all he beholds. And – a Lady Maxtondale!"

"You never expected that," remarked Chaney.

"I did not, sir! Nor anyone else. But when Sir Rupert arrived yesterday afternoon, in company with Mr. Ellerthorpe, everything was made plain. I was summoned; the housekeeper was summoned. We were informed that Lady Maxtondale would arrive from town last night, with her son and his nurse, and that everything was to be in readiness for their reception. And of course it was. And this morning, gentlemen, apart from the mournful necessities of the occasion, into the details of which I need not go, everything is going like clockwork! Sir Rupert is master; her ladyship is mistress. And," he added, with something very like a wink, "I should say they are both inclined to be very businesslike. Sir Stephen, now, he – well, he left things pretty much to me and the housekeeper. But these young people – ah well, gentlemen, one can't expect the good old days to last for ever."

Presently we saw Mr. Ellerthorpe, who received us in a small room which the late baronet had evidently used for business purposes. Chaney, after some perfunctory conversation, asked straight out what Mr. Ellerthorpe's further orders were. Did he wish us to remain in the neighbourhood or return to town? After all, said Chaney, the search for Batty, now in full working, was scarcely our job, and as for the previous affairs –

"I don't want you to leave just yet," interrupted Mr. Ellerthorpe. "I have had no opportunity of taking Sir Rupert's wishes on the matter, but I'll be responsible myself for further instructions. Stop here – near here – until the inquest on Sir Stephen is over, at any rate. That has been fixed for tomorrow. It will be held here – at the hall. I want you to attend it. Afterwards we will discuss the position. It may be that something will come out at the inquest which will throw light on the murder of Sir John Maxtondale, and in that case I may – I mean, I think Sir Rupert may – wish you to make further investigations. I understand that the Monkseaton police are actively searching for the man Batty. I don't think there's much doubt that he interfered with that bridge," concluded Mr. Ellerthorpe, looking from one to the other of us as if to seek our opinion. "But whether he had anything to do with the previous crimes is another question. However, come to the inquest tomorrow. I have been in communication with the Coroner already – he is a very downright and practical-minded man and I believe he intends to have things thoroughly thrashed out. By the bye, have you heard of a highly significant discovery made this morning at the cottage formerly occupied by the woman, Kitteridge, who was murdered with Robson?"

"We have not!" replied Chaney. "What was it, sir?"

"It appears that the cottage has never been locked up since the old woman's death," replied Mr. Ellerthorpe. "Strange – but so it is! This morning a man living close by took it into his head to have a look round. He went in for that purpose and in a room at the back found, under a quilt, thrown loosely across the bed, a saw which had been taken from the estate carpenter's shop. He had heard there was a missing saw, so he went straight to Weekes and told him of his discovery, and Weekes went to the cottage and now has the saw. This, I suppose, is the saw with which the supports of the bridge were severed."

"We'll call and see Weekes, sir," said Chaney. "I suppose he'll have already communicated with Mallwood."

"Well, don't forget tomorrow," repeated Mr. Ellerthorpe. "The opening of the inquest is fixed for eleven o'clock. Sir Stephen," he added, in a whisper, "will be buried in the family vault at Sedbury day after tomorrow; a very, very quiet and private ceremony, by his own often-expressed, particular wish."

We left the house. It was very silent, very funereal, very gloomy, with the blinds drawn down on all sides. Of the new baronet and Lady Maxtondale we saw nothing. But on the terrace the youthful heir apparent was joyously taking the air in charge of his French nurse.

As we stepped off the terrace to the road which crossed the park in the direction of the steward's house, Chaney turned to me.

"Camberwell!" he said, in a tone of voice I knew well. "That's a damned queer thing we've just heard!"

"Which thing?" I asked.

"The discovery of that saw in Mother Kitteridge's cottage this morning!" he replied. "I'll swear it wasn't there when we examined the cottage yesterday!"

"Sure?" I asked.

"Bet anything! Ellerthorpe says the man found it in a room at the back. That's the room that was Batty's, when he lodged there. Now, when we went into the cottage yesterday afternoon, we found that the bed in that room had been slept in and hadn't been made, hadn't been put straight again, since it was slept in. Ellerthorpe says this man found the saw under the quilt. But I moved that quilt yesterday!"

"You did?" I exclaimed.

"I did – when you and Mallwood and Chippendale were in the front room. Why I did I don't know. Unconsciously, mechanically, I suppose. Just twitched it off and threw it back. There was no saw there then. That's certain!"

"Then it would look as if somebody – Batty, maybe – had placed it there since we were in the cottage. Must have been Batty!"

Chaney made no reply. He began to rub his chin – a sure sign that he was thinking hard. And he remained silent until we reached the steward's house. Weekes was out – had gone out with Mallwood. They would be back very soon, said Mrs. Weekes; would we sit down and wait? We sat down, in the big pleasant dining room, looking out on the sunlit garden and lawns. Mrs. Weekes sat down too and picked up her sewing; she gave one the impression of having an itch for continual occupation.

"Nice changeable weather, ma'am," observed Chaney. "Change is a good thing, this time of the year. First shower, then sun."

Mrs. Weekes stitched steadily.

"Change?" she remarked. "There's nothing but change. Everything's always changing! Sir Stephen yesterday; Sir Rupert today. And now I hear that my daughter has married Sir Rupert in secret, and that they have a boy, five years of age. Lady Maxtondale of Heronswood Park! Well, neither me nor her father were consulted – nowadays young people don't think it necessary to consult their parents about anything. And Lady Maxtondale has not yet been to see her mother, Mrs. Weekes – the steward's wife!"

Neither of us felt disposed to make any reply to these remarks – fortunately Weekes came in just then, with Mallwood. We turned to a discussion about the discovery of the saw. But there was little to discuss. Both Weekes and Mallwood were as certain as men could be certain of anything that Batty was, or had been, somewhere about, and that he had left the saw on the bed in Mother Kitteridge's cottage.

"In that case, Batty can't be far off," remarked Chaney. "For if Batty did leave the saw on that bed, under the old patchwork quilt, he did so since yesterday afternoon at five o'clock, when it certainly was not there!"

Mallwood looked a little puzzled. Then he brightened.

"Must have been there last night!" he said. "He can't be far off, do you say? I'll have him! If I can only get him before the inquest begins—"

But when the inquest began, at eleven o'clock next morning, Mallwood had not got Batty, nor had he any news of him. Batty's name, however, very soon came to the fore. The Coroner, that same gentleman whose acquaintance we had already made a few weeks before, was in a very stern and uncompromising mood. He was determined, he told the jury of farmers, colliery officials, and small tradesmen, to get at the absolute truth of this affair and should adjourn his inquiry from time to time until he, or the police, did get at it. And, without any beating about the bush, he said that a certain name had been freely mentioned in connection with the affair of the bridge, and the mention of it would crop up again and again in the evidence which would be put before him and the jury. It would be well if the bearer of that name were present, but so far, he remarked, with a significant glance at his jury, earnest inquiry for him had failed. But he would take good care that nothing was suppressed, however long it took; however trying and wearisome the task, his determination was to get at the truth. Somebody was responsible for the death of Sir Stephen Maxtondale – who was it?

While these preliminaries were going on, I looked round. The inquiry was being held in the big ballroom of Heronswood Park; it was packed to the doors. Everybody of note in the neighbourhood was there. The new baronet and his wife were there. And so were Lady Maxtondale's father and mother. But Mr. and Mrs. Weekes kept their place – Lady Maxtondale sat by Sir Rupert's side in a privileged position.

Chapter 20

THE SAW

THE FIRST WITNESS TO be called after the usual preliminaries of identification and medical evidence had been got through was Samuel Freeman, an elderly man who described himself as a workman on the estate. Him the Coroner at once took in hand in a fashion which showed that he was going to get everything he could out of every witness that entered the box.

"Now, Freeman," he said, "I want you to be very, very particular about the answers to the questions I shall put to you; I wish everything to be as clear as daylight. Now, to begin with, I understand that on the morning of Sir Stephen Maxtondale's death you were working near Lady Sybil's Bridge?"

"Close by, sir."

"About how near?"

"Within thirty yards, sir, on the Heronswood side of the cutting."

"Were you alone?"

"No, sir, John Trippett was working with me. We were repairing a fence."

"Did you see Sir Stephen Maxtondale come along the path from Heronswood?"

"We saw him come out of the wood, sir – along the path."

"Did he see you?"

"Yes, sir. We touched our caps to him and he waved his stick at us."

"Now tell us exactly what happened after that, Freeman."

"Sir Stephen walked on to the bridge, sir. halfway across, he stopped and put his hands on the left-hand side railing. There was just a slight sound – a crack – and he plunged forward, head first, into the cutting. The railing went with him."

"That was almost as soon as he had stepped on to the bridge?"

"It was as soon as he stepped on to it, sir. At once!"

"What did you do?"

"I sent Trippett off there and then to Mr. Weekes, sir. I myself scrambled down the side of the cutting to Sir Stephen. He was lying in the roadway. The railing was partly under him."

"Was he alive?"

"Yes, sir – but I think he was unconscious. He never spoke again. I waited there till Mr. Weekes and several men came. Sir Stephen was carried away."

"Well, now, tell me this: when Trippett ran for help, how did he get across the cutting?"

"By the bridge, sir. The bridge itself was all right – it was only the railing that had gone."

"Had you and Trippett crossed the bridge that morning on your way to work?"

"Yes, sir. But we didn't touch the railings. I went over the bridge twice."

"Had you ever seen Sir Stephen cross that bridge before, Freeman?"

"Many a time, sir! Scores of times – I've worked on the estate for twenty years."

"Was it his custom to stop there?"

"I've seen him do the same thing often, sir. He used to stop in the middle, put his hands on the left-hand side railings, and stand there awhile, looking down the valley."

"And I dare say others than yourself have seen him in that attitude?"

"Lots of us about the estate, sir."

Weekes was the next witness. He told the court how he was fetched to the scene of the accident, how he found Sir Stephen lying in the roadway, unconscious, how he had him carried to the estate office, and how he died there, without regaining consciousness.

"Did he ever speak," asked the Coroner, "from the time you reached him till the time he died?"

"Not one word!" replied Weekes.

"I want to know, Mr. Weekes, what you did about the railings which had fallen with Sir Stephen and, according to the last witness, were partly under his body. Did you examine them at once?"

"No! I was too much concerned about Sir Stephen. I merely glanced at them. My first idea was that they were rotten – worn out. I left a man in charge of them, however, and as soon as the doctors came, I hurried back to the cutting. I then found that the railings had been sawn through, top and bottom, in four places, in such a fashion that the least pressure on the top rail would force them out of place and precipitate anyone leaning on them into the cutting."

"I suppose you pointed this out at once?"

"Yes, to the workmen standing by, and as soon as we'd carried the railings to the estate office, I showed them, first to the doctors, and then, when he came, to Superintendent Mallwood. I then locked them up in a spare room."

At this point the twelve jurymen left the court for a room close by in which the railings had been placed for their inspection. On their return the Coroner began a new series of questions to Weekes.

"Now, Mr. Weekes, I understand that you have a theory of your own about this sad affair, and I think we may as well have it put before the jury – it is no use keeping these things back. Is it true that you hold the opinion that whoever made the bridge unsafe did so with the express purpose of causing, not Sir Stephen's, but your death?"

"Yes, sir!" replied Weekes, with emphasis. "I do hold that opinion – and I stick to it! I don't think it was Sir Stephen who was meant, at all. It was me!"

"Sir Stephen, however, was known to cross that bridge, to linger on it, to rest his weight on the railings, every morning of his life. Had you any such habit?" asked the Coroner.

"I frequently crossed that bridge to meet Sir Stephen," replied Weekes. "Five mornings out of six I went to meet him. Sometimes I met him on his side – the Heronswood side. Sometimes it was on mine – the estate office side. Sometimes we met on the bridge. And we often stood talking on the bridge, and when we did, we used to lean on the railings."

"Still, you have other grounds than that for your theory, I think?"

"I have! My life had been threatened."

"You may as well say by whom," said the Coroner. "Let us have everything clear."

"That man Batty had threatened it," replied Weekes. "He's a man that has a bitter grudge against me, because I discharged him. He assaulted me in Monkseaton market-place and he got a month's hard labour for it. He threatened then what he would do when he came out. I believe he sawed through the bridge, expecting me to cross it next morning. And," continued Weekes, "I should have crossed it, and probably leaned on the railings, but for the fact that my wife called me back just as I was leaving the house, to look at some repairs that were being carried out. I was still there, in our kitchen, when they came to tell me about Sir Stephen's fall."

"But this man Batty – had you any reason to think he was in your neighbourhood?"

"I had, later in the morning. I found that a saw had been taken out of the estate carpenter's shop. That shop is always locked up every night. But Batty had – I mean he still has, wherever he is – a key to that shop. He ought to have given it up when I discharged him, but he didn't – he said he'd lost it. I think he came back after leaving prison, used the key to get that saw, and did what he did to the bridge with the idea of breaking my neck. And," concluded Weekes, with rising indignation, "I'll lay that's the truth and I think it's high time the police laid hands on him!"

"No doubt Superintendent Mallwood will do his best," remarked the Coroner. "As the rumours about him are pretty widespread, it is a somewhat significant fact that Batty, if he is innocent, is not here. But there is a witness here whose evidence I wish to take on the question of the threats Mr. Weekes spoke of."

A smart young policeman entered the witness-box and gave his name, rank, and particulars in the direct and staccato fashion which seems peculiar to members of the force.

"Were you present at Monkseaton police court when the man Batty was sentenced to a month's hard labour for an assault on Mr. Weekes?" asked the Coroner.

"I was."

"Did you subsequently convey Batty to prison?"

"I did."

"Did you hear Batty utter any threat against the prosecutor, Mr. Weekes, when he was sentenced?"

"Yes. He used threatening language then and subsequently."

"Can you remember and repeat any of the threats?"

The witness permitted himself to smile a little. "Some of them are not repeatable, sir! I can repeat those that are."

"Well – but if necessary you need not be too particular," said the Coroner. "I want to know their precise character."

"On being sentenced, sir, he said he'd settle Mr. Weekes when he came out, if he swung for it. He repeated this when, a little later, I took him his tea. Later on, when I conveyed him to prison, he said a good many things of the same sort. They were all of a threatening nature."

"All against Mr. Weekes?"

"Yes, sir. I never heard him mention any other person."

"He never mentioned Sir Stephen?"

"No, sir – in my hearing. He appeared to have a bitter feeling against Mr. Weekes."

"Can you remember any one distinct threat against Mr. Weekes?"

"Yes, sir. Just before I was handing him over to the prison authorities he said: 'You can tell that blank blank Weekes next time you see him that I'll put him where he'll think hellfire's a back number of the polar regions when I come out! – I know how to fix it!' Just those words, sir."

"Dear me!" said the Coroner. "Now, what particular significance did you attach to those words?"

"None, sir. But I bore them in mind."

The Coroner, who, I think, was a naturally inquisitive gentleman, reflected on the cryptic nature of Batty's threat for a moment; then he nodded to the witness, and the witness picked up his helmet and gloves and withdrew.

Next came the estate foreman carpenter, another elderly employee of the Maxtondale family.

"Mr. Weekes," said the Coroner, "has told us that a certain saw was found to be missing from the estate carpenter's shop when inquiries began to be made about the damage to the railing of Lady Sybil's Bridge, and that you reported the loss of it. When did you discover that loss?"

"Not so very long after the accident, sir. With Mr. Weekes I examined the railings when they had been brought up from the cutting, and I was so convinced that the severance had been made by a certain type of handsaw that I went off to the carpenter's shop and examined our stock. I found then that a saw which I myself had used the previous afternoon was missing. I made the very fullest inquiry about it from my men and came to the conclusion that the workshop had been entered during the night and the saw taken from it. It was a new saw with fine-set teeth. I am certain that it was the saw used at the bridge."

"You heard Mr. Weekes's evidence about Batty and a key to the workshop. Do you know anything about that?"

"Yes, sir. Batty had a key, as Mr. Weekes says."

"What was he doing with a key to the workshop?"

"He was – I mean, he had been before his discharge – doing extra work, sir. He was a very clever workman, a first-class hand, superior to any of my other men, if he'd only kept off the drink and owned a less violent temper. He was doing this extra work – some ornamental woodwork – at nights, so I let him have a key. We have – or had – three. Mr. Weekes had one; I had two. It was one of my two that Batty had. When he was discharged by Mr. Weekes, he didn't give the key up; he told Mr. Weekes he'd lost it."

The Coroner looked across at an official who was mounting guard over a brown-paper parcel; at his nod the official made haste to untie string and unwrap paper, and presently he produced a carpenter's saw and handed it to the witness.

"Is that the saw you have been speaking of – the missing saw?" asked the Coroner.

"This is it, sir," replied the witness promptly.

"How do you identify it? How do you know it from any other saw?"

"Easily, sir. It's got the estate office mark burnt on it, and also the date when I put it amongst the tools. That's the saw, sir."

"You're absolutely sure of that?"

"Dead sure, sir."

The Coroner turned to the jurymen.

"This saw, gentlemen, was found yesterday morning in a back room of the cottage formerly occupied by the woman Kitteridge, who was murdered in company with the late Mr. Robson, at Home Farm, one evening a few weeks ago. Call William Champness."

A young man – evidently, from his dress, a farm-labourer – looking somewhat sheepish, entered the box. The Coroner directed his attention to the saw at once.

"Did you take this saw to Mr. Weekes, the steward, yesterday morning?"

"I didn't take it to him, sir," replied the witness. "I fetched him to it."

"Where was that?"

"In Mother Kitteridge's place – back room. On the bed."

"What were you doing in Mother Kitteridge's cottage yesterday morning?"

"Well, sir, I hadn't anything to do then," said the witness, looking more sheepish than before, "but I was passing, and I'd heard the place was open, so I just went in and looked about. And when I saw that saw, I went and told Mr. Weekes about it, because I'd heard there was a saw missing from the workshop."

"Who'd told you that, now?"

"Don't know, sir. It was common talk. Some of the carpenters had talked about it."

The Coroner, apparently, had no more to say on this point. I nudged Chaney's arm.

"Are you going to tell them that the saw wasn't there when we examined the cottage?" I whispered.

"No!" he replied. "Leave them alone. Let them go their own way. We shall be hearing more soon."

The Coroner was talking to Mallwood, in whispers. Presently Mallwood left the room. He was away several minutes, during which the Coroner busied himself with his papers, the jurymen waited in stolid silence, and the spectators muttered to each other. Mallwood came back. Once again he and the Coroner put their heads together. Then Mallwood disappeared again, and the Coroner turned to his jurymen.

"An eleventh-hour witness has come forward, gentlemen," he said, "a witness who is evidently seriously afraid of appearing! We have, however, succeeded in reassuring her that she will come to no harm by telling us what she knows, and we shall now hear her evidence."

Mallwood came back at that moment escorting an obviously timid and shrinking woman whom I recognised as having seen once or twice near the cottages.

Chapter 21

MR. PILSEY'S SHOP

THE DEMEANOUR OF THIS new witness was so shrinking and frightened that the Coroner, before ever asking her for the necessary particulars of herself, considered it necessary to reassure her.

"Don't be afraid, my good woman!" he said encouragingly. "No harm can come to you from anything you say here, as long as you speak the truth. You're not frightened of telling the truth, are you?"

The woman hesitated, looking doubtfully round the court.

"I'm not sure about what might happen, sir," she replied. "I'd rather have kept quiet."

"You are frightened, then?" said the Coroner. "Who is it, now? Somebody been threatening you?"

"Why, not exactly threatening, sir, but Mr. Batty, he's that violent—"

"Oh, it's Batty, is it?" interrupted the Coroner. "Well, Batty is not here and he's not likely to molest you. The police—"

"The police can't be watching my cottage night and day, sir," said the woman. "And if Mr. Batty comes back—"

The Coroner turned in Mallwood's direction.

"How did you get hold of this information?" he said.

Mallwood pointed to a small boy who had been ushered into court behind himself and the witness.

"This boy says he saw Batty go to the witness's cottage the other night, sir," he answered. "The night before the accident to Sir Stephen."

"Is that true?" asked the Coroner, turning to the woman.

"Yes, it's true enough, sir. He did come there – and I wish he hadn't. I didn't want to have anything to do with Mr. Batty."

"You'd better go into the witness-box and tell me all about it," said the Coroner. "The police will see that you come to no harm. Name? Hannah Mallinson? Married woman? Widow? Living at the cottages, Heronswood Park. Well, Mrs. Mallinson, I understand that Batty came to your cottage the other night. What night was that?"

"Night before Sir Stephen's accident, sir."

"You're sure of that?"

"Positive, sir."

"What did Batty want? But, first, what time was it when he came to your cottage?"

"Just when it was getting dark, sir – I couldn't say to ten minutes, nor twenty. He came in through the door without knocking and gave me quite a turn. He wanted to know if I would let him have something to eat."

"To give him a meal, I suppose?"

"No, sir. He wanted something to take away with him – he said he'd pay for it. He said he'd come to fetch some property of his from Mrs. Kitteridge's cottage and was going to stay the night there."

"Did you oblige him?"

"Yes, sir. I got him a loaf of bread and some butter and cheese and a tin of salmon. He said he'd some bottles of beer in his pocket."

"Did you have any talk with him?"

"I didn't talk, sir – I wanted to get him away; he looked to be in a very bad temper. He talked a lot while I was putting the food together for him."

"What did he talk about?"

"Well, sir, it was principally about Mr. Weekes. He said Mr. Weekes had had his knife into him for a long time before he sacked him, but he'd have his knife into Mr. Weekes before long. And a lot more of that sort, sir."

"And you didn't reply, eh?"

"Why, I did say to him that if I'd been in his shoes, I'd have gone right away from Heronswood and never come back again – that was all, sir."

"And what did he say to that?"

"He said he'd leave Heronswood fast enough when he'd done what he wanted to do, sir."

"He didn't say what it was he wanted to do?"

"No, sir, not in particular. He muttered a lot about Mr. Weekes."

"Did you hear him say anything against Sir Stephen Maxtondale?"

"No, sir, not against him. The opposite, sir. He said Sir Stephen was a good old sort, but that Weekes, sir – he used language then which I couldn't bring myself to repeat, sir."

"Did Batty give you anything for the food you supplied?"

"He put half a crown on the table, sir."

"And went away then, I suppose?"

"Yes, sir."

"Did you see him again that night or next morning, Mrs. Mallinson?"

"No, sir, I've never set eyes on him since!"

There was nothing more to be got out of Mrs. Mallinson, except that she professed herself in mortal fear of Batty coming back to revenge himself on her for splitting, and presently, with another reassuring word, the Coroner let her go and began a whispered consultation with Mallwood. Eventually he turned to the jury.

"After talking things over with Superintendent Mallwood," he said, "I have come to the conclusion, gentlemen, that this will be a convenient stage at which to adjourn the inquiry. I shall adjourn for a fortnight – and it may be," he added significantly, "that we shall then only meet, formally, for a further adjournment."

The Heronswood butler was sitting next to me. He turned sharply towards my shoulder.

"What's he mean by that, sir?" he asked.

"He means that police proceedings may render any definite decision by a coroner's jury unnecessary," I replied.

"Ah, I see, sir, I see!" he said. "But they've got to catch somebody yet, haven't they?"

That catching of somebody formed the subject of a discussion between Mallwood, Chaney, and me as soon as we were alone, outside the room in which the inquest had been begun. For Chaney now thought he had better tell Mallwood what he knew about the finding of the saw.

"Look here, Mallwood," he said when we had taken the Superintendent aside, "you may as well know something that we know. About that saw, now. According to the woman, Mallinson, Batty went to sleep in Mrs. Kitteridge's cottage on the night previous to the affair at Lady Sybil's Bridge. Now, am I right in thinking that your conclusion is that during that night Batty, in possession of a key, went to the estate carpenter's shop, got out the saw, and sawed through the railings of the bridge? Eh?"

"Just about," admitted Mallwood. "Yes, I think that's my conclusion after what we've heard."

"And you think, further, that Batty, having done the necessary damage to the bridge, in the hope that Weekes would break his neck there, returned to the cottage and left the saw where it was found – on the bed in the little back bedroom? That right?"

"Yes, I guess so," said Mallwood. "Must have been."

"Well, he didn't!" retorted Chaney. "How do I know? Because the saw wasn't there, Mallwood, when you, Camberwell, and I inspected Mother Kitteridge's cottage on the afternoon of the accident. You didn't know, but when you and Camberwell went nosing round some of the antiques downstairs, I was examining the room upstairs which I knew, from certain things I saw there, to have been occupied by Batty when he lodged with the old woman. And I turned over the quilt which lay on the bed, and the bedclothes, and the pillows, and there was no saw there then. No, I hadn't any object in turning these things over – I just did turn 'em over, that's all. But there was no saw there that afternoon, Mallwood. The saw was put there during the night that followed our visit!"

Mallwood gave a sigh of relief.

"Oh, well," he exclaimed, "that's all right! Batty, of course, stopped a second night there. Maybe he'd had the saw hidden somewhere else. That's how I fix things."

Chaney remained silent a moment, regarding Mallwood with speculative eyes, as if wondering.

"Is it?" he said at last. "Um! Well, let's do a bit of supposing – favourite amusement of mine. Let's suppose that Batty stole the saw, sawed through the bridge, meant Weekes to break his neck, didn't care a damn if Sir Stephen broke his, too. We suppose all that – good! Now, are we to suppose that, having done this, Batty by nine o'clock next morning didn't know the results of his misdeeds? And are we to suppose that he then hung around the district – in danger of being seen? And that he came back next night to the cottage and put the saw on the bed he'd slept in the previous night, under the quilt? Are we to suppose all that?"

Mallwood began to look uneasy.

"What're you getting at, Chaney?" he asked, suspiciously. "Seems to me that you don't believe Batty put the saw there!"

Chaney stared at him.

"I don't!" he answered.

"You don't? Who did, then?" demanded Mallwood. "Who, now?"

"Damned if I know!" replied Chaney. "But I think we shall know before we've done. Well, what're you going to do next?"

"Do what we're already doing," said Mallwood, sulkily. "Comb the place out till we find Batty."

Chaney and I left him and went to our hotel at Monkseaton. During the rest of that day he remained strangely reticent, saying next to nothing about the events of the morning. The two youthful pressmen from the local journal had heard of our return and called to see us; they tried to get Chaney's ideas on the latest development. Chaney appeared to have no ideas to communicate. But I could see that he was thinking, and thinking hard; I knew, too, that in due time he would tell me the result of these mental exercises. In the mean time I stood by the old adage: Hurry no man's cattle.

Next morning as we were concluding a leisurely breakfast, a message arrived from Mallwood – would we go round to see him? We went round. Mallwood's car stood at the door of the police station; behind it was another car, in which were already seated two plainclothes men and another man in uniform. Mallwood was just coming out to us.

"Don't know if it's anything to do with our joint case," he said, "but I thought I'd let you know. We've had a report of a burglary at a village shop a few miles away, and from what we've heard, I've a notion that the burglar was Batty. However, we can soon tell – the burglar left some clothes behind him in exchange for a suit of the shopkeeper's.

We'll call at Heronswood and take along with us a man who can tell if the things were Batty's. Like to come?"

"In lack of anything more exciting, yes!" said Chaney. "What's missing from the shop besides the clothes?"

"That's what makes me feel sure it's Batty," replied Mallwood. "Food, chiefly. Tinned stuff. Looks as if Batty was hiding – and hungry."

We drove off and at Heronswood stopped to pick up a man from the carpenter's shop who assured us that he could readily identify any garment worn by Batty during the last year or two. Our course ran through the Sedbury woods, stretching for miles in an undulating countryside, to the village wherein the rifled shop stood – a little, out-of-the-way place called Wilferton, consisting mainly of one street, two or three farmhouses, a score or so of cottages, and the general store, at which our two cars pulled up and before the door of which stood the local policeman. He grinned widely as he saluted Mallwood.

"Not very much missing, sir," he said as we entered the little garden in front of the shop. "Only some bread and cheese and a tin or two of canned meat and suchlike. But Mr. Pilsey, he's mad because the thief's taken his best suit o' clothes, what he wears Sundays. He'd had 'em on last night, going to a meeting, and got 'em a bit wet, so he hung 'em before the kitchen fire, to dry, when he went to bed; and when he came down this morning, they'd vanished."

Mr. Pilsey, a round-faced man with a stubble of fiery beard on his aggrieved countenance, bore out the policeman's statement.

"Two tins of best ox-tongue, two ditto salmon, two ditto lobster, one loaf white bread, one ditto brown bread, two tea-cakes, one fruit-cake, a tin-opener, box plain chocolate – them," said Mr. Pilsey, waving a fat hand, "I only mention to show the precise nature of the depredations. Not of great value, to be sure – if I'd known the man was starving, I'd have imparted of my substance to him—"

"Any money missing?" asked Mallwood.

"Not my habit to leave money about," replied Mr. Pilsey. "What money there is in the shop at nightfall I take to my bedroom. No money, no – but a suit of clothes – good dark-blue serge for which I recently paid four pound, nineteen and six – clean gone! To say nothing," added Mr. Pilsey, sadly, "to say nothing at all of my Sunday boots – nearly brand-new – as was drying in the hearth!"

"Left something behind, I understand?" said Mallwood.

"Adding insult to injury, as the saying is," replied Mr. Pilsey. "Yes, sir, what the evil-doer cast off lay there on my favourite easy chair in the chimney-corner, just where he'd thrown them. But not for long, sir – this way."

Mr. Pilsey conducted us through a door at the rear of the shop, and through a sort of half-kitchen, half-living room, to another door which, being flung wide, revealed a scullery. On its brick floor, and ignominiously heaped together, lay a much-worn jacket and waistcoat, a pair of stained flannel trousers, and a pair of boots.

"His leavings!" said Mr. Pilsey, with a sniff. "Wonder I haven't burned 'em!"

Mallwood turned to the man we had brought from Heronswood.

"Well?" he asked.

"Oh, those are Batty's right enough," replied the man. "Swear to 'em anywhere."

He touched the grey flannel trousers with the toe of his boot. "Got that patch of paint in our workshop," he went on. "Trousers was newish then, and one of the lads splashed him in passing. Oh, yes, they're Batty's, those!"

Chaney had been listening in silence; he stood silent now, looking meditatively at the heap of discarded clothing. Suddenly he turned to Mallwood and the plainclothes men.

"Do any of you happen to know," he asked slowly, "if there's any gentleman in this neighbourhood who keeps a bloodhound or two?"

Chapter 22

BLOODHOUNDS

MALLWOOD'S EARS PRICKED UP at that; he turned on Chaney with a glance of admiring comprehension.

"Ah!" he exclaimed. "Good idea, that! You mean – run him down?"

"Just that," replied Chaney, dryly. "I've seen it done – once."

One of the plainclothes men stepped forward.

"Mr. Marston of Sedbury Manor keeps bloodhounds," he said. "I've seen 'em, two or three times, in his grounds."

"It's worth trying," remarked Chaney. "I dare say Mr. Marston would lend them. Bring them here, let them have a good sniff at these clothes, and then – well, then I suppose we should follow them."

"Excellent idea!" agreed Mallwood. "We'd better—"

But there Mr. Pilsey intervened. He had stood open-mouthed, listening with all his ears.

"I – I – do I understand you to say that you propose to – to hunt down this evil-doer – I'm not excusing him mind! – with dogs?" he asked in horror-stricken accents. "What, hunt a human being with fierce animals in a Christian country? Oh, I couldn't agree to that at all, gentlemen! It would be contrary to my opinions! Some other way, now!"

"Don't you want us to catch the fellow?" asked Mallwood. Then, with a wink at Chaney, he added, slyly: "Think of your best suit – Sunday suit, no doubt!"

"A very reprehensible thing to do, on the unfortunate person's part," responded Mr. Pilsey, "especially," he continued, with a glance at Batty's discarded garments, "especially as his own don't seem to have been so very much the worse for wear. But this dog-hunting—"

"Hounds!" corrected Chaney.

"Well, hounds, then – it seems an unchristianlike thing to hunt a man, however much a wrongdoer he may be," said Mr. Pilsey. "They – why, they might worry him! What're you going to do with those things?" he asked anxiously as Mallwood signalled to one of his men to pick up the clothes. "You see, if I got my suit back, he'd be wanting those garments."

"We're going to take care of them," said Mallwood. "Now, Mr. Pilsey, don't let's have any nonsense! This chap's got to be found; he's dangerous. He's threatened somebody's life – we've got to get him. Now, what I want is this – show me somewhere, a room, cupboard, anything in which I can lock up these clothes until I bring those bloodhounds here – if we can get them. We're not going to leave a stone unturned to get hold of this man – we've a very strong belief that he's a murderer already. Why, it's a mercy he didn't scrag you!"

This induced Mr. Pilsey to show us an outhouse communicating with the scullery and to produce the key of its door. He further volunteered the information that in his opinion the burglar had entered his premises by way of it, the window having been found open when he rose that morning.

"So much the better," said Mallwood. "The scent'll hang about there still, no doubt. We're going to have those hounds on the job, Mr. Pilsey, Christian or unchristian."

He put the key of the outhouse in his pocket, and we went back to the car, leaving the plainclothes men with the village policeman. Then the three of us set off for Sedbury Manor, a few miles away.

"You've seen bloodhounds at work?" said Mallwood, turning to Chaney. "I never have. Should like to. Interesting, of course."

"Seen it just once," replied Chaney. "Away down in Devonshire. Murder case – bad case. Love crime. Man had shot his old sweetheart and her new lover – popped 'em both off in the grounds of her father's house. He'd dropped a glove, a well-worn glove, this chap, at the scene of the murder. There was a gentleman living close by who kept bloodhounds, and they were fetched at once and put on to the glove and the trail. But that was an easy job – the fellow hadn't gone more than a mile away."

"Then they got him?" said Mallwood, eagerly.

"Got him – dead," replied Chaney. "He'd shot himself in a wood – where he and the girl he'd murdered had been accustomed to meet."

Mallwood was obviously disappointed at this tame conclusion. He shook his head.

"Still, they did get him!" he said. "Shows it can be done."

"Oh, it can be done," replied Chaney. "If Mr. Marston's got the right stuff, we'll run our man down."

We found Mr. Marston at home. Neither Chaney nor I had seen him since our return to the neighbourhood. He listened silently to our explanations.

"Um!" he said, when we'd finished. "You say the man left his old clothes behind him when he stole Pilsey's suit?"

"Coat, waistcoat, trousers," replied Chaney, "and boots."

"Well, there's always a pretty strong smell about a carpenter's clothes," remarked Mr. Marston, "wood, paint, and so on. Come this way."

He led us out of the back door of the house and across a big paved courtyard to a paddock at the back of his stables. There was a range of model dog-kennels there, and presently, under the care of Mr. Marston's gamekeeper, we found ourselves inspecting a crowd of dogs, pointers, setters, retrievers. Finally we came to a special kennel and were introduced to the bloodhounds, two magnificent animals which came to the rails at the keeper's call.

"Ah!" said Chaney, appreciatively, "beauties! The real thing, eh? Pure bred?"

"Oh, pure bred, sir," replied the keeper. "Couldn't find no better in all England. All our dogs and hounds are pure bred."

"What're the distinguishing features of these chaps, then?" asked Chaney. "Can you point 'em out?"

The keeper put a hand over the rails and began to point.

"Well, sir, to start with, that rich tan colour, with a dark saddle, no white showing, or, if there is any, the least show possible. Then a long and narrow head, with a round skull, and that peak at the top and back of the skull – occipital bone, that is, the vets call it. Then there's a third eyelid, what they call the 'haw' – that's what makes their eyes look bloodshot. Then the ears – they should be long enough to meet in front of the nose, but should fall straight on each side of the face. Those are the chief marks, sir. You'll notice that we've got 'em to perfection."

"Easily managed?" inquired Chaney.

"Um – not if they're roused up, sir. Like all hounds, they're a bit independent and contrary. But if they're well done by and know their friends, they're docile enough, and you couldn't find a better watchdog anywhere."

"Got names, I suppose, these two?" suggested Chaney.

The keeper pointed left and right.

"Bruce and Birdie," he answered. "Oh, yes, sir – all our dogs have names; Mr. Marston, he christens them as they get to a certain age."

Just then Mr. Marston called to us from the archway of the court-yard, where he was waiting for us with his car. The keeper brought Bruce and Birdie out on leads. Presently we in our car, and Mr. Marston, his hounds, and his keeper in his, set out for Mr. Pilsey's shop in the neighbouring village.

Mr. Pilsey was horrified at the sight of the bloodhounds, but Mallwood put him and his qualms quietly aside. The hounds were taken into the outhouse and introduced to Batty's discarded garments, the odour of which appeared to be of peculiar interest to them, and, the door being left open, were free to pursue their own investigations. Their first action on getting outside was to nose about the ground immediately beneath the window through which Batty was presumed to have effected his entrance, but they quickly returned to the door and, making a bee-line down Mr. Pilsey's back garden, broke through a gap in the hedge into the meadows at its foot. And after them we streamed, leaving instructions with our respective car-drivers to keep us in sight as far as they could.

We were very soon, however, quite out of touch with roads, by-roads, or lanes. Whether it was that Batty owned a peculiarly strong scent, or that any sort of scent held well that morning, I don't know, but Bruce and Birdie went strong and steadily until we were well out of the village and in a thickly wooded bit of country. Across meadows, alongside deep hedgerows, through a coppice here, a plantation there, the hounds nosed along, with ourselves, as deeply interested followers, a little in their rear. That was a lonely stretch of country; we were going steadily away from village or outlying farmstead. Presently Mallwood, who from long experience knew the lie of the land, spoke.

"Bet a pound to a penny I know where he made for," he exclaimed, "for these hounds are making a bee-line to it!"

"Where?" asked Chaney.

"Highcastle Crags! There's a piece of as wild country there as you can find in all the Midlands. Rocks – ravines – caves – scrub – heather – that sort of thing. A man could hide there for a long time."

We were some distance away from Pilsey and his shop by then. And we went still farther, getting at every half-mile into wilder and wilder country. At last we came to the place Mallwood had spoken of. It was a deep ravine in the midst of old, dark-timbered woods, and on one side of it there was a great rampart of limestone rock, pierced here and there with cavernous-like openings. Mallwood pointed to them.

"They say you can go in at the mouths of some of those caves and come out at the top of the woods, high above!" he said. "I've heard – ah, you see, those hounds are making up there!"

The hounds were turning up the side of the ravine beneath the limestone rampart. They went on and on, seeming never at fault, until they were immediately at the foot of the great grey masses. And suddenly they turned into the mouth of one of the caves, and we, hurrying up the slope, followed them inside.

We saw at once that wherever Batty might be at that moment, he had tenanted this cave within the last few hours. There, carefully arranged on a ledge of rock, were some of Mr. Pilsey's canned goods: ox-tongue, salmon, lobster. There, too, were bread and fruit-cake and the tin-opener of which Mr. Pilsey had told us. And there were evidences, too, in the shape of crumbs and fragments, that Batty had made a meal. He had done himself very well with ox-tongue, bread, cake, and chocolate; it required no microscope to see that. But Batty himself was not there.

We looked into matters a little more closely. In Mallwood's opinion – and we agreed with him – Batty had made that cave a sort of head-quarters. There was a quite comfortable bed in one corner, made of dried bracken and heather, with some old sacks and rugs – horse-rugs probably stolen from a neighbouring farm – for covering. And the floor was strewn with used matches, and there were several emptied cigarette cartons and two or three candle-ends. But – no sign of Batty.

But the hounds had not done. They did a good deal of sniffing and nosing in and about the cave, and suddenly they were off again, with ourselves in pursuit. This time they followed a narrow track beneath the rampart of limestone, until they came to where a gully in the rock led up to the high ground, thickly wooded, above the ravine. Straight through the woods they went and suddenly emerged on a wide stretch of open grassland, at the farther side of which rose the gables and chimneys of a big house. We stopped, staring.

"Good God!" exclaimed Mallwood. "Heronswood! We've worked round to it!"

The hounds went straight ahead now. Ten minutes more, and at a close-shut door in the walls of the older part of the house they stopped and suddenly began to bay loudly.

Chapter 23

THE AMBASSADOR'S CUPBOARD

ALTHOUGH I HAVE SAID a good deal already about Heronswood, I have not yet said anything about its history or architectural features. Long before it came into possession of the Maxtondale family, it had been a monastic building – Heronswood Abbey, dating from the thirteenth century. The modern house dated from about the time of James I and had been remodelled, improved, restored at various dates since the Civil War. But joined on to it, at the rear and along one side, were the old monastic buildings, still in a wonderful state of preservation; some of them, indeed, were still in use. The greater part of them faced a big courtyard, enclosed by a high wall. It was to a doorway in this wall that the bloodhounds had led us. And the door at the foot of which they now stood baying was shut – a great, formidable barrier of oak, heavily studded with square-headed iron nails.

"What's this mean?" asked Mallwood, as we came straggling up. "Surely Batty hasn't come here? Here, of all places!"

Mr. Marston hurried to the front, calming his hounds.

"Try the door!" he said.

Chippendale, who was nearest, seized the big latch and, with an effort, lifted it; the door swung slowly open, revealing what I believe would be correctly designated as the cellarium of the old Abbey – a long, low, corridor-like arcade of stone with a groined roof. And over the flagged floor of this the hounds went forward, nosing the worn stones. Again they came to a door, set in the left-hand wall and closed, and again they began to bay.

"Try that, too," commanded Mr. Marston.

That door, also, yielded to Chippendale's eager hand; we trooped up the steps in front of it and into a small, stone-paved, stone-wall-lined hall, in one corner of which was the opening to a stairway of more steps, worn to a hollow in their centres. There were two inner doorways in that hall; the hounds sniffed and nosed from one to the other. Chaney pointed to an iron chain which hung down the wall near the foot of the stairs, from an opening in the roof.

"Probably a bell up there," he said. "Pull it, Chip."

Chippendale pulled, gently, then more insistently. The chain, rusty from long disuse, creaked and squeaked. Then, somewhere above us, a bell began to sound. From the faintness and far-off-ness of that sound, I knew the intervening walls were of enormous thickness.

"Keep on pulling," said Chaney. "Somebody'll hear it – eventually."

Mr. Marston and his gamekeeper were pacifying the hounds. The baying ceased, but they still whimpered, restlessly.

"Never been in this part of the place before," remarked Mr. Marston. "Part of the old monks' property, I suppose. But whatever has that fellow been doing here? That he's been here is certain. Not so long since, either."

"Pull again, Chip!" said Chaney. "Louder!"

Suddenly, somewhere up the winding stair in the corner, we heard a door open – it was evident, from the sound, that the hinges were seldom used and needed oiling. Then steps on the worn stair, and round the corner of the newel came into view the wondering, half-scared face of a footman. At sight of Mr. Marston, however, his face cleared.

"Butler anywhere about?" demanded Mr. Marston. "Rabbage?"

"Mr. Rabbage, sir?" said the astonished footman. "Yes, sir – in his pantry, sir. I'll fetch him. Will you come up, sir?"

"No, bring him here," replied Mr. Marston. "You know me – tell Rabbage I want him."

The footman hurried away. Some minutes elapsed; then Rabbage, looking even more astonished than his underling, came into view, and at sight of men and hounds stared open-mouthed.

"Come down!" said Mr. Marston as Rabbage paused on the stairs. "Look here – you've had a burglary in here!"

"Good Lord, sir, you don't say so!" exclaimed Rabbage. "Not to my knowledge, sir. Nothing been heard of it, Mr. Marston."

"Bet you have, anyway," said Mr. Marston. "That fellow Batty, who's suspected of cutting the bridge. He broke into Pilsey's shop at Wilferton during the night, and these hounds of mine have tracked him here. He must have been here – may be about here now. Anything missing? Money – plate – valuables?"

"I – I really couldn't say, Mr. Marston, sir," replied Rabbage. "I – I haven't heard of anything, sir. Nor have I missed anything myself, sir. To be sure, I've had no time to notice things this morning, Mr. Marston. We're that busy, getting things ready for Sir Stephen's obsequies tomorrow morning, that—"

"You'd better have a look round," interrupted Mr. Marston. He turned to his gamekeeper and gave him an order about the two hounds, now secured in leashes.

"Here!" he went on. "We'll come up with you, Rabbage. Where's Sir Rupert this morning?"

"Sir Rupert and her ladyship are with Mr. Ellerthorpe in the library, at present," replied Rabbage. "Shall I call Sir Rupert, sir?"

"No, I'll go to him," answered Mr. Marston. "I know the way – when I once get out of this rabbit-warren! Where do these steps lead?" he asked, as we followed the butler up the newel stair. "Never been in this part before."

"No, sir, very few people ever have," said Rabbage. "We're in the very oldest part of the house, sir. This, sir, leads into what I'm told was the monks' dining room – the refectory, as they termed it, sir – and from that into the new part of the house. This way, gentlemen."

We emerged into the refectorium (still in such a fine state of preservation that I would willingly have lingered to examine it) and from it passed by a door and a vaulted passage into the modern house, in the main corridor of which Mr. Marston left us. Rabbage looked wonderingly at the rest of us.

"Do you really think Batty's been in here?" he asked. "Burgling! Well, I never heard anything, and I don't think—"

"You'd better look round, Rabbage," said Mallwood. "Your pantry, now, where you keep the plate. But, then, I expect you sleep there?"

"Well, sir, as a matter of fact, I don't," replied Rabbage. "I used to – a butler's supposed to do so, I know. But our pantry, gentlemen, is of limited dimensions, and of recent years, by my late master's orders, I have slept elsewhere. Of course, I take the key of the pantry to my bedroom every night – but I'm afraid it's a very ordinary lock, gentlemen, and a burglar who knew his job—"

"You'd better have a look round, Rabbage," interrupted Chaney. "Batty's been in this house without a doubt."

Without more ado Rabbage led the way to his pantry. It was, as he said, a somewhat small room, its wall space pretty well filled up with drawers and cupboards. In one corner, sunk into the wall, was a safe.

"All the old, valuable silver is kept in there, gentlemen," said Rabbage. "It's a very old safe, one, I should think, of the very earliest ever made, but I fancy that even a modern cracksman would find it a bit difficult to get into – sound stuff, gentlemen. Then there's more silver – the sort we have in daily use – in these drawers and cupboards – I don't think anything's been touched," he continued, as he began opening these receptacles and peeping into them. "I see no sign of any robbery."

"Any loose money left lying about anywhere?" asked Chaney.

Rabbage suddenly started. He moved across the room to a shelf in a corner near the fireplace.

"Oh, well—" he said. "Yes, there is—"

The next moment he turned on us with a horrified face.

"It's gone!" he exclaimed. "Gone!"

"What's gone?" asked Mallwood. "What?"

"Money!" gasped Rabbage. "Bag – with money in it. Money I drew from the bank a day or two ago for the servants' monthly wages. I left it there, on that shelf last night—"

"How much?" interrupted Mallwood.

"A hundred pounds," replied Rabbage. "The wages come to between eighty and ninety – I always draw a bit extra for loose cash. And I've left the bag there, in that very corner, scores of times! Always left it there till wanted."

"It's gone now, anyway," said Mallwood. "You don't think it's been moved by any of the servants?"

"They couldn't get in, Mr. Mallwood. The door's always locked and the key in my pocket," replied Rabbage. "But it's such a simple lock – I've often said to Sir Stephen that we ought to have a new and stronger one. But—"

Just then Mr. Marston came back, with Sir Rupert Maxtondale and Mr. Ellerthorpe at his heels. Mallwood told of the butler's discovery.

"Better have other places examined," said Sir Rupert. "But – how should this fellow Batty, if it's his work, have got his knowledge of the house? How should he have known which was the butler's pantry? Every door in this corridor is alike as far as I know."

"Batty was doing work here not so long since, Sir Rupert," replied Rabbage, who was now nearly on the verge of tears. "He saw me in this room – I gave him his instructions here. He was here not – not so long before the affair of the late Sir John, gentlemen – he came to do some repairs in the south drawing room."

"South drawing room!" exclaimed Sir Rupert. "Good heavens! – that's where the Ambassador's cupboard is! Here, we'd better go there at once!"

He left the room hurriedly, followed by all of us, and, turning down the corridor and across the great entrance hall, led us through a succession of rooms, all darkened, to one that filled a corner of the big house on the southwest side. All the blinds were drawn there, too, but Sir Rupert switched on the electric light, and, that done, made for a certain glass-panelled door sunk into a wall near the great fireplace. Behind the glass panel something glittered.

"No end of treasures in this cupboard," said Sir Rupert as he approached it. "You know all about it, Ellerthorpe. It contains the various gifts and presents made to my great-grandfather, Sir Horace Maxtondale, when he was Ambassador at one or other of the European courts. Rings, snuff-boxes, reliquaries, all sorts of valuables – worth, I dare say, thousands of pounds. I used to tell my father – hullo, look here, now!"

He was in front of the glass-faced cupboard by that time and he suddenly turned on us, pointing at the same time to the top panel. In its lower left-hand corner a square had been cut clean out of the glass. And, that done, nothing could have been easier than for the man who did it to put in his hand and wrist and help himself to the contents of the cupboard – anyway, to such of the contents as he could reach.

Chaney went closer to the cupboard and tried the door.

"Locked!" he said. "Of course he's taken whatever caught his fancy through this hole. Made with a glazier's diamond, that – probably he carried one. Lots of carpenters do. Have you a list of what was in here, Sir Rupert? The contents should be checked."

"There's a list somewhere," replied Sir Rupert, gloomily. "It'll be amongst my father's papers, no doubt. I see that one thing's gone, anyway. The Emperor's snuff-box! That was given to my great-grand-father by a tsar of Russia. Solid gold, set with diamonds. Ridiculous, to leave it here! But all this stuff has always been kept here – it's a wonder no burglar's ever been at it before."

Rabbage permitted himself a gentle cough.

"I've heard my late respected master say there was a hundred thou-sand pounds' worth of valuables in that cupboard, gentlemen," he said deferentially. "Still, nothing has ever been missed – in my time."

"There's something missing now, anyway!" growled Sir Rupert. "Ellerthorpe, you and I had better look for the inventory – I know there is one."

He was turning away as if to leave the room when Chippendale, who had been wandering about, suddenly spoke.

"There's a window unfastened here!" he said. "And I see footprints on the soil outside."

Chaney, Mallwood, and I hastened over to the corner of the big room in which Chippendale had made his discovery. There were some twelve or fifteen tall windows in that room, stretching from floor to ceiling and opening on the terrace. But beneath the edge of the terrace paving and the foot of the outer hall was a strip of flowerbed, and, as Chippendale had been quick to notice, there were footprints, two distinct footprints in it. And they both pointed *away from the window*. Chaney was as swift to act as Chippendale had been to see.

"Chippendale," he said, "run round to Mr. Marston's gamekeeper in the courtyard. No – not through that window, my lad. Find your way back through the house. Tell the keeper to bring the hounds round here – outside, of course."

Chippendale hurried off; Sir Rupert and Mr. Ellerthorpe came back. We waited until the gamekeeper and Chippendale came round a corner of the house with the bloodhounds. Mr. Ellerthorpe, a nervous man at all times, let out an exclamation of something like fear, at the mere sight of them.

"Dear, dear!" he said. "And – and they have actually followed this man – all that way? And you think—"

But no one paid any attention to Mr. Ellerthorpe; we were all watching the hounds. Released from their leashes, they began nosing around. Suddenly they picked up the scent again and were off – across the terrace, down a flight of steps, out into the open park. And those of us who had followed them before, followed again.

We had not followed far when this new track led us into the old one – at the farther edge of the park. And along the old one the two bloodhounds pressed forward. Chaney began to get uneasy; it seemed improbable that Batty would have returned on his own tracks. But, as I pointed out, it was also quite probable that he had used the cave as headquarters and had not only set out from it on his burgling expedition, but returned to it. Anyhow, back to the cave the hounds led us. And there Chippendale, first up in the chase, made a startling discovery. The food-supply, which we had left there only two hours before, had disappeared! Of course, as somebody pointed out, some person other than Batty might have been there. But it was not likely in that lonely spot. And the hounds soon settled that point. Once more they picked up a scent, and a new one. This time they made off in another direction, which took us into the thickest part of the woods on one side of Heronswood Park, and kept us there by unfrequented ways until we wound up at the back of Home Farm – Robson's place. There, for some reason which neither Mr. Marston nor his gamekeeper could understand, the scent failed. I had my own suspicion as to the failure: since Robson's death his farm had been neglected, and the mephitic odours from a fold which had not been cleared for some time and was reeking under a hot midday sun were enough to destroy the scent of a human fugitive.

But there was no doubt Batty had been at his cave that morning and had afterwards made for Home Farm and been in its precincts. And the question was – where was he now?

Chapter 24

BOLTED, BARRED, SHUTTERED

Brought up against the gateway at the rear of the big fold of Home Farm, we stood looking in on a scene of neglect and desolation. The gamekeeper had opened the gate and admitted the bloodhounds. They had followed a trail up to our side of the gate plainly enough; once within the gate they seemed to be at an utter loss. They made a cast or two here and there, wandered about a bit, sniffed the air – foul enough from the accumulated and rotting refuse and garbage – and came back to us, whimpering. Clearly, the scent had failed. And yet, up to that point, there had seemed to be no doubt that we were hot on Batty's track.

"Queer!" muttered Mallwood. "They seem to be at a loss here."

"No wonder!" growled the gamekeeper. "There's more smells than one in this place. Look there!"

He pointed to a loathsome-looking mass lying a little way inside the fold. Some animal or animals had disinterred from the manure the body of a dead pig; over it a cloud of flies hovered. And as that was a hot morning, with the sun pouring its rays out of an unclouded sky...

"Whole place looks lost," said Mallwood. "It used to be spick and span enough in Robson's time. And he hasn't been dead that long – but things soon go to rack and ruin when there's nobody to look after them."

I remembered the general aspect of Home Farm at our first visit to Heronswood, and I was surprised to see how neglected it now looked. There was not a sign of life about the place. The fold itself was a mass of manure, mud, and refuse. The buildings surrounding it were destitute of horses, cattle, sheep, pigs; the only sign of life visible was in the pigeons fluttering about the old dove-cot. We could see little of the house from where we stood, but I gathered from what I saw of the top storey, seen above the roofs of the stables, that all its windows were closely shuttered. The whole place – house, buildings, orchard, garden – wore an air of desolation.

A man suddenly came out of the wood on our left – a labourer, evidently bent on crossing the meadow in which we stood. Mr. Marston hailed him, and he came slowly and wonderingly towards us.

"Anybody about here?" asked Mr. Marston.

The man shook his head as if surprised at the question.

"Been nobody about since the sale, sir," he answered. "It's all shut up."

"Nobody in the house?"

"No, sir. The housekeeper, she went away day before they sold the furniture, and it's all locked up."

"That's three weeks since," remarked Mallwood. "I remember the sales – stock and implements one day; furniture another. Who's got the keys of the house?" he went on, turning to the man. "Anybody about here?"

"I did hear that Mr. Robson's brother, him that had everything sold up, took the keys away with him," replied the man. "I don't know as how anybody else might have a key, unless it would be Mr. Weekes, the steward."

Nobody asked him any more questions, and he went on his way. Mr. Marston said we'd better have a look round and bade the gamekeeper try the outbuildings, stables, and so on with the hounds. He himself went with them; the rest of us went across the evil-smelling fold, through a stack-yard, now innocent of grain, hay, or straw, to the house.

The house looked as deserted as its outbuildings. Every window – and there were a great many of them, for it was a big house – was closely shuttered; every door, front, back, and sides, locked and bolted. There was no way of entrance except by a key – whoever had finally closed the place after the sale of the late tenant's effects had taken good care that everything about it had been made secure. The steward's house was not far away; we sent Chippendale down there to see if Weekes had a key. Chippendale came back empty-handed; the keys of the house were in the possession of Robson's brother, who was also his executor, and who lived some distance away, in another county.

So we drew a Home Farm blank. The bloodhounds found no trace in the outbuildings or around the house. Brought back to the gate of the fold, they showed an inclination to return on their tracks towards the cave in the other side of the woods. But it was inconceivable that Batty should have come as far as the farm and then turned back on his own path thither; besides, according to our reckoning, he could not have done so in the time we calculated upon. Mr. Marston and his gamekeeper went off to Sedbury Manor with the hounds; Mallwood went to see Weekes; Chaney, Chippendale, and I returned to Monkseaton, pretty well tired out with our morning's work.

"Lay anything Batty is hidden somewhere about that place!" said Chaney, as we went off. "Mallwood ought to put a ring of men around it. Lots of safe hiding-places about there, I'll be bound."

"Queer thing about the scent, though, Mr. Chaney, isn't it?" suggested Chippendale.

Chaney made a face expressive of disgust.

"Not with that fold about, my lad!" he said. "Pah! – I can smell it now!"

Going into our hotel at Monkseaton, we met old Mr. Portinscale coming out. He paused, turned back, motioned us to follow him into an empty room.

"Any luck?" he inquired.

"In what way?" asked Chaney.

"News travels fast in these country districts," replied Mr. Portinscale. "You've been out with Mr. Marston and his bloodhounds – man-hunting!"

Chaney told him all about it then. Mr. Portinscale began to look wiser than ever when he came to tell of our deadlock at Home Farm.

"Ah!" he said. "I know that place – knew it well, years ago. I don't know what might be the result of putting bloodhounds into it, but otherwise a man might hide there in that house for weeks! As, indeed, men have done, in the old days. There's a priest's hole there."

"What's that?" asked Chaney.

"Secret hiding-place used by fugitive clergy in the old penal days," replied Mr. Portinscale. "Most ingeniously contrived and hidden, it is, too, this one. That Home Farm, you know – parts of it – dates back to James the First."

"Place was barred, bolted, shuttered," said Chaney. "But we'll tell Mallwood."

However, we did not see or hear of Mallwood again that evening. Indeed, we heard no further news and did not know what Mallwood and his men were doing. I went to bed early that night and left Chaney and Chippendale talking. I had been on my legs in the fresh air nearly all day, and I slept soundly – until I was aware that somewhere a big bell, deep, heavy-toned, was ringing, ringing, ringing. Then there came a thump at my door.

Chapter 25

GRANDMOTHER'S BUREAU

I was half-dazed with sleep when that thump came, and still dazed when the door opened and some hand, switching on the electric light, let a flood of light into the room. Then, as I staggered up in bed, blinking, Chippendale's voice broke on my confused senses.

"Mr. Camberwell! Get up, sir! That's the fire-bell. There's a big fire on, somewhere outside the town," he said. "Mr. Chaney says it's somewhere out Heronswood way. Look!"

He was pulling up the blind as he spoke, and, jumping out of bed and joining him at the window, I saw across the roofs of the town a dull red glare, spreading upward in the sky. And it was Heronswood way, as Chaney said. Without a word I turned back into the room and half-mechanically began huddling on some clothes.

"Mr. Chaney's dressing, too," said Chippendale. "I'll go and finish mine – I'm to get a car. He thinks it may be Heronswood. He—"

A great rush and racket from the street outside the hotel stopped him. Again we made for the window and looked out. The fire-engine, manned by men in brass helmets and drawn by big, powerful horses, went rattling by at top speed. And already the Monkseaton people were leaving their beds and rushing into the streets – there was a perceptible streaming down the road towards Heronswood.

"I'll be ready in two minutes, Chippendale," I said. "Hurry up and get the car – best you can find. Try the garage round the corner."

In less than ten minutes I was down at the front door; the hotel boots was up, had let Chippendale out, and now stood on the steps of the front door, staring at the red glow in the sky, which was spreading rapidly. Chaney came hurrying down the staircase, joined me and the boots, and stared, too, in silence.

"They say it's Heronswood Park," said the boots, suddenly. "Lord! – and they're burying Sir Stephen today!"

Chippendale came round the corner with the car; all three of us bundled into it, bidding the driver to get along at top speed. Flashing past the police station a minute later, we saw Mallwood and some of his men climbing into his car; they came after us. Outside the town, where our own merged with the other main roads leading in the direction of Heronswood, other fire-brigades dashed up, one horse-drawn, the other, more modern, motor-impelled. There was by this time a regular stream of traffic in the direction of the fire. And over the tops of the woods, now in the full leafage of early summer, the red glow in the sky grew wider and higher.

Chaney said nothing until we had passed Sedbury Park and were getting near to the boundaries of Heronswood. Then he spoke, sharply.

"Camberwell!" he said; "this'll be Batty's work! We've heard of his threats. And it won't be Heronswood we shall find ablaze. It'll be Weekes's place!"

I hadn't thought of that. And before I had time to think of it, we had cleared a corner of the plantations and swept round a bend of the road that brought us close in front of the fire. Weekes's house, yes, and everything about it! Above the rattle and clang of the fire-engines, of which there were now at least three on the spot, and the shouts of the people flocking as near to the scene as they could get, we heard the steady, relentless roar of the flames. They shot right up into the darkness, mingling with gigantic columns of smoke.

There was plenty to feed the flames. In addition to his stewardship, Weekes farmed a goodly piece of the estate for its proprietors, and on one side of his house lay a stack-yard, in which, despite the fact that winter, the usual threshing-time, was long past, there still stood a number of big stacks of wheat, barley, oats, to say nothing of sundry valuable stacks of hay. All these were on fire and blazing furiously. Then, on the other side of the house, between it and the carpenter's shop and the estate office, stood a wood-yard, filled with great piles and stacks of seasoned and seasoning wood. That, too, was burning steadily in every part – and as we raced up we saw the flames leaping from the blazing timber to a range of outbuildings and to the fringe of the wood which shut the whole place in.

That there was no hope for the house itself we saw at a glance; it seemed to us, as we jumped from the car and got as near as the heat allowed, that the very garden and orchard were on fire. Weekes's house, modernised though it was as to its interior arrangements, was a very old one, with a lot of timber in its composition, and, in addition to that, a thatched roof. It was by that time a mere shell, white-hot.

We raced up to a group gathered at the edge of the stable-yard. There were Sir Rupert and Lady Maxtondale, half-dressed; there was Ellerthorpe; there was Rabbage; there were other faces that I knew, servants, workmen. And on a sort of stretcher, her daughter bending over her, helpless to do anything, lay Mrs. Weekes, moaning fitfully.

Ellerthorpe pulled Chaney and me aside.

"She's badly burned and badly injured," he whispered. "Some of the men who got here first say they could have got her out safely, but she actually fought with them to get to some room in the house from which, I suppose, she wanted to rescue something. Then a beam fell on her, and they dragged her away – and there she is. Dying, I think – I wish a doctor would come!"

"Weekes?" asked Chaney. "And the rest – the servants?"

Ellerthorpe pointed to a couple of women who had evidently escaped in their night-clothes and had been supplied with coats from some of the workmen's shoulders.

"The two girls got out," he said, "but nothing's been seen of Weekes. He must have been overcome by the first outbreak – he's not about, at any rate. This is that fellow Batty's work, Chaney!" he went on. "One of these men tells me that there was a lot of petroleum, paraffin, and other inflammable stuff stored in an outhouse built on to the wall of the house, and that the fire started from there and in the stack-yard and the wood-yard at the same time! A diabolical outrage! – Is this the doctor?"

A car came dashing up; a man jumped from it and came hurrying to where Sir Rupert and Lady Maxtondale were bending over the injured woman. We went quietly after him and stood near. . . .

Suddenly we heard Mrs. Weekes speak. Whether she was delirious or not, I have no means of knowing; but I heard what she said.

"Weekes – he knew nothing of it," she muttered. "Weekes—"

Then she was silent again. Chaney and I looked at each other. What was it that Weekes knew nothing of? Was it – ?

Just as suddenly Mrs. Weekes spoke once more. This time her voice rose almost to a cry. "The bureau! Let me get at my bureau! That room—"

The cry died as suddenly as it had risen. The doctor bent lower – still lower. Then he straightened himself and turned towards Sir Rupert. There was that in his face which made the rest of us turn away.

"Gone!" said Chaney.

He turned away presently and, going amongst the groups of watchers, began to make inquiry for the men who had got Mrs. Weekes out of the burning house. One of the estate carpenters stepped forward.

"I got her out," he said. "Me and Jim there. And a nice job we had with her! We could have got her out unhurt, but she screamed and struggled, ay, and fought with us. She wanted to get at something in a back room – an old bureau or something of that sort – she said something about valuables. She fought like a wildcat to get away from us to that room—"

"It was an old secretaire, a sort of bureau that was in there," interrupted one of the rescued women-servants. "She kept it locked up, did Mrs. Weekes, but I've seen her looking into it many a time. It was her grandmother's, so I've heard her say."

"Did she get at it?" asked Chaney.

The carpenter shook his head.

"She did not!" he answered. "She did her best, though. She broke loose from me and Jim in the hall and darted back, and she'd got halfway down a passage when a big beam crashed right down atop of her. We dragged her out from under it and carried her out here, and a nice job we had!"

"Weekes?" asked Chaney. "Did you see anything of him?"

"Never a sign, mister! Saw nothing at all of him from first to last. He's in there somewhere," continued the man, nodding at the holocaust. "And he'll be no more than a cinder by this time."

"Who saw the fire first?" asked Chaney.

"Tom Dukes saw it first," replied the carpenter. "That's his cottage, across yonder. The glare shone into his windows. He got up and roused the rest of us hereabouts. It had got a fine hold by the time I got round here. And I saw enough to see it had been started in three places. There was a lot of inflammable stuff, petrol, paraffin, oil, and so on, in that shed at the end of the house; that was blazing proper! Then the stack-yard had been fired, too, in two or three places. And a light had been put to a big pile of shavings in the wood-yard. Lord bless you! – there weren't a chance from the first! The roof – all dry thatch, that, mister – was blazing finely within five minutes of my coming, and the flames were already coming out of some of the windows. There's a bit of a fire-engine, an old-fashioned thing, down at the Hall, but it was no more use than a toy squirt at a do like this."

"It's burning itself out now," said another onlooker. "There's be precious little left of either house or buildings."

The night merged into morning; by daylight the fire had died down to a dull glow, from which now and then a sudden flame leapt to life. When day finally broke and the sun came out, the scene was one of utter desolation. Not a single stack of wheat, barley, oats, straw, was left in the stack-yard; the piled-up wood in the timber-yard was a heap of grey ash; the house a mass of smoking ruins. But, thanks to the efforts of the fire-brigades, one wing had suffered less damage than others, and from this, as the heat of the fire died down, the men began the work of salvage.

It was nearly two hours after noon of that day when the carpenter who had told us of his adventures with Mrs. Weekes suddenly drew our attention to a half-burnt-out room, now rapidly cooling. He pointed to an old desk which stood in a corner.

"That's the thing Mrs. Weekes wanted to get at," he said. "So, at any rate, the servant says. Grandmother's bureau, she says."

He turned away to another part of the ruins, and Chaney and I, with Chippendale in attendance, went over the fallen timbers and examined the object just indicated. It was a good, solid specimen of an eighteenth-century bureau, in polished birch-wood, and, though seared here and there by the flames, had suffered very little damage in the fire. Chaney began to examine the lock of the sloping top.

"Simple sort, this," he said musingly. "If I've a key that'll fit it—"

He drew a bunch of keys from his pocket and began to try one after another. Suddenly the lock gave way, and he lifted the lid.

"Usual sort of thing," he remarked. "Small drawers, pigeon-holes, and so on. Now, what was that woman so keen about? She must have kept something here. Plenty of papers, to be sure – household receipts, most of 'em, I reckon."

He began to turn the papers over. Suddenly, amongst a mass of letters, he caught sight of a signature and with a sharp exclamation turned to me, pushing the sheet of paper into my hand.

"Look at that, Camberwell!" he exclaimed. "That proves what I've been suspecting! Mrs. Weekes knew, if nobody else did!"

I looked at what he pointed to – a signature at the foot of a letter. "Your affectionate daughter, Ettie Maxtondale." I turned the letter over – the address was Malmesbury Mansions, the date only a few weeks back.

I handed the letter back to Chaney.

"Yes," I said, "that's plain enough. Mrs. Weekes knew!"

Chaney was busily examining other letters. Chippendale was eyeing the old bureau as if appraising its value.

"My father has an old desk like this," he said suddenly. "His has a secret drawer. Not so much of the secrecy business about it, though. It only means that there's a little drawer concealed behind another bigger one. You draw one out, like this, and there's a false bottom, and – why, this has just the same thing! Look!"

He had pulled out one of the small drawers as he spoke, and then from behind it drew out another smaller one. That was filled with –

But the next instant all three of us saw what filled it. There was a wash-leather bag, full of diamonds, cut and uncut; a gold watch and chain; a wad of banknotes, some letters and papers. . . .

From staring at these things, we stared at each other – in silence. There was now a common knowledge between us; we knew whose hand had fired the shot that killed Sir John Maxtondale.

Late that night, over a last pipe before we went to bed, Chaney and I discussed the events of that exciting day. After his wont he was very matter-of-fact about them and also about the mysteries which had preceded the final catastrophe.

"There's precious little mystery about any of these things, Camberwell," he said, "if only one can hit on a centre-point in good time. If I'd known – but then, how could I know, how could anyone know? – but if I'd known when we first came here that Mrs. Weekes's daughter was secretly married to young Rupert Maxtondale, I'd have solved the problem of Sir John Maxtondale's murder and the two subsequent murders in five minutes! For, of course, Mrs. Weekes was the murderer – she shot 'em, all three. The thing's obvious. Sir John comes back; on his way to the ancestral hall he encounters Mrs. Weekes, who, born and bred on the estate, knows him at sight. Probably they talk – but Mrs. Weekes is thinking. Sir John's back; Sir John may be married; anyhow, her daughter's chance of becoming Lady Maxtondale is weakened by Sir John's return. And Mrs. Weekes has her gun in her hands, for she's gone out to shoot rats. She shoots Sir John then and there – she was just the sort of woman to make up her mind quickly and to act on her decision."

"Chaney," I said, "do you think she'd no accomplice in getting rid of the body?"

"No!" he exclaimed. "I don't! She needed no accomplice. She was a strongly built, wiry woman. She'd have no difficulty in fetching and carrying those weights, one at a time; no difficulty in dragging the body that short distance to the water. But I'll tell you what I do think – I think the old woman, Mother Kitteridge, probably witnessed the murder of Sir John, and that she endeavoured to blackmail Mrs. Weekes and then went to Robson's, to tell him what she'd seen. I think Mrs. Weekes followed her there, overheard the conversation through the open window, and promptly shot both of them. That, Camberwell, is, in my opinion, the plain truth. Mrs. Weekes was a woman of – shall we call it character?"

"There's another cross-current, Chaney," I said. "Batty?"

"Oh, Batty!" he replied. "Batty? I never believed for one instant that Batty had anything to do with the three murders we've been talking about. Batty's sole motive was revenge. It was Batty, of course, who set fire to Weekes's house."

"The bridge?" I whispered.

"The bridge? Oh!" he answered, "you may lay your last shilling that Mrs. Weekes did that too! It was her hand that sawed through the timbers, Camberwell, and hers that put that saw where it was found – in the cottage in the wood. Mrs. Weekes took full advantage of what we may call the Batty legend. She'd finished off Sir John; she'd settled the possible witnesses or possessors of her secret; all she'd got to do was to settle Sir Stephen, and see her daughter Lady Maxtondale! Of course! But you remember that she called her husband back to see to something in the kitchen when he was setting out to meet Sir Stephen? Yes, sir – Mrs. Weekes had four murders on her soul! She was, I repeat, a woman of character. You're a scholar, Camberwell – I'm not; but weren't there women in history who were of that sort? – women who'd stop at nothing, nothing whatever, to gain their ends?"

"A good many, Chaney, from time immemorial!" I said. "Heaps of 'em!"

"Well, I reckon they aren't extinct," he remarked thoughtfully. "A woman, Camberwell, is a very queer being, very queer indeed. You don't know what a woman is capable of!"

"Well, anyhow, Batty got the Emperor's snuff-box," I said.

"And a good deal besides, I dare say," asserted Chaney. "And I think the police'll have a tough job in finding Batty. Batty, this time, has taken care to make himself very scarce. But we aren't employed in any Batty business. Batty, Camberwell, has had enough sense to go speedily and secretly to – wherever it is he's gone to."

He was right there. Up to the present I have not heard that the authorities have succeeded in tracing Batty, and Chaney says they never will.

Q.E.D.
by Lynn Brock

There's Death in the Churchyard
by William Gore

Murder of the Ninth Baronet
by J.S. Fletcher

Dead Man Manor
by Valentine Williams

The Man in the Dark
by John Ferguson

The Dressing Room Murder
by J.S. Fletcher

*Glory Adair and the
Twenty-First Burr*
by Victor Lauriston

The Tunnel Mystery
by J.C. Lenehan

Murder on the Marsh
by John Ferguson

The Fatal Five Minutes
R.A.J. Walling

*The Crime
of a Christmas Toy*
Henry Herman

Death of an Editor
Vernon Loder

Death on May Morning
Max Dalman

The Hymn Tune Mystery
George A. Birmingham

The Middle of Things
JS Fletcher

The Essex Murders
Vernon Loder

The Boat Race Murder
R. E. Swartwout

Who Killed Alfred Snowe?
J. S. Fletcher

Murder at the College
Victor L. Whitechurch

*The Yorkshire
Moorland Mystery*
J. S. Fletcher

Fatality in Fleet Street
Christopher St. John Sprigg

The Doctor of Pimlico
William Le Queux

The Charing Cross Mystery
J. S. Fletcher

Fatality in Fleet Street ePub & PDF
FREE when you sign up for our
infrequent Newsletter.

Printed in Great Britain
by Amazon

42345435R00111